To

Rhett ♥ 4/06

UP THE DEVIL'S BELLY

a novel by

RHETT DEVANE

RABID PRESS   *AUSTIN, TX 2005*

Rabid Press, Inc.
P.O. Box 4706
Horseshoe Bay, TX 78657

Design and layout by Peterson Design
petersondesign@mn.rr.com

Library of Congress Control Number: 2004118315
ISBN 978-0-9743039-2-5

Printed in the United States of America
First Edition, September, 2005

ACKNOWLEDGEMENTS

By the grace of God, I have been allowed to share my stories with the world.

A special thank you —

~ To all of the readers who have waited patiently for this book. I do not forget for one moment that you spend your hard-earned money to purchase my writing.

~ To manuscript proofreaders, Ann Macmillian and Joy Hevey.

~ For the expert guidance of Editor David Baker of Rabid Press.

~ For the diligence, patience, friendship, and perseverance of Rebecca Gruelich, Marketing Director of Rabid Press.

~ To my wonderful family, for putting up with me over the years. To my mother, the most Divine DeVane.

~ To Denise Fletcher, for her devotion and support, and for hauling me and cases of books from pillar to post.

~ To law enforcement experts: Dick Barnes, Cathy Kennedy, Chris Garrison, and Kelly Walker.

~ To nursing experts: Mary Menard, RN, Tonya A. Harris, RN, MN, Associate Professor of Nursing(retired).

~ To Leigh Ansley for heading up the cheering section, and Stefanie Shippy for providing her bizarre wit. To Lillian Tilford for shining forth her brilliant light. Special thanks to John Gandy and Cathy Bell.

~ To my boss, Dr. Bill Cooke, and all of my coworkers.

~ And, to all of my friends and patients who have continued to encourage me through it all.

Thank you, thank you, thank you! I'd kiss each and every one of you right on the lips if I had the energy.

For my mother, Theresa DeVane
- my hero, my friend, and my biggest fan.

UP THE DEVIL'S BELLY

"There are two kinds of devils – the ones you know and the ones you don't. The devils you don't know are the ones you want to look out for. They'll put a hurtin' on you every time."
   Piddie Davis Longman

PROLOGUE

Sarah Chuntian Lewis

LULLED BY THE MONOTONOUS DRONE of the jet's engines, I drifted into a clammy, drooling sleep. The twenty-four-plus hours spent traipsing the globe from China to Los Angeles to Atlanta throughout the previous day and evening finally provided the dead-out exhaustion to override my normal resistance.

Beside me, Sarah Chuntian Lewis dozed peacefully on Holston's lap while he scribbled in a small notebook. Miniature bubbles of saliva formed at the corners of her rosebud mouth. We marveled at her ability to wall herself off from the turbulence of the world. Perhaps the noisy, crowded orphanage where she'd spent the first seven months of her life had steeled her to the jangling din of human voices.

From the moment Holston and I had met Sarah at the orphanage in the Jiangxi province, we had fallen desperately in love with her round, ever-smiling face and sunny disposition. I had imagined she would hold a deep, abiding sadness for her unfortunate introduction into a country so overpopulated that its rulers dictated the number of offspring per family, and whose society valued male children over its female counterparts.

UP THE DEVIL'S BELLY

As a newborn, Sarah had been found late in September in a reed basket on the stoop of the orphanage, wrapped in a soft pink, hand-woven blanket, amid handfuls of wild daisies. A hand-scripted scrap of paper attached to a corner of her clothing contained the Chinese character for the word *chuntian - spring* in English.

A subtle change in the pitch of the engines nudged my awareness. I opened my eyes and studied Holston's profile in the dawning light. The shadow of beard stubble accentuated the lines of his strong chin. A wisp of dark brown hair hung over his gentle dark eyes. Often, I marveled over this tall, dark, and handsome man. By any standards, I was average; five-four, medium-length brown hair, hazel eyes. Nothing special. But, Holston Lewis loved me to absolute derision. I thanked the heavens on a daily basis for whatever good karma had sent him my way.

"I can't wait to tell Jake you actually slept on an airplane," he said.

I yawned and stretched as far as possible in the cramped space. "He'll just bug you to find out how much Benadryl you had to give me to knock me out." I nodded toward Sarah. "Can you believe her? She's slept practically the entire trip."

The intercom crackled. *"Ladies and Gentlemen, we'll be landing shortly in Tallahassee. Weather conditions this morning...sunny, clear, 68°, highs expected in the upper 80's with around 75% humidity. We'd like to take this opportunity..."*

"Here's how I see it. Devil's got hisself a meanness meter — say one to a hundret. Little mean acts like pilferin' your neighbor's mornin' paper or thinking how fat Elvina's behind looks in her new skirt, they may be a five or ten. Devil don't take much mind of them, 'less they start to pile up and happen more regular. Then, he sets his sights on you. Sends more temptations to do meanness. Pretty soon, meanness seems normal, and you plumb forget what it felt like before. That's when the Devil has you by the short hairs. The darkness comes a' ridin' into your soul in a fire-snortin' gallop."

    Piddie Davis Longman

CHAPTER ONE

A BIBLE OF SOUTHERN ETIQUETTE would contain a psalm on appropriate food gifting occasions: *And it came to pass that a decree was sent out unto the land that each person should bring, according to his or her due, a casserole.*

During times of stress — good or bad — the residents of Chattahoochee came bearing glassware and aluminum pans filled with homemade comfort food. The entrees included chicken'n'dumplin's, pot roast with potatoes and carrots, green beans with french-fried onion topping, tuna and English pea salad, and, always, one container filled with an unnaturally colored unidentifiable mixture topped with a melted mat of cheddar cheese.

With the aid of Aunt Piddie and her longtime friend and fellow little-ole-lady-hotline nemesis, Elvina Houston, folks from the three surrounding counties knew of our return to the farmhouse on the Hill. They politely waited one full day to allow us to settle in. Then, they came. By the afternoon of the second day, the refrigerators in the country kitchen and the pool house were filled to bursting with offerings. I bugged my sister-in-law Leigh, my cousin Evelyn, and our down-the-lane neighbors, Margie and John, to take food home with them. The congratulatory cards were piled high on the kitchen island waiting for thank-you notes to be penned and sent in the return mail.

Jake Witherspoon's rear protruded from the refrigerator as he poked under the aluminum foil lid of a pottery bowl. "Tuna casserole — I'll bet Julie at the Homeplace made that one. Hmmm…lasagna! That'd be Angelina Palazzolo's." He removed a large milky-blue glass covered dish. "Whose dumplin's?"

I shrugged. "Ginny Pridgett, I think. The card's over there somewhere."

"Ewww! Can I have some? She makes the *best* chicken'n'dumplin's. But, don't dare tell Piddie I said so. It'd eat her alive."

"Help yourself. We've gotten so much food, it'll go bad before we can eat all of it. You want to take the tuna casserole home with you? I detest the stuff. And Julie, bless her heart, always brings it. I think she got the recipe from Mandy at the Cut'n'Curl."

Jake wagged a thin finger. "Triple C Day Spa and Salon, Sister-girl. The Cut'n'Curl is a thing of the past. Just call it the Triple C for…" He snapped his fingers with an upward flourish. "Cut, curl, and coddle."

"You're really getting into this thing, aren't you? I mean, considering you're not *really* working there."

Jake propped his hands on his slender hips. "Beg pardon, missy. I'm the creative designer, overseer, and grounds manager. Actually, with Jolene in place at the Dragonfly Florist, I've spent more time at the Triple C than uptown." He clapped his hands together. "I can't wait till Saturday. The grand opening and welcome-home-baby-Sarah party is going to be *the* social event of the late spring season!"

4

"No doubt about that, with you heading up the planning committee." I shook my head and smiled. "Evelyn made the most amazing little playsuit for Sarah to wear."

"The one with the appliquéd gold dragon?"

"There's more than one?"

Jake piled a paper plate with a congealed lump of dumplings and shoved it into the microwave. "Does your cousin ever go half-way with anything? She's made five different oriental influence outfits for Sarah. Two are silk — obviously *not* for everyday spit-up wear."

The microwave beeped, and Jake settled onto a cushioned barstool at the island counter with his plate. "You haven't seen her house since you've gotten home, then?" he asked around a mouthful.

"Let me guess. Red, black and gold? Chinese characters as wall hangings? Maybe some bamboo curtains and rice paper lanterns?"

Jake's nose wrinkled as he grinned. "Piddie would say you have ESPN."

"Poor Joe. He just finished hanging the nautical kitchen wallpaper before we left for China."

Jake moaned with pleasure. "Gah, this is *so* good. Sure you don't want some?"

I shook my head. "Not unless you want me to blow up. I've done nothing but eat since we got home. So, Evelyn has redone their entire house since we left for China?"

He stabbed the air with his fork. "Actually, no. Just the kitchen and den. She's been too busy. Her ongoing home redecoration fetish has paled with the demands of her new designer clothing business. We had planned on having a small display area for her gowns and outfits right behind the reception desk at the Triple C. Since she needed more space, she and Joe outfitted an old pantry off the mudroom for her work area. She has cutting and layout tables, two old sewing machines, and one new computerized model that, I'm sure, set Joe back several thou."

"What about Aunt Piddie? She can't stay home alone all day."

Jake swallowed a gulp of iced tea, then dabbed delicately at the corners of his mouth. "Pid's going to run the reception desk for the spa. She's all psyched up about it. Said it'd beat sittin' around at home. As long as we have a TV so she can watch her soaps and Oprah, and an extra phone line so she can keep up with Elvina's goin's on, she'll be happy."

He chuckled. "You should see Joe. He's like a new man. Since Evelyn's been so busy making clothes for the shop, she hasn't had time to cook. He's been eating out most every meal, and he's even put on a little weight! I haven't seen him this happy since the Alaskan cruise."

How Joe had tolerated Evelyn's lack of culinary skill for all the years of their union was beyond me. My cousin was famous for her bad cooking, but it didn't stop her from experimenting on her husband and mother. Evelyn's state-of-the-art kitchen contained every gourmet tool known to the modern world and a library of over fifty cookbooks. My cousin's downfall was her tendency to embellish the printed recipes with her own strange spins. My Aunt Piddie had been living with Evelyn and Joe for the past few years since her balance had deteriorated and swore that Evelyn's bad cooking *kept her regular.*

"Oh…let me show you the business cards Jon designed for Evelyn." Jake fumbled in his wallet and produced a small, pale green card with a line drawing of a smiling elf holding a needle and thread. One end of the thread looped to form the logo ELF-Wear.

I rolled my eyes. "*Elf*-wear?"

"For her initials…Evelyn Longman Fletcher. ELF-wear."

I laughed. "Clever."

Jake smoothed a wrinkle from his tailored shirt. "She's working on a line of infant clothing. I think the whole thing with Sarah, and of course, little Josh, has inspired her. She's made the cutest little kimono outfit for him to wear to the party. Josh is such a chunk, he's going to look like a Sumo wrestler in it!"

I pushed a strand of stringy hair from my eyes. "I'm going to feel underdressed."

Jake carried his utensils to the sink. "Actually, you won't. She's made satin kimonos for the whole dang family and staff. You should see mine! It's a luscious shade of deep purple."

"You know, kimonos are Japanese. They don't have them in China."

Jake stopped midway between the sink and the dishwasher. "Don't you dare point that out to Evelyn. She'll be devastated. Kimonos look oriental...that's all that will matter to folks around here. No need to get technical."

"Suppose you're right. By the way — did you ever get the scoop out of Piddie as to why that sleaze-ball Hank Henderson tried to block the rezoning petition for the mansion?"

"Not a clue. She says she'll *take it to her grave*. Must've been something good, though. He changed his mind so fast, the city council's still reelin'!"

I plopped into my favorite chair, a threadbare overstuffed recliner long past its prime. "I don't get why he has it in for you. It worries me."

"Sister-girl, not everyone's gonna love me. My *queerness* offends a lot of folks. Especially if they don't bother to get to know how incredibly enchanting I am." He smiled wide enough to show off his twin dimples.

"Humble, as well."

Jake executed a stiff bow. "Humility is one of my finest girlish qualities."

"There's just something about Hank that creeps me out." I shuddered involuntarily.

"Well, he keeps that young Williams hoodlum off the street, anyway. Since he's been doing odd jobs and errands for Hank, he's not looming around town looking like a drug deal waiting to happen."

I swept a scattering of breadcrumbs from the countertop. "I've wondered about that, too. Hank always has kids coming and going. How could he possibly have that much footwork to do here in this small town?"

"Dunno." Jake shrugged. "Maybe he's trying to make points with the city council by helping the underprivileged. He's the type to always have some kind of agenda. Whatever he's doing seems to be lucrative. Elvina Houston told me she heard he'd ordered a new Mercedes."

"The one he has doesn't look that old!"

"Different priorities, I suppose."

"Oh, by the way, I wanted to thank you again for picking us up at the airport. I still can't fathom how you and Jon managed to slip off to Tallahassee without half of town in tow."

"Jon convinced everyone that y'all would be exhausted from the trip, and that it might overwhelm poor little Sarah if everyone came at once."

"Bless you!" I kissed him on the cheek.

Jake's boyish features had changed little since grade school – same calm blue eyes, impish smile, and pleasant face with a scant dusting of freckles across the nose and cheeks. A few faint lines around his mouth belied the constant pain he had lived with for the past few years.

"My pleasure. I'll make sure to bring you a copy of the video Jon took of you three coming off the plane." He cocked his head. "You unpack my present yet?"

"Nope. Paul Wong is shipping a big box over for us. You'll just have to wait."

Jake snorted.

Holston and I had purchased silk lounge jackets similar to Japanese kimonos for the entire family. Jake's red coat sported a black dragonfly resembling the logo for his West Washington Street flower shop.

Jake jabbed my arm. "One little hint?"

I shook my head. "Nada."

"After all I've done for you, Hattie Davis Lewis! Slaving away at this farmhouse, doling out daily affection to your poor pooch and puss. Taking both of the cars out for drives to keep their little batteries alive!" He dabbed his eyes dramatically.

I patted him on the head. "It will be worth the wait. I promise."

Jake slapped his brightly-painted art deco walking cane on the floor. "Well, I'd just love to stay here and see who we could drag across the coals next, but I've got a few last minute touches to add to the Triple C before tomorrow. Oh, by the way, Evelyn asked me to tell you to have your little family at the Salon in the morning by 8:30, the latest. She'll have your kimonos ready. Just wear plain black pants and a white top."

Jake shuffled toward the front door. "The Homeplace is catering lunch. So, all you'll need to bring are Sarah's bottles and supplies. The open house will run until around 4:00 PM. Evelyn has cribs set up for Sarah and Josh for baby naptime in case they get fussy. Toodles! Love and kisses to Prince Charming and little sweetpea."

"Sure you don't wanna stay a little longer? Sarah'll be up from her nap any minute now, and I'm gonna wake Holston. I thought we'd take John and Margie's ATV to the fishpond."

Jake hesitated a moment. "I'd really love to. A little peace would be great about now. Mandy, Melody, and Stephanie have worked themselves into a high rollin' boil over the *whore-derves*. Someone could end up in the ER if I don't get on back and referee." He grinned. "I can't believe you haven't dragged that baby to the pond yet...or yourself, for that matter."

I looked at Jake like he'd lost his last remaining piece of sanity. "Can I remind you that we just got home from half-way around the globe day before yesterday?

We slept the entire first day home, and the masses started bringing food today."

Jake cocked his head to one side. "Poor baby. Tough to be admired so much, isn't it?"'

Jake artfully dodged the wet kitchen towel I threw in his direction before sticking out his tongue as he stepped out of the front door.

The four-wheel all-terrain vehicle kicked up puffs of dust in its wake as we crossed the five-acre field behind the farmhouse. Once a cultivated patch of field corn and acre peas, the barren land had begun to show signs of reclamation by the surrounding woodlands. Clumps of broom sedge and weeds were interspersed with volunteer pine seedlings. The small pines held the promise of maturing into tall sentinels that would whisper secrets into the passing wind.

At the edge of the field, a small cleft in the tree line revealed a narrow, one lane rutted path leading to the fishpond. Briars and wild honeysuckle vines draped across the canopy of trees like leftover New Year's party crepe paper streamers. Holston negotiated the winding lane, occasionally blocking a low-hanging branch before it slapped the human intruders in the face.

The fishpond was nestled in a small depression at the base of two hills where three natural springs converged. In the middle of the wide earthen dam, the lean-to shed listed precariously to one side, barely shading two rusted lawn chairs. A twenty-gallon drum with a cement-weighted lid held commercial catfish food. On the cleared slope, a series of steep steps led to the water's edge. Heavy spring rains had washed the foundation from the final step. Holston jumped down, then held his arms up to retrieve Sarah. I landed with a thump beside him.

"We've really got to fix the steps this summer," I said. "Jake won't be able to make it down here at all."

Sarah giggled and cooed at our mutt rescue-dog Spackle as he jumped up and licked her stubby toes. He dashed to the water's edge and plowed into the water, yapping and biting at the small frogs and minnows that fled in terror.

I spread an old quilt on the soft grass.

Holston studied the wooded slopes surrounding the water. "Bobby and I were discussing the pond yesterday. Jake has sketched a design for a covered gazebo and multi-layered deck. He didn't think it was a good idea to put it on the dam. Maybe on one of the hills overlooking the pond."

"Jake loves this pond almost as much as Bobby and me. He's been coming down here since he and I were kids. He spent a lot of time down here after the assault. Called it his healing time."

"Well — it's your and Bobby's land. Do you want it changed?"

I picked up a smooth stone and skipped it across the water. "I think Mr. D and Mrs. Tillie would love to look down and see us enjoying the pond they built. Did Bobby say what he and Jake had in mind?"

Holston smiled. "I don't know that I can explain it with quite the flamboyance Jake did…but…it would sit on the hill overlooking the pond to one side, kind of a treehouse type of thing. Bobby even suggested screening in part of it so that the mosquitoes wouldn't keep us from using it during the summer months."

"Good idea. They're not too bad yet, but give it a few weeks, and they'll tote you off."

Holston motioned to the opposite shore. "Jake suggested a set of stairs with landings at a couple of points. Maybe a staggered series of decks."

"That must've been the part of the conversation I overheard in the kitchen this morning. Leigh was saying something about buying some new rocking chairs. We already have several on the porch at the Hill. I wondered what she was referring to."

Holston nodded. "Bobby wants to widen the road leading down here, too. It's getting so overgrown, even the ATV gets scratched trying to dodge the limbs and briars."

I hugged my knees to my chest. "Good idea. I think it would be fantastic to have a place here by the pond. It's the one spot on the Hill where I feel closest to my parents."

"Bobby said something about starting to clear out a spot next weekend… if it's okay by you."

I nodded absently. A small blue heron waded at the far edge of the pond. As I watched, it jabbed its beak into the water and emerged with a struggling minnow.

Holston rested his arm around my shoulders. "I forgot one detail — Jake's idea, naturally. He wants to build a small waterfall next to the gazebo to provide *the music of running water*. Bobby was more inclined to see the benefits of the aeration it would provide, especially during the hot part of the summer."

I nuzzled the soft spot beneath his ear. "Hmmm…sounds beautiful to me. It'll seem almost like being in the mountains."

Sarah played with a lime green grasshopper that had joined us on the quilt.

"Oh! No!" I called out.

Spackle bounded directly to Sarah, then shook himself silly to remove the muddy pond water from his coat. Sarah held her hands toward the spray and giggled, babbling in baby language.

Holston wiped a spatter of mud from his face. "Maybe we'll take a dip in the pool when we get back, since we're already wet, thanks to our hound."

The small fenced-in pool was the one modern addition my father had made to the farmhouse.

"It'll be dark soon. The water's warm." I smiled playfully. "We could always skinny-dip."

"There're two times in a person's life where she has life figured out — as a child and as an old woman. Trouble is, nobody much listens to either one."

Piddie Davis Longman

CHAPTER TWO

THOUGH I HAD KNOWN SARAH just shy of a month, there was clearly one major difference between us. She, like Holston, was a chirpy *Rebecca-of-Sunnybrook-Farm* morning human who greeted each day with bouncing enthusiasm. Holston immediately assessed the disparity in our approaches to awakening. He and Sarah giggled their way through breakfast, while I schlepped around, sleep-matted hair hanging over my eyes, a cup of strong coffee in hand. The house rule — no one spoke to me until after my second dose of caffeine.

My family of origin had been similar. My mother, Mrs. Tillie, and brother, Bobby, hit the floor in high gear. My father, Mr. "D", and I groused like spring-stunned black bears, cranky at being upright and mean-hungry. Had my middle sister survived, she would've tipped the balance of family dynamics. Bobby and Mama chirped *good mornin'* to each other and discussed everything from world news to local affairs. Dad and I struggled to avoid colliding with the furniture. As long as each person remained with his respective dive partner, no one got hurt.

My normal low morning energy level was magnified by the remnants of jet lag and the general lack of spunk I'd felt since the cancer surgery. Fortunately, my massage therapy practice would allow the freedom of scheduling appointments later in the day. Being the compassionate boss, I frequently gave myself a day off. Holston could tend Sarah in the mornings, writing while she slept or played at his feet. When his body rhythms crashed in the afternoon, I planned to take my shift.

Shammie and Spackle quickly became Sarah's animal guardians. Spackle, the devoted slobbering canine, immediately cherished the baby. He loved anyone who would show him kindness. Shammie's initial feline disinterest melted after the first few days. The cat code of ethics demanded that she not welcome us home with open paws. A mandatory period of martyrdom over being deserted for an extended length of time forced her to wait two full days before succumbing to Sarah's charms. From that point, Shammie was never far from the baby and slept curled in a tight ball on the rocking chair by the crib.

On the morning of the open house/welcome home party, Holston had showered, dressed, fed and clothed Sarah, packed the diaper bag, and fed the animals before I emerged from the shower. I climbed into the black slacks and white shirt I'd ironed the previous night, ran a comb though my wet hair, and grabbed a cup of coffee in a travel mug. Make-up was not an issue. I rarely wore any.

Regardless of the name on the property title, the sprawling white house on the corner of Morgan Avenue and Bonita Street would forever be referred to as the Witherspoon Mansion. Jake's mother, Betsy Witherspoon, had been the wealthiest woman in the history of Chattahoochee high society. The Greek revival style antebellum residence her husband Beau had built for his wife and young son made Tara's columned house from *Gone with the Wind* look like a sharecropper's shack in comparison.

The house was tucked between towering stands of short-needle pines, flowering dogwoods, mimosas, and ancient Spanish moss-draped live oaks. Banks of azaleas surrounded many of the trees, with moats of grass providing pathways between the vegetation. By the time Jake inherited the property following his mother's death, the once-proud showpiece was in a state of accelerating decay. Sheets of curled paint and extensive wood rot threatened the integrity of the exterior walls. The grounds were weed-infested and overgrown.

To Jake's dismay, his mother's inherited family fortunes had dwindled, and her flamboyant, expensive tastes had amassed mounds of unpaid credit card debt. The sale of the family homestead left Jake, after settlement of the estate, barely enough money to purchase the flower shop and a second-hand delivery van. Until he and I opened our business uptown, The Madhatter's Sweet Shop and Massage Parlor, Jake had camped out in a cramped storage room in the rear of the Dragonfly Florist. Upon my insistence, and because we needed the shop space for expansion, Jake relocated to the Hill.

Holston had purchased the mansion following his extended stay in town while he worked on his novel about Jake's assault. After Holston and I married, Jake renovated the second level of the mansion for his private quarters. Holston depended on him to oversee the building and grounds in exchange for room and board. Jake and Mandy, the owner of the Cut'n'Curl, came up with the idea to turn the expansive lower level of the house into a day spa and salon. Stephanie, a former waitress at the Homeplace Restaurant, had received massage therapy training and planned to set up shop in the newly appointed clinic space. Melody, Mandy's nail care specialist, won a prized spot in the main hair salon.

Holston pulled Betty into the Triple C's main entrance off Bonita Street, then took the paved delivery driveway to the rear door. The Dragonfly Florist van stood next to the ramp with its side door ajar.

Jake shuffled from the back door and waved when he saw us pull in. "Hey! Glad you got here early. Help me with these pots of bamboo for the front parlor, and I'll give you the three-dollar tour before we have to get into our party frocks. Evelyn's busy steaming the last minute wrinkles from the kimonos…like there *are* any!"

Holston removed Sarah from the car seat. She was in her usual effervescent *I'm-just-a-baby-so-I-don't-know-enough-to-be-cranky* mood.

"You are one cute kid." Jake cooed at Sarah, who blew spit bubbles in reply. "You'll be an asset today for the grand opening."

"We'll all try to do our part," I said, sarcastically.

Jake raised one eyebrow. "Eww…is *Evil Rita* with us today? Or is it my friend, Hattie?"

"She just needs more coffee," Holston said.

Jake grabbed my elbow, leading me inside as he patted my arm. "There, there, sweet girl — my little *sweetie-poots*. Jakey has a fresh carafe of Colombian special dark blend just for you."

The kitchen buzzed with activity. Mandy, Stephanie, and Melody were putting the final garnish on four round platters of cheese and fresh fruit. When Melody opened the commercial-sized refrigerator to rearrange the layered trays of cold cuts, I spotted an intricately-carved watermelon shell filled with melon balls in summer sherbet shades of green, peach, and red.

Melody handed a stack of napkins to a pretty, petite black girl. "Just put these on the small, round table by the door, Tameka honey."

"Anything I can help with?" I asked.

"Nope," Jake said. "You and your crew are guests today." He handed me a steaming cup of strong black coffee.

Holston nodded toward the parlor. "Who's the little black girl?"

"That's Tameka Clark. She and her older brother, Moses, are going to be helping out a little around here." He lowered his voice. "I'll fill you in on the details later. Mrs. Lucille Jackson told me about them. The kids live with their grandmother, Miz Maizie, and she's been pretty sick here lately...out of work. I figured we could use them for odd jobs. Any amount of money will help them put food on the table. Moses planted a lot of the meditation garden. They're both good kids. And...don't worry. It's legal and above board. I checked on permission for the two of them since they're underage. All of the paperwork is in place. It's not such a big issue right now, with them out of school for the summer."

Holston nodded. "I'd never doubt your judgement, Jake. Not for one second."

Mandy clucked. "Hattie, Hattie, Hattie! Your hair looks like a rag mop. Give me twenty minutes with you in the salon, and I'll make you presentable."

"I didn't realize it was that bad."

"Trust me..." Jake nodded. "It is."

"Give me a few minutes to show them the house and grounds, then she's all yours." Jake ushered us out of the kitchen. "Besides, it's only a matter of time before Evelyn comes sniffin' around."

I glanced into the front parlor. "Is Aunt Piddie here yet?"

"Joe's bringing her over a little later. Evelyn came in pretty early to make sure the Elf-wear display was perfect and her workshop was straightened up a bit. She's been working like a mad woman to get ready for today."

"Leave the little dumplin' with us!" Mandy held her arms out to receive Sarah. "Can she have a chunk of cantaloupe, Mama?"

"Sure. She has a few teeth. Just make sure it's not so small that she'll choke on it. She mostly just sucks the juice out, anyway. There are bibs and baby wipes in the diaper bag. Whatever you do, don't let her mess up Evelyn's new outfit. I'll never hear the end of it!"

"Don't you worry, Mama. Auntie Mandy'll take good care of her." Melody and Stephanie hovered nearby, anxious for their turns to hold the baby.

Built-in baby sitters — not such a bad thing. Holston and I followed Jake into the front parlor.

Jake motioned us into the spacious waiting area. "I know you saw some of this before you left, but we've added a few touches."

Upholstered high-back chairs lined the walls, interspersed with teak occasional tables. A richly-hued Oriental rug covered a large portion of the highly polished hardwood floors. In one corner, a bubbling rock fountain provided the soothing music of trickling water. The floor to ceiling windows were shaded by almond-toned plantation blinds, opened slightly to allow the soft morning light into the room. The Spa's logo, three gilded C's connected to form a triangle, was centered on the far wall so that it was the first thing a salon patron would see upon entrance. One long wall displayed two bold modern paintings, art work commissioned especially for the Triple C. The artist, five-year-old Ruth Hornsby, was the adopted Chinese daughter of our friends, Patsy and Rainey Hornsby of Tallahassee.

"I found most of the small bric-a-brac at a discount store in Tallahassee." Jake motioned to a set of blue and white ginger jars and a stone planter containing a Jade plant.

Two ornamental parlor palms and a standing ivy topiary added live greenery to the room.

"It just feels like the sort of place you'd come to relax and indulge yourself," I said.

Jake pointed to the next door. "That's the idea....now...this, of course, used to be the dining room. Now, it's the reception area and display room for Evelyn's Elf-wear."

An antique mahogany desk and armoire held court in a corner next to a glass and wood display case filled with Stephanie's chosen line of professional skin care products. The majority of the room was occupied with long painted poles suspended from the high ceiling. Evelyn's gowns and casual ensembles hung in artful display.

Holston whistled. "Wow! She has been busy."

Jake threw one hand into the air. "Positively a maniac. She's had all three of her sewing machines going, sometimes two at once. That computerized model acts like it has a mind of its own. She plugs in a design disc, positions the material, and the thing just takes off all by itself. She'll be hemming on one machine and it'll be over there, just sewin' away without her!"

Jake waved toward the kitchen. "Of course, the kitchen's like it was when we first started to renovate. It won't be open to the public. Just *us girls.*" Jake cocked his head coquetishly to one side. "We didn't change a thing in your private office and bedroom, Holston. If you want to redecorate your space, just say the word."

The hair salon combined two smaller rooms, divided by a large arched doorway. "One area is Mandy's. The other is Wanda's."

I had been curious to meet the woman with the New Jersey accent since Jake told me Mandy had hired her. "Is Wanda here yet?"

"Unfortunately, no. The sale of her condo down in Naples hit a hitch. She's closing on it Monday of next week. She should be up in a few days. She just won't be able to make it for the grand opening. She's supposed to be an expert with African-American hair design and care. Mandy's excited about her coming on board."

Jake waved toward the far corner. "Melody has a little niche for her fingernail care and pedicures near the rear of the hair salon. We installed a strong exhaust fan so that the acrylic fumes won't bother her or the patrons."

Jake continued toward the back of the lower level. "We put Steph's massage therapy room back here — nice and quiet, away from everything."

I admired the spacious treatment room. The pale blue walls and ceiling were painted with fluffy, white clouds. Blue-gray slate tile covered the floor. A soft, tufted wheat-hued rug cushioned the area surrounding the massage table.

I spotted the electric lift levers. "She went all out, didn't she? An automatic adjustable table! I'd kill for one of those."

Jake nodded. "Steph says she's gonna have to do a lot of hard labor to pay for that piece of equipment. It was…I believe, close to three thousand dollars by the time she added the extras."

Built-in floor to ceiling cabinets concealed rows of stacked linens, massage lotions and creams, a small stereo system, stacks of compact discs, and aromatherapy supplies. Soft lighting from the linen-draped windows gave the room a peaceful, Mount Olympus ambiance.

Holston asked, "You design this room?"

"Natch," Jake flipped back. "Now, let's go see the wet treatment room. Then, we'll tour the meditation garden."

The 14 x 14 mudroom had once been strewn with gardening tools, wet boots, and every manner of household overflow. The cleared area now contained a cushioned wet therapy table for use in sea salt scrubs, seaweed body wraps, and mud exfoliation treatments. A long water pipe with a line of shower nozzles was suspended over the table.

"What's that for?" Holston asked.

"Visshyshower. Amazing experience. After a full body scrub and exfoliation, the patron lies on his or her stomach — draped with towels in the appropriate private places, of course. Then the circular shower curtain is pulled around like so… and these jets send a warm spray of water down the back, all along the spine. Most delightful!"

Except for the freestanding etched Plexiglas shower stall in one corner, the remainder of the room was barren. The floor sloped slightly toward a central drain. Three fluffy white guest robes hung from a silver rack near the shower stall.

"The tiled floor and walls will allow Stephanie to wash down the room after each treatment. Keeps it all clean and fresh," Jake said.

"Are you up to code as far as handicapped accessibility?" Holston asked.

"Absolutely. We have ramps at all the entrance doors, and all three of the bathrooms used by patrons were enlarged and fitted with handrails and wheelchair accessible fixtures." Jake looked around. "That's about it for the first level — except for Evelyn's workroom. The upstairs is pretty much unchanged. I've been too dang busy down here to update my own space. You know, the plumber's sinks are always clogged. Eventually, we can use the upstairs as guest quarters for weekend retreat patrons."

Holston raised his eyebrows. "You moving sometime soon?"

"Not right away. At some point in the future, Jon and I would like to have a house somewhere in town. Don't worry. I won't leave you with a mess on your hands. I'll be the overseer whether I live here or not." Jake motioned us to hurry outside. "Let's tour the garden before Evelyn gets involved. Folks have a tendency to go in to her workroom and never come out."

The meditation garden filled the majority of the area within seventy feet of the rear double doors and wrapped one side of the house to the edge of a thicket of uncleared land that marked the posterior border of the lot.

"Kelly from Native Nurseries in Tallahassee designed the layouts for the plantings, and her coworker, Sheila, planned the water garden feature. They delivered the plants, and we've all taken turns plugging them into the existing landscape. Moses dug the hole for the koi pond, and I talked him through the instructions for installing the liner, pump, and aquatic plants. He's going to be in charge of grounds maintenance. Miz Lucille sure did us a favor by sending those kids over here. Tameka is learning to help Mandy with the interior work, and Moses is a whiz with the plants. He installed most of the ferns and the entire butterfly garden right by himself."

Jake chuckled. "It's a good thing we have a laundry room on site. He looks like a mudball when he finishes. I've had him bring a change of clothes so we can soak the ones he wears. Take some of the work off his grandma, you know."

Jake guided us onto a slate pathway, pointing to the newly distributed plants. "I'll try to remember the names without looking on the plan drawing. Moses will be along 'terectly, so if I miss anything, I'm sure he can tell you exactly."

Beneath the shade of a Southern magnolia, the koi pond was nestled between banks of ferns. A submerged pump pushed water over stacked slate rocks to form a series of waterfalls. Jake pointed to each clump of vegetation, calling them by name.

"Sheila said that there would be moss growing on the rocks before long. It'll look more natural then." Jake motioned toward a small stand of shrubs in the shade of a massive live oak tree. "The bird area is over there in the semi-shade."

Three feeders were suspended from overhanging branches of a massive live oak. A boulder with a carved-out bowl depression served as a birdbath. Saw palmettos and berry-producing plants lined the periphery.

"Now, follow the slate path. It's wide and smooth enough for wheelchairs, by the way — Piddie did the test run for us. It leads to the butterfly/hummingbird sanctuary."

Three large cement urns contained mixtures of purple-leafed sweet potato vine, wild petunias, black-eyed susans, and clumps of dye flower coreopsis, Florida's official wildflower.

I pointed to a shrub with pointed dark green glossy leaves. "Is that a tea olive bush?"

"Sure is. Good eye, Sister-girl. Kelly's tried to incorporate native species — like this rhododendron here — with low maintenance plants that are drought and temperature resistant for north Florida. The tea olive will provide flowers even in the winter when other plants are dormant. There's a night blooming jasmine over there, too."

"I remember that plant! Aunt Piddie had several in the back yard of her little house on Morgan Avenue. It blooms only at night with the sweetest, most heavenly scent. Too bad they can't bottle that aroma. I'd buy a case."

"What I really like about this whole deal, other than the use of plants from the area, was that she worked around the established trees and shrubs. We had to remove a few of the old diseased azaleas, but we've kept pretty much everything else. Kelly found an old rose bed of mother's that had gone wild. Said it contained a lot of antique varieties, and she's going to keep the spot like it is — maybe put in a sitting bench.'"

Jake pointed to a series of iron trellises at the rear of the garden. "There are several flowering vines planted, too. We'll add to the plantings as time and money allow."

Jake motioned to the dense thicket. "We'd like to continue the slate path through the woods. My goal is to make the entire lot one enormous garden, all handicapped-accessible."

I turned in a slow circle, studying the layout of the lot. "I never realized how big this property was."

"We have over four acres to play with. The Triple C will be a Southern showplace when we're done with it. Maybe we'll get written up in *Southern Living* magazine! It could happen. A girl has to have a dream!" Jake batted his eyelashes, then reached over and ran his hand playfully through my damp hair. "Now, Sister-girl, we'd better get you back inside so Mandy can tackle your coiffure before the party starts."

"I heard it said that the Devil's in the details. Reckon that's why some lawyers love them so much."

    Piddie Davis Longman

CHAPTER THREE

Daniel "Hank" Henderson, Attorney

THE INTERCOM BUZZER SOUNDED on Daniel H. "Hank" Henderson's private phone.

"Yes, Maxie?"

"Umm…Mr. Henderson…umm…there's a Mr., what was your name? A Mr. Alfonso Williams here to see you."

Dumb blonde bitch secretary. Why the hell Janice had to go and get herself pregnant again at age forty, and leave was beyond his comprehension. How could a woman her age actually choose to have a clinging brat to take care of? Well, it was her husband's deal to pay her way, now. None of his concern. And, this latest broad…Maxie…jeezus! It had taken her two freakin' weeks to learn to use the intercom instead of popping her cow face through the door every time someone came in for an appointment.

"Mr. Henderson?" Maxie's voice prompted.

"Send him in!" Hank snapped.

"Right away, sir."

The hurt in his secretary's voice was immensely irritating. Alfonso Williams bound into his office like he was tuned in to the hard driving bass rap beat Hank despised with all of his being.

"Shut the door!" Hank said.

A brief flash of white-hot hatred fleeted across Alfonso's dark eyes before his features returned to their normal state of disdainful disinterest.

"Where the hell have you been?" Hank asked. "I sent word for you two days ago!" Damned black boys. If he could find one poor white-trash teenager to corrupt, he would be blasted if he ever had to deal with the likes of Alfonso again.

Alfonso Williams shrugged and shuffled over to Hank's mocha brown leather couch. Hank watched in disgust as the youth flopped onto the buttery soft upholstery and slung his filthy high top sneakers onto an armrest. The muscles popped and churned on Hank's temples as he clenched his teeth to avoid striking the insolent teen.

"*Mis*ter Williams, I have some work for you to do. Some errands. Important errands."

Alfonso ran his tongue across his new front gold crown. "I got a new boy for yo' yard. I ain't doin' the yard work no more."

Hank hoisted his belted pants over his distended belly. "I don't give a good *gotdamn* about the yard, boy."

Anger flickered in Alfonso's eyes.

"You need to be by my house today around 2:00 PM. to pick up a load of...," Hank hesitated, enjoying the charade, "...clothes to donate to the local Goodwill store."

"Yeah. Right." Alfonso nodded.

The *clothes bags* would contain a combination of stereo components, laptop computers, hand guns, jewelry, possibly a Ziploc bag of black market amphetamines or painkillers; all overflow from the evidence room in Midview's Police Department's headquarters, compliments of Hank's cousin, Lamar Mason.

Hank lit a cigar and blew the thick blue smoke toward the couch. "Who's this new boy?"

Alfonso's eyes watered. He blinked to clear his vision. "Moses Clark."

He motioned with the lit cigar. "What came of that other kid? I don't remember his name."

"Marcus. His daddy said he can't work for you no more."

Hank slammed his fist on the walnut desk. "Since when do *any* of you turn down money? Half y'all live in stinking one room shacks a rat wouldn't set foot in!" Hank stood and peered out at the small garden patio beyond the double doors of his private office.

How was he supposed to help these people if they couldn't get off their lazy butts long enough to work a decent job? They'd rather steal for a living. All of 'em — thieves. Every last damn one.

Alfonso's dead stare bored into the back of Hank Henderson like a jagged, rusty knife, deeply cutting the white man's heart out of his greedy chest. "Moses stays with his grandma. She's got high blood and can't work much. He need the money."

Hank brushed a piece of lint from his tailored pants. "This Moses. He got any brothers or sisters?"

"One sister." Alfonso glared at Hank, awaiting his next question.

"Reckon she might need money, too?"

"She's just eight."

Hank's sleazy grin slid over his features like an oil spill spoiling an overdeveloped strip of beach. "That never seemed to stop 'em before. Money's money, Alfonso, my boy. I'll pay her well for her...services."

Alfonso frowned. "Moses ain't gonna go for none of it."

"Moses doesn't have to know. Tell him I'll pay him three times what he'll get elsewhere. When he gets used to the cash, he won't worry so much when his sister starts coming 'round." Hank flipped through his phone number file and snatched the receiver from its cradle. "Don't be late. I want that stuff out of my house today."

Dismissed, Alfonso slowly rose and shuffled from the room.

"Maxie!" Hank barked into the intercom. "No more visitors today. I've got one call to make, then I have to leave for the day."

After a brief call to his cousin in Midview, Hank slicked his thinning dark gray hair back with a comb, checked his capped teeth in a mirror, and grabbed an oxblood red leather briefcase.

As an afterthought, he turned toward the secretary and flashed a smile before he pushed his way through the glass double doors. "You can go on home early today, honey. I won't be back in this afternoon. Why don't you take yourself over to the new spa and enjoy a little of the grand opening? That's where I'm headed."

Maxie's expression brightened. "Thank you, Mr. Henderson!"

Hank flipped the keyless entry button on his gold keychain. The Mercedes flashed its lights once in a seductive wink to announce the deactivation of the alarm. No need, really, to arm the system here at the office. The location next door to the Chattahoochee Police station assured safety. He just liked the feeling that he *could*.

A self-satisfied smile teased his lips. Mercedes — the mark of someone who's made it. At least his business endeavors allowed him to drive a fine piece of German machinery. Not like the Detroit pieces of shit the local hillbillies called transportation.

The new sedan he'd ordered would put this whole county in awe — a black opal metallic Mercedes 500, S class series with gray leather interior. He mentally tabbed through the list of options: sport package, command system, brake assist, killer sound system, active suspension, and a GPS that would alert Mercedes if the air bags deployed. The impressive automobile would rack up at least $100,000 by the time tax, title, and destination charges were added.

Just a few more months to make sure his distributors had paid his foreign bank accounts, one or two more deliveries from his interbred screwball cousin in Midview to top off the coffers, and he'd have ample means to take the sweet automobile on his last ride out of this hick town. He'd see the rural blight from its best vantage; retreating like a shot cur dog in his rear view mirror.

Hank started the ignition and wheeled the Mercedes into the street. Pausing once to check his reflection in the lighted vanity mirror, he grimaced at the thought of attending another dull Chattahoochee business opening.

"If I didn't need to keep an eye on that Piddie Longman biddy, I'd blow this off and go to Destin for the night. Hell, maybe I'll just head on down there after I check things out…as long as Alfonso shows up like he's supposed to."

There'd always be some easily-bribed female tourist ripe for the picking on the strip of beaches the locals called the *Redneck Rivera*. Drive a fancy car, whip some cash around, and they would fall at your feet; anxious to please and stupid as a stick, just the way Hank liked them.

The Triple C Day Spa and Salon

In her usual tradition, Elvina Houston was the first party guest to arrive. Piddie Longman maintained that Elvina came first and left last so she wouldn't miss a thing or provide an opportunity to be talked about. Elvina wore a bright blue, yellow, and hot pink hibiscus-print cotton sundress accessorized with a straw purse and large-brimmed sunhat tied with a yellow grosgrain ribbon.

"Mornin', Elvina," Piddie called from her station at the receiving table. "Don't believe you'll need that sunhat this mornin'. Too cloudy. You look like you're gettin' ready to meet the love boat to Jamaica."

Fully armed for the nice/nasty form of southern-women banter she lived for, Elvina smiled and cocked her head to one side. "And, you look like somethin' out of a Susie Wong movie, shuga…"

Piddie smoothed the satin material. "Ain't this red kimono beautiful? Evelyn made one for each of us — different colors to suit our personalities. She's quite talented, my Evelyn."

Elvina sniffed. "It's a good thing for Joe that she's turned away from cookin'. I heard he's eatin' out at the Homeplace near every day at lunch." Elvina looked around the front parlor. "Lordy mercy! If this isn't a lovely place now! It's every bit as grand as when Betsy Lou Witherspoon first moved in."

Piddie nodded. "Better. She had the tackiest taste this side of the Mason/Dixon line…kinda like Elvis Presley and Graceland. Don't you remember the time the old bat redid her kitchen to look like a 40's diner?"

Elvina swatted the air with one hand. "I had forgotten all about that! She gave that fancy tea, remember? That was when Sissy Pridgeon was still alive. Lawdsy, I can still see the look on Sissy's face when she walked into Betsy Lou's kitchen. As I recall, it was a most ungodly combination of colors."

Piddie chuckled. "Betsy Lou was colorblind, you know. That's why her clothes never matched just right. She had the money to hire a decorator, but insisted on doing it herself and *allowin' the experience to overcome her.*"

Elvina smiled and adjusted her hat so that it tipped flirtatiously over one eye. "Good thing Jake had some fashion sense. He was, I believe, around ten or eleven at the time. He told his mama what no one else in this town dared — that the colors were downright tacky! She let him redo the entire house after folks went on about how he saved the kitchen. Amazing, isn't it? That his talent showed up at such a young age."

Piddie shrugged. "Not really. I'm sure you and I were naturals the very first time we held a phone receiver in our hands."

The two old women dissolved into fits of laughter.

"What are you two cackling about?" Jake asked. He placed a bamboo-trimmed handmade book on the table by Piddie.

Piddie winked at Elvina. "Just reminiscing 'bout old times — somethin' you do when you get to the point where there's more life a-layin' behind you than stretched out in front."

Jake pecked Piddie on one heavily rouged cheek. "I hope you'll have many more years out in front." He patted the towering sides of Piddie's coifed hair. "Your hair is positively a work of art today, Pid. That color goes perfectly with your kimono."

Piddie's hair, due to her last color rinse, was a pale shade of shell pink. Small oriental fans were stuck between the tall layered mound of stiff curls. Delicate dangling gold fan earrings and red satin slippers complimented her ensemble.

Piddie batted her eyelashes. "You're such a charmer, Jake Witherspoon. If I was sixty years younger, and you leaned toward the female side for your philanderin's, I'd take you under my wing and show you a thing or three!"

"That's damn near enough to scare him straight," Elvina said. She pointed toward the table. "What's the little book for?"

"It's a guest sign-in keepsake for little Sarah. One of Jon's friends in the ER over at Tallahassee Memorial made it," Jake said.

"Well…that's nice. Where is Jon?"

"He's upstairs grooming Elvis. You're goin' to love his outfit! Evelyn made him a little doggie kimono for the party. That little Pomeranian was, I remind you, the 2000 Georgia Calendar Dog for December."

"I'd heard. But, is that altogether sanitary…havin' a dog in here?"

Elvina wrinkled her nose like she smelled something foul.

Jake smirked. "It's only for the grand opening. He's great at meetin' and greetin'. Otherwise, he'll be confined to the upstairs private quarters when Jon's visiting. Besides, that canine probably takes more baths than most people in this town. I know Jon spends more time on Elvis' hair than I do mine. That little dog wouldn't know a flea if one slipped up and bit him on the behind!"

"I don't know how Jon stands to drive every day in that Tallahassee traffic," Elvina said. "Why...just last Wednesday, Miz Lucille and I rode over to an interfaith women's mission meeting at the Ramada, and some lady pulled right out in front of me. I stood the car on its nose tryin' to keep from hittin' her! And the funny part? She had one of those bumper stickers that said *GOD IS MY COPILOT.* I told Miz Lucille that, judging by the way that woman was slingin' her car around, she maybe oughta move over and let Him do the drivin'!"

Jake plucked a ladybug from the floral arrangement on the entrance table. "The other day when I was over there picking up some supplies for the party, I saw some fella in one of those big ole SUV's almost run over a biker on Thomasville Road. The poor guy was in the designated lane especially for bicycles. You know what the SUV's bumper sticker said? *SHARE THE ROAD. BIKES BELONG!*"

Elvina leaned in, a conspirator with a mission. "I reckon Jon will move on over here once he starts his job with Hospice, then?"

Jake propped his hands on his hips. "Sure doesn't take long for things to get around!"

Piddie punched him playfully in the arm. "Aww...c'mon, Jake. You've lived here long enough to know there ain't any secrets. At least, not as long as Elvina and I can draw a breath."

"That's right," Elvina said. "Besides, the Bible teaches for you to love your neighbor like your own self. How you supposed to do that if you don't know what's happenin' to them?" She tapped the brim of her hat. "I think I'll go on back and look around before the crowd arrives. Oh! I almost forgot!" She dug around in her straw bag and retrieved a small wrapped package. "This is a little somethin' for the baby."

Jake pointed to the far side of the parlor. "There's a gift table set up over by the fountain."

"Let me say that I think it's wonderful what you're doin' to help out those Clark children. Their Grandma Maizie's a fine woman. It's a cryin' shame she's havin' to take on the responsibility of raisin' those younguns. I suppose it happens a lot, nowadays. The younger generation's too busy out druggin' and drinkin' to mind the babies they've spawned."

Jake sighed. "Yeah. We see it a lot around here — particularly with the folks that don't have a lot of money to live on. Moses and Tameka are a pleasure to have around, and a big help."

"And, at least you're not lookin' for a public pat on the back like that oily Hank Henderson." Elvina sniffed.

"Well, I gotta flit around a bit. Make yourself at home, Elvina." Jake headed toward the kitchen.

Elvina reached down to pat her old friend on the hand. "Piddie, I'll come back and draw up a chair to keep you company after I tour the spa."

Piddie grinned. "Alright. That way, we can see everything's goin' on, and talk about people as they come by."

"My thoughts exactly, shuga."

Hattie

I settled into one of the cushioned high-back chairs next to Aunt Piddie. As the morning progressed, more townsfolk filtered in to view the newly redecorated mansion. Leigh and Bobby brought little Josh at 11:00. In his tan and black elfwear kimono and diapers, my nephew resembled a miniature Sumo wrestler. His chubby, solid body had earned him the nickname *Tank,* a label that would no doubt stick with him until he was a burly, testosterone-infested linebacker for the local football team: Tank Davis, first string linebacker for the Chattahoochee Yellow Jackets.

The babies entertained themselves on a handmade quilt spread in the center of the front parlor, purposely far removed from any breakable decorations. People stopped to say their first hellos to Sarah, who looked delicate and fragile in comparison to her newly acquired first cousin.

"How you holdin' up, gal?" Piddie asked.

"Fine. I thought Sarah would be fussing for a nap by now, but she seems to thrive on the attention and activity."

"I love my little Chinaberry!" Piddie waved and cooed toward the quilt.

Sarah had been fascinated with my elderly aunt from their first meeting. Whenever Piddie was near, Sarah's eyes periodically sought her out, as if she was checking to make sure my aunt was still there.

"Goo-gah!" Sarah giggled and pumped her arms in our direction.

Piddie waved. "Goo-gah to you, my little Chinaberry!" she called out. Then, to me, "I do believe that's the sweetest little nickname Sarah's pinned to me. Don't have a clue what Goo-gah means, but if she's picked it out, then that's who I'll be."

I studied my aunt's wrinkled profile. "Evelyn says you haven't been feeling well."

"Honey, at my age, if I get up in the mornin' and somethin' don't hurt somewhere, I figure I've died durin' the night."

"Evelyn seems pretty worried about you."

Piddie swatted a hand in the air. "She worries if I chip my nail polish. I've just been a little tired and short'a breath lately. I guess that's to be expected at ninety-eight years of age. I ain't no spring chicken."

We sat in silence for a moment, watching the babies play amidst the milling crowd.

Piddie heaved a sigh. "Evelyn's set up an *appoint-mint* next week with some fella in Tallahassee. Supposed to specialize in *jerry-actricks*. You know what they'll write on my chart when I go in there, don't you?"

"Hmm?"

Piddie stuck her chin in the air. "L.O.L."

"What does that mean, Pid?"

"It stands for *little old lady*, and it means they won't lissen to a thing I say!"

I chuckled. "You know, you probably aren't too far from the truth."

"Well, I'll go on over there to humor Evelyn. It won't be so busy here at the spa they can't handle the reception desk for a few hours while I'm gone." Piddie stared at the front entrance with keen interest. "Well...if it ain't the devil's apprentice, hisself. God knows — Satan has a pitchfork warmin' up for that man, just waitin' for him to kick the bucket and come to claim it."

We watched as Hank Henderson oozed into the room and immediately glommed onto the Mayor.

"Jimmy T.! How ya doin', son?" Hank said in a loud voice. He pumped Mayor Jimmy T. Johnson's hand like he was trying to siphon water from a deep well.

The mayor beamed. "Mr. Hank Henderson, where you been keepin' yourself?"

Hank pushed his hands in his pockets and rocked back and forth on his heels. He puffed his chest out like a banty rooster. "Keepin' busy. A lot to do for folks in this area, you know."

"You sure are a dedicated citizen. I was just talking to a couple of the council members just t'other day. You're 'bout due to receive the golden key to the city — what with your work with the underprivileged youths in the black community."

Hank flashed a saccharine-laced smile. "I do it *purely* out of love for this fine little town, Jimmy T."

The mayor dabbed a trickle of sweat from his pudgy face. "Your daddy would've been proud. He always was involved with civic projects when he was alive. This town sure lost an asset when he passed."

"Why, thank you, Mayor. It's always good to hear such fine words. 'Scuse me, let me go over and say hello to the guest of honor."

"Certainly, Hank. You stop by the city hall sometime, and we'll go grab some lunch." He patted the attorney on the back.

Piddie and I watched Hank approach the quilt where Sarah and Josh were playing, oblivious to the milling crowds surrounding them. The hair on my neck prickled. When Hank reached down to touch Sarah's face, she let out an ear-piercing shriek that made several of the older party guests reach to fine tune their hearing aides. Clearly shocked, Hank snatched his hand away.

The room fell silent. Thirty pairs of eyes watched the small drama on the center stage.

"What'd you do to that child, Hank?" Mayor Johnson asked. "Quote her your fees?"

A ripple of laughter rolled around the room.

"I…I don't rightly know. I just love little girl babies. They usually take to me right off!" When he reached for Sarah the second time, she squealed louder than before and crawled off the quilt toward us. Josh reached over and bonked Hank's hand with a slobber-laden plastic pop bead.

I scooped Sarah into my arms. She turned her head and studied Hank with huge dark eyes.

Jimmy T. came to Hank's defense. "Must'a been your boyish charm, Hank."

"Come here to Goo-gah, little Chinaberry." Piddie settled the baby onto her lap. Sarah whimpered and reached up to pat Piddie's wrinkled face.

Hank shrugged. "I guess not all women can handle my good looks." He chuckled nervously and left the room in search of someone more easily impressed.

Jake appeared behind us. "What was *that* all about?" he asked in a low voice. "I heard Sarah squeal from the back of the mansion."

"She knows what we all know about Hank Henderson," Piddie said. "There ain't enough money in the world to buy class."

By the end of the afternoon, many of the residents of Chattahoochee, Sneeds, Greensboro, and Mt. Pleasant had stopped in to say hello and tour the Triple C. My friends from Tallahassee, Chris, Kelly, and Kathy, had driven over, promising to visit us on the Hill. The appointment books had filled for the first two weeks. Both of the Bed & Breakfast owners had discussed adding a spa package to their vacation specials, and the new owners of the local golf course took a stack of business cards for the clubhouse. Though Wanda Orenstein had yet to arrive, the members of the black community who attended the open house had expressed interest in her rumored expertise with hair weaves. Jake and Mandy's dream of providing a haven for all members of the surrounding communities was taking shape.

Evelyn's kimonos were a big hit. She took ten orders for the oriental influence designs. Several infant elf-wear designs were purchased for upcoming baby showers. Melody proudly displayed her new line of *scenes from the inner city* nail polish and handed out free samples of cuticle remover and conditioner. Stephanie borrowed a seated massage chair from one of her friends in Tallahassee and spent the day giving ten-minute shoulder and neck massages. Clad in a bright yellow satin kimono, Mandy flitted between her hair salon post and the kitchen, making sure Tameka and her brother kept the serving platters filled.

After the last of the lingering guests departed, we crowded into the front parlor. Bobby and Leigh took Moses and Tameka home, laden with platters of leftover food for Grandma Maizie.

"Whew!" Mandy plopped down on a cushioned chair. "I don't know about you guys, but my dogs are tired." She removed the satin slippers and rubbed her feet.

"Amen on that one, honey," Jake said. "Poor little Elvis fell asleep right in the middle of the hair salon. Jon's upstairs asleep. He has to pull an eleven-to-seven tonight. I'll be so glad when he's through with hospital shift work."

"It had to be good for him to be introduced around to everyone," Stephanie said. "There're a lot of folks here who will probably be patients of his some day."

Jake smirked. "Well, thanks to someone we all know and love — I won't mention any names, but she has tall pink hair — everyone in town knows that Jon's nickname is *sugar monkey*. Course, they've shortened it down. Everyone's calling him *Shug Presley*!"

Piddie grinned. "He didn't say it was a gospel secret. I figured it was all right to tell."

"It would've got out, eventually, Jake," Mandy said. "Besides, *Shug Presley* kind of has a nice, warm, nurse-y ring to it, don't ya think?"

Jake shrugged. "Maybe. I'm just too tired to dwell on it right now. Jon doesn't seem to mind."

Mandy sat bolt upright like she'd been stabbed with a straight pin. "That slime ball Hank Henderson! You won't *bee—lieve* what he said to me!"

Jake smirked. "Somethin' politically incorrect, no doubt. The man's an absolute cretin."

"Well...he was watchin' Tameka carry a plate of cheese balls into the front parlor, and he says *who's the pretty little pick-a-ninny?* Well... I said, *I think that saying went out with the Civil War. If you can't say African-American, or just, black, don't say anything at all!*"

"That jerk," I said.

Mandy frowned. "He launched into this long song and dance about how *everyone's so sensitive these days...squealing sexual harassment over what used to be considered fun.* It was disgusting...and, the way he looked at Tameka. It gave me the heebee-jeebee's."

Aunt Piddie huffed. "Don't you worry. I'll be keepin' a watchful eye over Mister Henderson!"

"That goes for me, too," Elvina said.

"I never thought I'd see the day when the wing part of a chicken would be so popular. Used to be, that was the part I'd eat to save the good pieces for ever'one else."

   Piddie Davis Longman

Hattie's Devil-Hot Wings

2 ½ lbs. chicken wings, cut up
½ stick of margarine or butter, melted
½ cup Louisiana hot sauce
1/8 cup lemon juice
½ tsp. dried basil
1 pkg. Good Season's Italian Dressing Mix

Broil lightly salted wings until crisp on each side. Switch oven from broil to 400°. Marinate wings with sauce mixture above as they cook, turning to coat both sides. This will take about ten to fifteen minutes depending on the size of the wings. Lightly sprinkle cooked wings with additional hot sauce after cooking if hotter wings are desired. Serve warm with carrot and celery sticks and either ranch or bleu cheese dressing as a dipping sauce.

CHAPTER FOUR

The Davis Homestead

LATE SPRING WEATHER in the northern panhandle of Florida is unpredictable. Some years, the allotment of low humidity and mild temperatures lasts for a mere two to three weeks. The heat builds and the very thought of venturing outside after ten AM or before eight PM can send even the hardiest native into a full-blown sinking spell.

This year, we were blessed with three months of temperate days and cool nights. The home improvement stores geared up to cash in on the biological fact that human psyches are wired for spring yard work. Some mechanism clicks *on*, and a soothing voice beckons — *go dig a hole in the yard…several of them! Don't worry about what you'll put in the holes. That will come.*

I was happy as a fat feeder pig in mud — up to my armpits in hoes, shovels, and fertilizer, digging holes all over the Hill. Clumps of narcissus, lirope, and daylilies needed to be divided and replanted, which created even more holes to fill with loads of top soil hauled in from — yet, another gaping hole I'd created at the edge of the woods.

Holston found his property maintenance niche in the form of a shiny new green and yellow John Deere mulching riding mower. He and Bobby left early one Saturday on an expedition to locate the perfect piece of machinery to properly trim the three acres of grass lawn surrounding the farmhouse.

Several hours later, they bounced up the sandy lane with the new mower lashed into the bed of Bobby's faded blue pick-up truck. After carefully unloading the machine via the ramps Bobby had thoughtfully provided, the two men took turns slicing wide arcs into the lawn, stopping often to grunt over some newly discovered adjustment. The first time they mowed the acreage, it took three times longer than necessary. A great deal of male bonding had to happen between the breaks for actual work.

Being female (and, therefore, obviously an idiot in their eyes), the one thing I couldn't quite fathom was the need for headlights on a riding mower. Why would you possibly ever mow at night during the time of year when daylight extended from six in the morning till almost nine at night? Perhaps, if your buddies stopped in late for a visit, the bright beams would come in handy, allowing you to demonstrate the amazing qualities of the machine without running over the dog in the dark.

Like most of the discrepancies in the male/female view of life, things evened out in the long run. Holston and Bobby couldn't wrap their male minds around the fact that Leigh and I could go shopping for new black pumps when we already had, between us, seven pair. Or, that we could cuss and discuss daytime soap opera plots and players as if they were members of the family. I'd somehow allowed myself to be drawn into the daytime dramas' tangled web during recuperation from surgery. Now, I was right up there with Jake and Aunt Piddie, either watching or recording my shows, and Oprah, with a single-minded vengeance I'd previously reserved for football games.

One area where Holston and I were similar — our notion of the sovereignty of the remote. Late in the evening when Sarah was settled into her crib with Shammie keeping diligent watch over her dreams, we drew straws for the title of the *official remote ruler.*

The only occasion it was nonnegotiable was during a Florida State football game. As soon as I left the room for a potty break, Holston would blatantly flip the channel to some science-based documentary on whale sex. The fact that there were two perfectly good remote-controlled televisions in the house made little difference. The kitchen was the place to be. The most comfortable easy chairs were there, and the refrigerator. The bathroom was only six steps away. Holston and Jon were convinced that, if Jake and I could insert do-it-yourself catheters for a televised football game, we'd eliminate *that* annoying break altogether.

Counting the VCR, television, and cable box, we had three separate remotes with which to contend. I drew the line when Holston noticed a remote-controlled ceiling fan at the Home Depot. Limits have to be set.

On one occasion, I removed the main channel control batteries. Standing behind the kitchen island counter, I strained against laughter as I watched my usually sensible, calm husband try to change the station. He shook the control, moved closer to the TV to try again, frantically pushing buttons and scratching his head like a frustrated ape trying to peel a rubber banana. When I confessed my prank, he claimed it was *the meanest, lowest thing I'd done to him since we'd known each other*. He was waiting until I relaxed my vigil, then he'd strike back with an evil revenge of his own.

"You want popcorn tonight?" Holston asked, buttering me up to make me watch a Home and Garden show instead of ESPN.

"Is it the no-fat kind?"

He studied the package. "Butter-rich, movie gallery…," he read.

"In that case, yes." I could watch Bob Villa for a half-hour.

At eleven, bleary-eyed from staring at the television and a full day of putzing around the yard, we finally surrendered the day.

Nothing can pump a gallon-sized squeeze of adrenaline straight to your heart like the ring of the bedside phone at two AM.

"Hattie?" Joe's voice was tinged with urgency.

"Joe? Wha…something's wrong?" I fumbled for the small halogen reading light above my side of the bed. Holston rolled over and squinted with one half-opened eye.

Joe's voice quivered. "Hattie…it's Piddie. Evelyn's gone with her in the ambulance to Tallahassee."

I was fully awake now. "She okay? What's wrong? Stroke? Is it a heart attack?"

"Hattie," Joe interrupted. "They think she may be going into congestive heart failure. She woke us up about a half-hour ago. Said she was having trouble catching her breath. I'm getting ready to leave and go on over in the Towncar. I just thought you'd want to know."

"Yeah…thanks." I turned to Holston. "We've got to go to TMH. Aunt Piddie's heading to the ER. It's her heart. I've got to call Bobby… and Jake!"

Holston, always the calming influence, rummaged around the bedside chair for his shorts and shirt. "We'll need to call someone to watch Sarah. You know how emergency rooms are. It could be hours while we wait on a doctor's diagnosis."

I grabbed the phone. "Margie. I'll call Margie. She'll come."

By the time we dressed, made the necessary calls, and located the keys to Betty, Margie appeared at the kitchen door.

"Y'all go on, now. Don't wake Sarah. I'll just sleep on the couch. I spent many a night here after your daddy died, before Miz Tillie felt okay staying alone. Call me as soon as you hear something."

"Okay. Sarah's cereal is in the cupboard…there's milk, and she likes bananas crushed up…." I struggled to call up baby-related details.

Margie smiled and patted my arm. "Honey, I raised four of my own, and I'm workin' on spoiling the grandkids now. I'll make do. Go on and be with your family."

I hugged her hard. "What would I do without you?"

"Just roll over and die, I reckon. Now, git!"

The interstate drive between Chattahoochee and Tallahassee took forty minutes between the Hill and the first set of capital city exits. Except for an occasional eighteen-wheeler beating a lonely path in the blackness, little traffic shared the road. The three-level parking garage in the block adjacent to the hospital was deserted when Holston pulled Betty into a spot. We hustled up the ramp to the hospital's rear entrance.

"Liddyanne Longman?" I asked the check-in nurse.

Before she could answer, Joe appeared behind us. "Piddie's back in room five.

Evelyn's with her. They'll only allow one family member in with her at a time."

We followed Joe to the waiting area. The usual raging hubbub of human activity was absent this early on a weekday morning. Fridays and Saturdays were the opposite. Hoards of wounded, beaten, and sick people filled the plastic molded chairs. Many had several family members in tow. Unless you were bleeding profusely, or fell out on the floor, you waited and waited and waited.

"Do you know anything yet?" Holston asked.

Joe raked a hand through his thinning hair. "Just that she was in congestive heart failure. Her lungs had all but filled up with fluid before she let on that anything was wrong. A little longer, and she might not've made it."

"Lasix…did they give her Lasix?" I recalled the medication's name from the time of my father's heart ailment.

"A lot of it on the way over here…through an IV. She's comfortable now. They'll probably move her to the third floor cardiac unit as soon as the doctor writes the orders."

My friend Mary Mathues stuck her head into the waiting area. "I thought I recognized your aunt's name, Hattie."

I rushed to hug my dear friend. Her nursing skills and compassion had helped me and my family through some tough spots in the last few years.

Mary smiled at Joe and Holston. "I'll try to get some details for you guys. How's Sarah? I hated missing the open house at the spa. I had to pull a double shift the night before the party, and I was shot! Maybe I can call, and come over one weekend soon."

"We'd love that. You're always welcome. The baby's great. We left her with our neighbor, Margie. I know you'll just fall in love with Sarah — like everyone else has."

"Can't wait to meet her. Now, y'all sit tight, and I'll go snoop." Mary pushed through the swinging doors and disappeared down the long hallway.

Several minutes later, she returned. "Dr. Ketchler is with her. She's going to be admitted to the cardiac unit." Mary reached over and held my hand. "Many people live with congestive heart problems. There are medications to help, Hattie. They'll probably run tests on her tomorrow and figure out the best regimen."

If you want to know anything in a hospital, ask a nurse. "Thanks, Mary."

"Let me get on back to work before I'm missed. My shift ends at seven, and I'll come find you."

Evelyn's face appeared in the window of the door separating the emergency ward from the waiting area. She stuck her head out and motioned toward us.

"One of y'all want to go on back and sit with Mama for awhile? They won't let two of us stay back there with her at one time. She's just waiting for a room upstairs, and I need to use the little girls' room."

I nodded. "I'll go in. She's in five, right?" I waved toward Holston and Joe, then slipped past the security guard who could've passed for *Mayberry, RFD*'s Barney Fife's younger brother.

Piddie looked peaceful when I opened the door. For a brief moment, I thought she was dead.

She opened her eyes and smiled. "Did I scare you? Ever'time I would drift off to sleep, Evelyn would panic." She patted the side of the gurney. "Come sit yourself down a spell."

An IV was connected to her left wrist. Electrode wires hung like Christmas tree lights from the monitor beside the bed. The LED screen displayed her vital signs.

I leaned down and kissed her wrinkled cheek. Even in the green fluorescent glare of the overhead lights, she looked healthy and substantial. "I was so scared, Pid."

"How'd you think I felt? *Am-boo-lanch* sirens scare the beejeezus outta me anyway! Much less havin' to be on the inside'a one!"

I eased onto a seat beside her gurney. "You seem to be breathing okay."

"That *Lay-sticks* is a miracle drug. Only bad part — I'm peeing like it was the best idea I ever had! I've used the bedpan five times already."

Piddie noticed the fear in my eyes. "Honey, my old heart's just about shot. Lordie, I'm ninety-eight years old. They gonna put me upstairs and run a gob of expensive tests. They love to do that! They gonna tell me what I already know — I'm just plain wore out."

"Now, Pid..."

She held up a pudgy hand. "Don't you go patronizin' me, now. I won't abide it! It's only natural that my generation takes leave'a here eventually. It'd get real crowded down here if some of us didn't go on *Home*."

Tears burned my eyes.

She patted my hand. "Now...don't tune up and start, Hattie. Even if I died right now, I'd have nothin' to complain of. I've lived a long life full'a family and friends. I've seen ever' single episode of Oprah she *ever* made, and I've gotten to watch men set foot on the moon!"

The corners of her pale mouth drooped. "I did want my letter from the *Prezedent* for makin' it clean to a *hunnert*, though."

"Maybe you still will if..."

Piddie rolled her eyes. "If frogs had longer legs, they wouldn't scrape their butts when they hopped. C'mon, Hattie!"

I shrugged my shoulders. Sometimes, there are no answers — not even ones you invent to make you feel like you have a modicum of control. "Is there anything you need? Or want?"

Piddie adjusted herself on the stack of pillows. "There. My hind end was goin' to sleep. There're some things you can do for me."

"Just name them."

Piddie leaned over and whispered, "Evelyn gets herself all worked up when I try to talk to her about my passin'-over time. You'll have to help me get a few things past her…without creatin' a stir."

"Okay."

She grinned. "I want a birthday party. I've been thinkin' on it. We can have a big whoop-de-doo at the Woman's Club. Maybe a covered dish. We got some good cooks in town. We can call it *Piddie Longman's Damn Near A Hundred Birthday Party*."

I covered my mouth with one hand to stifle a laugh. "That sounds like fun… but, are you sure you don't want to wait till the real thing?'

Piddie crossed her hands over her chest. "Hattie, you and I both know I more'n likely won't be around to see that. If, by some miracle, I do — we'll pitch another shindig! But, just in case — I want a big ole celebration as soon as they'll let me break out of this joint." She pointed her finger. "And, somethin' else…"

"Yes?"

"I want to be cremated and my ashes scattered in the garden behind the Triple C."

"Wha…?" I stared at my aunt, my mouth agape.

"Close your mouth. You'll catch flies." She tapped my chin. "I ain't never wanted to be planted. Takes up perfectly good ground space. Let's face it, no one comes much to a cemetery after the first few years. Too damn depressin'. If I'm at the spa, all kinda folks'll come by to see me in the garden. Tell Jake to sprinkle me in a nice sunny spot and plant some daisies over me. I do so love daisies! I can be fertilizer for the flowers. I like that idea much better than being all gussied up in a coffin. Always seemed silly to me — layin' there all propped up wearin' your Sunday best like you were expectin' to go somewheres."

Piddie nestled down into the stack of pillows. "Now, get Reverend Thurston Jackson, Lucille's husband, to preach me a good callin'-down-God funeral — right there at the Triple C. None of that mopey, white folk, sad garbage. My life's been a pleasure and a celebration. I'd like for my leavin' to be the same."

Piddie patted me on the hand. I was too stunned and sad to respond. "I know it's a lot to lay on you, honey. But, Evelyn's fractious about this kinda thing. She just falls all to pieces. You're the only one I trust to see it's done up right!"

Piddie grinned. "I been thinkin' on something else, too." Her voice grew low and conspiratorial, though we were alone in the room. "I want y'all to put me a headstone up at the church at the homeplace in Alabama, right next to Carlton's spot."

The puzzled expression on my face sufficed as a reply.

"It's all family history, Hattie. I ain't got enough wind left in me to tell the tale. I got it all recorded in one of my journals, somewheres. Your great grandma Docia had two graves, one she was actually buried in next to my grandpa — the other was just a headstone her daddy put up in the Jones family cemetery. We always called it her *vacation grave.*"

Piddie shifted her weight a little to one side. "I realize my rightful place of rest should be up by Carlton, but I love Chattahoochee so much, and all my friends are there...what's left of them, anyways. If it's done the way I want, folks will see my marker in its dutiful place next to my husband, and I can still be scattered at the spa where everyone can come to visit me."

I released a heavy sigh. "Okay, Aunt Pid."

She patted my cheek. "I knew I could count on you, gal. I'll have me a vacation grave I can float off to if I get tired of hangin' around all of you!" Her bright blue eyes twinkled.

We sat in silence for a moment before she spoke. "One more thing."

I couldn't stand the weight of another barrage of funeral plans.

She gestured with one pudgy hand. "Bring me one of my gowns from home when you come over next time. Evelyn and Joe dashed off without my good bedclothes. These hospital frocks are a bit airish in the rear."

I laughed. The big knot of fear inside of my chest dissolved under the pressure of Piddie's humor. "Know what you mean. When I was in here, I flashed a few unsuspecting people in the halls when I was doing my daily walk with the rolling IV pole."

My aunt Piddie winked as if we were conspirators in a murder mystery. "If I pass over and figure out a way 'round it, I'll let you know I'm a'watchin' over you all."

The vision of Piddie as a winged guardian angel with a two-foot high mound of pink hair made me smile.

"Sometimes, I get to going so hard, I wisht I could fall down. Least then, I could rest while I was gettin' up."

   Piddie Davis Longman

CHAPTER FIVE

Triple C Day Spa and Salon

THE CUSTOMER WAITING AREA at the former Mandy's Cut'n'Curl beauty salon had consisted of three folding directors chairs, one overstuffed high-back seat upholstered in a faded blue and hot pink cabbage rose print, and a wooden magazine rack. With the exception of an occasional patron lulled to sleep by the drone of a professional hair dryer, everyone in the 12 X 60-foot mobile-home-turned-hair-salon joined in the ongoing conversation. While seated underneath the dryer bonnet with a head full of plastic curlers, the local females had mastered the Elvina Houston turn-one-ear-out method for overhearing the chatter.

A well-known Southern tradition dictates; no matter how grandiose or modest the establishment, the closest friends enter through the side door. The Triple C Day Spa and Salon followed in the barefoot steps of its predecessor. Though patrons entered the elegant double doors, they bypassed the formal front parlor and made a beeline to Mandy and Wanda's expansive hair salon. Within three days of the official grand opening, the once barren double workroom was filled with a scattering of kitchen chairs, new color-matched tone-on-tone director chairs, and a few upholstered seats pilfered from the front parlor. Only the vacationers, the *out-a-towners*, graced the reception area.

Wanda Orenstein chewed a piece of Double-Bubble gum like it was her life's sole purpose. She lifted a newly-colored hank of Mrs. Lucille Jackson's hair and cocked her head to one side. The air bubbles she'd artfully trapped into the elastic wad snapped like miniature popguns when she closed her mouth. "You ever think 'bout maybe a short bob, hon?" Wanda made eye contact with the black woman's reflection in the gilded mirror.

"Wouldn't that be a little...young for me?" Mrs. Lucille asked.

Wanda flipped her hand through the air. "*Young* is all in your mind, Miz Lucille. Besides, them that has it, don't know what they got till they're older...and realize it's lost to 'em."

"Uh-huh." Mrs. Lucille nodded. "I heard that."

Wanda tilted her head to one side. "Let's try cutting a little fringe around your face. It'll soften your natural crease lines."

"That another way of saying wrinkles?" Mandy laughed. "I kinda like that!"

"Can't claim it as my own." Wanda popped her gum. "Piddie said it first. I'm just borrowin' it."

Elvina Houston stood in the threshold of the stylist room. "That figures. Sounds like Piddie Longman."

"Hey, Elvina!" Mandy called. "Have you heard from Piddie? How's she gettin' on?"

Elvina sniffed and settled onto an oak kitchen chair. "I'm in constant contact. You can rest assured of that. She'll be comin' home, most likely tomorrow after her doctor makes his rounds. She's holdin' up pretty good for an old woman."

Mandy grinned. "Not that you'd know anything 'bout that, huh?"

Elvina chose to ignore the comment. "I've come to share something with you all. If you don't want to hear it, I'll just mosey on and find some folks that do."

Mandy threw the hairbrushes she was scrubbing into the sink with an exaggerated clatter. "Aw, c'mon, Elvina. You know we depend on you. Do tell!"

"Well…seems Piddie Longman's decided she wants to shock the clock and have her 100th birthday party — let's see — a full year and two months early."

"Shoot, if you get to choose, I think next year — I'll be thirty, again," Wanda said.

Elvina leaned forward, her voice dropping into a low conspiratorial tone. "She don't think she's gonna make it to a hundred."

Mrs. Lucille batted the notion away with a flip of her hand. "That's nonsense, if I ever heard it. Only the good Lawd knows when a person's time on this earth is done. My friend Piddie Longman's strong as an ox. We'll all be pushing up daisies afore she passes on to her reward."

Elvina sniffed. "I'm just tellin' you what she said. Hattie and Evelyn's already talkin' 'bout rentin' the Woman's Club. I think it'll need to be at the fellowship hall at the 1st Baptist Church 'cause it's bigger. They're gonna have a dinner-on-the-grounds. Let everyone bring a covered dish."

Ginny Pridgett, who had one-eared the conversation from her perch underneath dryer number two, perked up. "I'll make my red velvet cake! And some chicken'n' dumplin's."

"You best make the cornbread, too, Miz Ginny." Mandy spoke loudly to overpower the whine of the dryer motor. "If you don't, we'll all have to eat that gummy mess Harriet Olsen passes off as fittin' to eat!"

Ginny Pridgett nodded so hard, her curlers clacked against the dryer dome.

Elvina said, "Be sure y'all tell Stephanie, now. Melody, too."

"I'm listenin'!" Melody called from behind her partition. She rolled her manicurist's chair backwards and leaned over to peer into the stylist salon. "Long as I'm not running this blasted exhaust fan, I can hear okay."

Wanda shook her finger at Melody. "You'd better run it! It'll keep you from bein' higher than Georgia pine off them acrylic fumes!"

"Yeah. Yeah. Yeah," Melody parroted. "I can bring some ambrosia fruit salad…maybe a plate of sliced home grown tomatoes outta Daddy's garden." Melody's blond head bobbed like a cork caught in a trout's mouth. "Creamed corn. I can bring some fresh creamed corn."

Mandy tidied her workspace in preparation for her next patron. Ladonna O'Donnell, local beauty queen and model, was due in shortly for a root touch-up. "Don't you just love this time of year when the fresh vegetables start comin' in? I had my first vine-ripe tomato yesterday. It was so full of acid, it almost turned my mouth inside out! Gah! It was G-double-O -D, Good!"

Vanessa Whitehall woke with a start from underneath dryer number one. The large bag of Dove chocolates and a super size potato chip bag were balanced on her wide double-knit upholstered lap. "I'm tryin' this new diet I saw in a magazine I was readin' the other day. You eat the same stuff for four days, then you get three days off to eat whatever you want. It's supposed to melt away five pounds a week." Vanessa sank back into her warm cocoon and sipped from a liter-sized Pepsi. Her pudgy hand was crammed deep into the potato chip bag.

"Must be one of them *off* days," Elvina said. A titter of laughter rippled through the room.

Mandy's precisely-plucked eyebrows knit together. "I wonder if Evelyn's talked to her kids about coming to the party. Suppose she's tried to contact Karen?"

The room was dead silent.

Lucille cleared her throat. "Well, I'm sure they'll let Byron and Karen know 'bout the party. It wouldn't seem right if Evelyn and Joe's kids weren't here."

Elvina puffed herself up, full of privileged knowledge. "Actually, Piddie and I talked about this very issue just yesterday. Seems Byron and Linda can't come in from Ohio 'cause the boys are involved in some kind of summer science camp.

They're plannin' on comin' down for Thanksgiving. It's not easy to come from so far away on such short notice, after all. Now…as to Karen…"

The women leaned forward intently. The only sound came from the hum of the hair dryers.

Elvina frowned. "Piddie is certain that Evelyn will invite Karen. We all know that gal won't come."

Lucille sighed. "It's a cryin' shame 'bout that girl. Imagine moving off to a big city like Atlanta, changin' your name, and pretendin' to be someone else entirely? I still can't get my mind wrapped around it."

Wanda raised her hand like a first grade student trying to gain the teacher's attention. "Will someone kindly fill me in? Once again, I'm totally lost."

Elvina picked up the gossip game ball and ran it in for a touchdown. "It's the weirdest thing, and nobody talks about it, on account of it hurts Evelyn so much. But…her daughter, Karen, moved off to Atlanta pretty soon after she graduated college. Changed her name to Mary Elizabeth Kensington, started talkin' like she was from England, and no longer even lets on like she knows any of us!"

"That is *so* bizarre. And, here I thought all the real kooks were in South Florida," Wanda said.

Mandy laughed. "I can't believe you said that, when we've lived all our lives with a mental hospital on the main street."

Wanda shrugged. "Well…there's that. I guess I'm tryin' to say that it's strange when it's someone everyone knows."

"I've seen Miss Karen on the TV," Lucille said. "She works for that public television station up there — does those documentaries and such. It's the oddest thing, hearin' her talk with that British accent. You'd never know she come from the South."

Mandy wiped the sweat from her brow. "I reckon whatever will be, will be.

It should prove interesting. That's for sure."

Elvina took a deep breath. *"Any*way… Hattie and Evelyn's plannin' on luggin' a heap of extra chairs from the Hill with Pearl, and they'll need even more to accommodate ever'body. I don't think the church has enough to hold all of Piddie Longman's friends."

"We'll all pitch in, of course. I got a whole shed full of folding yard chairs," Mandy said.

Wanda propped her hands on her hips. "I'm starting to feel like a complete idiot. Who's this Pearl I've been hearin' about? And, is it Betsy? Who's she? Do we see them in here?"

Elvina shook her head. "Betty — not Betsy. They're Hattie's two trucks. Betty's the gold sports utility vehicle she bought before she and Holston Lewis were married. Pearl is her old red pick-up truck. She's had Pearl for goin' on… five, maybe six years or so."

Everyone stared at Wanda, watching for her reaction. She dropped the section of Mrs. Lucille's hair she was holding ready to wrap on a curler. "The folks in the South sure have some weird ways."

"You just gotta understand Hattie Davis Lewis. She always names her automobiles." Elvina tapped her forehead to shake her memory loose. "I don't own as I remember all of 'em. Piddie could tell you."

Mandy stepped up to bat. "As I recall, Elvina…Pearl was the reason you and Piddie had one of your biggest fallin's out."

Elvina squirmed in her seat. "Well, I've since rectified that bit of unfortunate misinformation."

Wanda's auburn eyebrows shot upward. "What was it all about?"

Mandy's green eyes twinkled as she warmed up to deliver the answer. "Elvina spread it around town that Hattie was gay…on account of her drivin' up out at the Davis farmhouse in that little red pick-up truck! It was before Miz Tillie died — that was Hattie's mama — and before Hattie and Holston met and married. Kinda blew that fish clean outta the water, what with Hattie sleepin' with and marrying someone of the opposite sex, huh Elvina?"

"Suppose I was due a lesson in humility. God sends us those lessons, you know." Elvina dug in her straw bag and resurrected a lace-trimmed hankie. She dabbed at the beads of perspiration on her liver-spotted forehead. "It was only natural to assume such at the time. I mean…Hattie was over forty, unmarried, and just so…headstrong! She comes drivin' up in a brand spankin' new pick-up truck, wearin' blue jeans and a mannish flannel shirt. Why, anyone would have drawn the same conclusion."

Mandy stood with the water spray nozzle aimed in Elvina's direction. It took all she could do not to aim it dead on at the busybody's face. "Personally, I don't find anything wrong with the whole homosexual thing. It's not like the whole dang planet's not crowded enough. We should be relieved to let some folks choose their own sex — less babies that-a-way. And, just look at Jake and Jon. You'd not meet two better folks than them. Who cares what goes on in someone's bedroom, anyhow?"

Elvina sniffed. "Well…I reckon a lot of folks have changed their tunes around here on account of Jake Witherspoon. He's just downright decent."

"Judge not lest ye be judged," Lucille said. "It's up to the creator to look each of us over and decide if we've led lives of service and compassion toward our neighbors."

Except for the low hum of the dryers, the room was quiet for a few moments; each woman lost in her own private thoughts.

"Hattie's first car was a dark blue Mustang named Sally — Mustang Sally. Hattie and I took some wild rides down Thrill Hill in that car." Mandy's gaze looked dreamy as she reminisced. "Thrill Hill used to be a whole lot more fun before they planted those three stop signs at the top."

Wanda popped her gum. "I went over Thrill Hill once — years ago. I was here visitin' my cousin Susan. Her brother, J.T. — he got killed in Vietnam — took us over the hill in his folks' Pontiac. It was a load of fun! We used to go slidin' around the Hadley Hills back home in Michigan in the ice and snow, but it still wasn't nothin' compared to that. We bottomed out the shocks when we landed!"

Wanda settled Mrs. Lucille under dryer number four and adjusted the setting. "That was the summer I realized I wanted to move to the South when I got old enough to leave Michigan."

Elvina frowned. "I thought you was from New Jersey."

Wanda handed Lucille a stack of magazines. "Not originally. My folks lived in Michigan when I was growin' up. I lived in Jersey for a few years before I met my second husband and moved to south Florida."

Elvina smiled. "You got a trifle sidetracked, didn't you gal?"

"Yep. I followed three different men to three places I didn't want to live until I finally came to my senses and made it back to the best part of the country."

"And she even has a new admirer — a *rich one*." Mandy winked.

"Do tell!" Ginny Pridgett called out over the roar of her dryer.

Wanda slashed her hand through the air. "No one I'd ever want to brag over."

Elvina stabbed the air with a bony finger. "Who? I'll find out sooner or later. You might as well give."

Mandy had stood it as long as she could. "Seems our town attorney-at-law has been making eyes at his favorite new stylist!"

Elvina's eyebrows shot up. "Lawd! Hank Henderson?!"

Wanda propped her hands on her hips. "Now look, I don't want any of this getting out. I'm not encouraging the man. He kinda gives me the creeps. Although, he is cute in a good ole' boy sort of way."

"It won't make it out of this room," Elvina lied. She'd break her neck sprinting to the phone. Tallahassee Memorial wasn't a long distance call, and Piddie *did* need something to take her mind off her ailments.

Wanda shrugged. "It was strange, really. He kept telling me he could get me anything I needed to make my life more pleasant…stereo…TV…that type of thing. It wasn't like he was offering to buy it for me — more like he was a slick-Willie salesman on commission."

Elvina felt the tips of her fingers burn with the need to pound numbers on the keypad of her new cordless phone. "What you reckon it's all about?"

"I don't know. I didn't get any great romantic feelings. More like I needed to go wash my hands and check for some kind of infestation."

Elvina stood and smoothed her linen skirt. "Well, I've got other errands to run. Be sure to tell Stephanie about the upcoming party so she can start plannin' her covered dish or dessert. Maybe her Hummingbird cake. That's one of Piddie's favorites."

"This a private conversation? Or can any old body join in?" Ladonna O'Donnell propped against the antique door arch at the entrance to the salon. The leggy blonde's shorts were so tight they left no crease to the imagination. Ladonna made no attempt to hide her beauty-star light under a bushel basket.

"We're always open for new blood, hon." Mandy patted the operator's chair seat. "Come take a load off those million dollar legs."

"Whew!" Ladonna eased into the leather chair and pealed the bandanna from her hair. A mass of bleached blonde tresses dropped and swirled around her bare tanned shoulders. "My roots are shinin', Mandy."

Elvina turned to leave. "That ain't all that's shinin'," she muttered under her breath.

▼ ▼ ▼

Hattie

Crowded under the sink in our master bathroom are seven brands of antiperspirant/deodorant, fresh scent baking soda body powder, and two types of disposable flower-fresh wipe tissues. That's only on my side. Holston has an equal number of manly-scented products, body colognes, and aftershave lotions. Neither of us have pathological body odor. A fact of the humid, sultry, wilt-your-fifty-dollar-hairdo South: one day you're dry and smelling like a powder fresh, mountain spring, dew drop, and the next, using the same concoction, you could, as Aunt Piddie so colorfully put it, scare the buzzards off of day-old road kill.

A survey I'd like to see:

BODY ODOR
VS.
SOUTHERN HEAT AND HUMIDITY

Circle the best answer.

1. How many brands of deodorant/antiperspirant do you currently have?

   Less than 2   3-5   10+   Can't count that high

2. What type of delivery system do you prefer?

   Roll-on liquid   Solid white   Clear gel   IV drip

3. How many times within a summer season do you switch products?

   Never   1-4   5-10   Every dang day

UP THE DEVIL'S BELLY

Spring had faded in north Florida. Rather, summer had barreled in and sat on its fragile head. The temperatures were licking into the low 90's, with the promise of 100 degrees looming on the horizon. By midafternoon, waves of radiant heat rose in shimmering waves from the sticky asphalt on the newly-resurfaced parking lots of the uptown antique district. Any woman silly enough to wear spiked sandals found her heal tips permanently gummed into the semisoft tarry pavement. Elvina Houston told it around town that Ladonna O'Donnell had already ruined a brand new pair of hundred dollar cherry-red pumps. Not one of my issues. I had switched to low comfortable footwear in my early thirties.

In the aftermath of Aunt Piddie's wild ride to the emergency room and brief hospitalization, our lives settled into a comfortable routine. On the days I scheduled clients at the Madhatter's Massage Parlor, Sarah accompanied Holston to his office at the Triple C. The baby was content to play at her father's feet on a tufted pallet Evelyn designed. With the slew of built-in baby-sitters, she seldom spent time amusing herself.

Piddie and Sarah often manned the front desk. The combination of jolly, beehive-haired, elderly woman and slobbering, giggling, oriental baby touched the heart of even the most stoic spa patrons. Aunt Piddie had taken to decorating Sarah's hair with silk butterflies, ribbons, or flowers to match the adornments in her own manicotti mound of curls. Between phone call updates from Elvina, daytime soap opera dramas, talk shows, and postal deliveries, Piddie answered the business line and scheduled appointments for nail care, hair styling, massage therapy, and full body scrub/exfoliations. She delighted in reigning order over the four salon operators' schedules, piecing the business hours together like a three-thousand-piece jigsaw puzzle.

Tameka Clark slipped between the front office, spa, and kitchen replenishing the freshly brewed coffee, tea, and finger pastries from the Madhatter's Sweet

Shop. She restored stacks of clean, bleached linens to the massage treatment rooms and tidied the stylist salon between patrons. Since Tameka's Grandma Maizie had fallen ill, Wanda reserved time during the week to help the child clean and tame her long, thick, unruly hair. As a surprise reward for tidying and stocking Wanda's work area without being asked, Wanda planned an elaborate braided hairdo for Tameka featuring handmade pottery beads, just in time for Piddie's party. Tameka and Moses had been hired by Evelyn and Joe to help decorate, attend guests, and clean following the anticipated social function of the summer season.

Evelyn stuck her head around the corner of Holston's private office. "You busy?"

"I can take a break." Holston removed his reading glasses, rubbed his eyes, and pushed back from the computer desk. "My eyes start to cross after awhile."

Evelyn settled into a white wicker rocker. "How's the book comin'?"

"Good. Just making a few last minute revisions. The manuscript's due to my editor in New York next week."

Evelyn leaned toward the computer monitor. "You got Hattie and little Sarah in this one?"

"That's what I'm adding in, actually. I believe it makes the book more personal to relate our adoption story. My editor agreed. Following the case histories from the Tallahassee area adoptive families, our story will take up the final chapter."

Evelyn rocked back and forth and closed her eyes for a moment. "I'm sure it will be just delightful. That book you did on Jake's beatin' was so touching. I cried all over again when I read it, and we all lived through it."

The old rocker creaked in rhythm as she gently swayed to and fro. "I could near 'bout go to sleep right here. There's just somethin' 'bout the sound of a rocking chair that takes the fire right out of a person."

Holston smiled. "Why don't you crawl up in the back bedroom and take a nap?"

Evelyn's eyes snapped open. "Can't do that! I'm putting the finishing touches on Mama's dress for the party. Then, I got to stitch up the linen cloth for the front table where the family'll be sitting."

"Do you know how many people are coming?"

Evelyn blew out a sigh that would've sailed a small boat clean across Lake Seminole. "Lordy-be! At last count, around two hundred! And, that's without mailing out any written invitations. We might as well just run an ad in the newspaper. *Have you ever known Liddyanne Davis Longman? If you have, bring a covered dish and come to her party!*"

"It's an idea, Evelyn. It'd save you some postage."

Evelyn jumped up and pecked Holston on the cheek. "*You* are my favorite Yankee genius! I knew if I laid it out to you, I'd see a way through! Mama can call the folks she wants to invite personally, and we'll put out a — what's it called? An APB? — to invite the folks we might miss."

Holston watched Evelyn head for the door. "Was there anything else you needed? Some other unsettling dilemma I can stumble upon an answer for?"

She spun around so quickly, her multicolored skirt resembled a rabid wildcat caught in a blender. "I'd dang sure lose my head if it wasn't tied on! Mama wants to record her memoirs for the party. Hattie said you have some kind of little tape recorder. Can we borrow it?"

"Certainly. A new box of tapes, too. You're welcome to them. I bought them with the intention of recording my thoughts to transfer to the computer later on, then never touched them. I guess I just like to put pen to paper. I usually end up scribbling notes to myself on anything available, then I use the word processor to edit and help with my spelling."

Holston rummaged in the bottom drawer of the computer armoire and removed a small cassette recorder. "The mike's built in. Just push here and start speaking. I'm no technology geek. It's a no-brainer to operate."

She rested one hand on his shoulder. "You're an answer to prayer, Holston. I'll get this back to you as soon as she's finished with it. Also, I have a number of old family pictures of Mama and Daddy when they were younger, some of the cousins from up home, the grandkids, and folks Mama's known over the years. I wanted to do some kind of presentation at the party. You know, to surprise Mama."

"That, I can help with. Between Hattie and me, we have enough computer knowledge and software to put the pictures on disk. Hattie, I'm sure, can put together a PowerPoint show that will tie them all together, complete with captions."

Evelyn clapped her hands together. "Wonderful! I think this is goin' to be fun! I didn't much warm up to the idea at first...but, Mama's dead set she wants her hundredth birthday party right away."

Evelyn stared out Holston's window into the meditation garden. The magnolia blossoms hung like oversized white cotton balls on the branches next to the house. "She's got it in her head that she's not gonna make it to see a hundred." Evelyn's bereft expression betrayed the anticipation of grief.

"Evelyn, none of us have any guarantees on how long we'll be here. If your Mama wants this party, the best we can do is kick up our heals and celebrate with her. Every year we live is just icing on the cake, anyway."

Evelyn nodded. "Yeah...well. I've gotta get back to my sewin'. It doesn't do it by itself." She chuckled. "Although — Joe swears that new computerized machine has a mind of its own. He won't even stay in the room when it's over there sewing up a storm all by itself."

"When you get to be my age, even circlin' the drain is exercise."
   Piddie Davis Longman

CHAPTER SIX

From the *Twin City News:*

Piddie Longman's "Purt Darn Near A Hundred" Birthday Party

FRIENDS AND RELATIVES of Liddyanne Davis Longman, fondly known to all as Mrs. Piddie Longman, are invited to attend a covered dish dinner in her honor. The social event will be held at the Fellowship Hall of the First Baptist Church of Chattahoochee on Main Street, Saturday, July 21, 2001 at 12:00 noon. Anyone planning to attend must RSVP with Evelyn or Joe Fletcher at 555-2098 by July 14th. Please plan to bring a covered dish or dessert to share.

Housework is the closest thing to perpetual motion on God's Green Earth. My mother had passed that tidbit of wisdom down from my maternal grandmother, Ida Gwendolyn Brown Gibson. Since my mother was forty when I pushed my way into the world, my memories of my grandmother were dim — a frail, sweet woman with a downy-soft halo of white hair, already paralyzed on her left side from a stroke. Her nursing home room had been dotted with school pictures of her grandchildren and great grandchildren. Ida remembered names, dates, and the tiny minutiae of our lives until her death at the age of seventy-five.

Bobby and I grew up hearing the wisdom of Miss Ida. Always make your bed and wash your dishes before you leave the house every day — then, your place will look decent in case someone stops in for a visit.   Pretty is as pretty does.

Wear clean underwear and wash behind your ears. Never forget to praise God on high for the good that comes your way, less it will take another path.

Though I resisted her wisdom in my know-it-all youth, Ida's legacy became mine. Through my single years, I kept a tight reign on clutter — not quite to the point of pathology, but pretty dang close. The kitchen was always clean; a place for everything, and everything in its place.

The addition of a child into our household tossed the Good Housekeeping Award right out the window in its gilded frame. At first, I battled to maintain the previous level of order: toys in the toy box, dishes in the dishwasher, and soiled clothes in the hamper, sorted and awaiting laundry day.

One afternoon, I tilted. Relaxed. Let go. Let the air out. I was the Wicked Witch of the West after Dorothy doused her with water. *Melting...I'm melting... all this beauty. What have you done?*

Holston and I became accustomed to picking our way through a minefield of pop beads and rattles. Shammie nestled into her new niche amidst the discarded stuffed plush monkeys, bears, and bunnies. Spackle learned to post himself near Sarah, awaiting dropped cookie goo and spit-up strained split peas.

Leaving the house took hours of preparation. We needed a team of hired workers to clean and dress Sarah and to round up the assortment of toys, bottles, diapers, extra clothing and bibs and anything else in the house we might remotely require to keep us sane and Sarah from looking like a *throw'd-away.*

The morning of Aunt Piddie's party, I had the additional burden of preparing food. By the time we loaded Betty with Sarah's supplies, extra folding chairs, the computer, and two boxes containing the contributions to the feast — two apple pies, spinach lasagna, homemade garlic rolls, and a hummingbird cake — it was ten minutes till twelve. The Lewis family unit would walk in precisely at noon. By that time, Jake would be in an absolute high rollin' boil.

UP THE DEVIL'S BELLY

❡ ❡ ❡

The First Baptist Church Fellowship Hall

A Southern *dinner-on-the-grounds* covered dish party can only be fairly compared to a cruise ship midnight buffet on steroids, minus the ice carvings. The cavernous fellowship hall of the First Baptist Church was fully decorated to resemble a French sidewalk café, if one was to somehow be magically deposited in Chattahoochee in the middle of the summer. Three rows of small round white linen-draped bistro tables were interspersed with larger tables with seating for up to eight. Clusters of tall parlor palms and Boston ferns created intimate niches between the seating areas. A backdrop of ivy-laced white trellises fostered the illusion of a garden party, or perhaps a spring high school prom sans the rampant hormones and rock band.

The order-from-the-fancy-scripted-menu façade was shattered by the presence of three long rows of buffet tables in the middle of the room. Two separate side tables held drink selections: iced tea so sappy sweet it could make your fillings ache, soft drinks, water, and strong brewed coffee. A twelve-foot sideboard awaited the deluge of homemade cakes, pies, pastries, and gelatin desserts. At the end of the room, a long table reserved for Piddie and the immediate family was draped with Evelyn's handmade tablecloth. A large projection screen was positioned in the corner, awaiting Piddie's surprise this-is-your-life video presentation.

Promptly at noon, the food-laden guests began to arrive. Jake and Stephanie flitted between the buffet tables, making sure the casserole dishes were plugged precisely into the culinary jigsaw puzzle of meats, main dishes, vegetables, starches, breads, and desserts.

Jon *Shug* Presley greeted us at the side door of the fellowship hall. "I'm glad you guys are here. Maybe you can calm Jake down a little."

Holston unloaded the baskets of food from Betty's rear compartment. I handed Sarah to Jon and grabbed the computer case. "Anything wrong?"

"He keeps checking his watch and wringing his hands. Most of the food and guests have arrived and Piddie's not here yet. Joe came on up with their food, but Evelyn's still at home helping Piddie get ready. Seems she's moving kind of slow today."

I smiled. "Probably doing her hair. You know that takes some time."

Shug Presley shook his head. "I don't have a good feeling, Hattie. Piddie's color hasn't been right the last couple of times I've seen her."

"Pid's an ox, Shug. She'll make it, congestive heart failure be damned. Besides, it's my understanding that a person can live for several years with all the new medications they have now."

Jon shrugged. "I suppose I'm just being a mother hen again. Can't help it. The nurse in me won't give me any rest."

"You bring Elvis today?"

He shook his head. "Too many people. Some folks might not take too kindly to a little dog being around all the food. Anyway, this day should belong to Piddie, and Elvis demands so much attention. I left him at the mansion with a new chewy bone. He's perfectly happy."

The noise level inside the cavernous fellowship hall had reached a fever pitch. Jake stood at the end of a buffet table, gesturing wildly and barking orders to Stephanie, Tameka, and Moses. Laughter and chatter mingled into a joyous din. Clusters of folks dressed in their Sunday best dotted the room waiting for the arrival of the party-girl guest of honor.

Jake scuttled toward us. He wore a black tuxedo with a floral print cummerbund and matching bowtie. A shiny black cane with a carved silver handle completed the ensemble.

"You look like Gene Kelly," I said.

He propped both hands on the cane and swayed from side to side. "And you, I suppose, are Ginger Rogers. Sister-girl, *you* are late!"

"C'mon, Jakey. Calm yourself. Pid's not even here yet. Show me where to set up the computer, and I'll be ready to roll in five minutes, tops. Holston's taking care of the food, and Shug has absconded with my child."

In the few minutes it took to connect the laptop computer and test run the PowerPoint presentation, the room filled to capacity with casserole-bearing guests. I spotted my police officer friends from Tallahassee — Chris, Kelly, and Cathy — as well as a good number of Tallahassee Memorial Hospital staff, our friends Patricia and Rainey Hornsby with their adopted Chinese daughter Ruth, and my ex-lover, Garrett Douglas, with his daughter Jillie.

A murmur of surprise followed by applause wafted from the far side of the hall. Evelyn wheeled Aunt Piddie, resplendent in a flowing yellow chiffon gown with appliqued daisies, into the room. Evelyn was smartly dressed in a linen skirt with a matching sleeveless jacket in a muted shade of lemon yellow. When a beaming Mandy stepped into the room behind them, the reason for the delayed entrance was clear — Piddie's hairdo. Dyed to match her dress, the ice cream cone-shaped mountain of buttercream yellow curls reached a height of two feet. Dainty silk daisies were interspersed between the layers.

My aunt's hair had long been her one true trademark; the stamp of individuality. The towering style was commonly referred to as a beehive, but Aunt Piddie's coif went far beyond the capabilities of any bee nature had ever invented. Her style was reminiscent of a termite mound's towering architecture; layer upon layer of carefully constructed curled and sprayed locks reaching toward heaven.

Piddie set up shop by the front door, welcoming friends and distant relatives as they milled into the hall.

I made my way through the press of bodies to stand behind her wheelchair.

"You look like the best part of a summer morning," I whispered in her ear.

She patted her temple with a bejeweled hand. "Like it? Mandy had a little trouble with the color. Kept comin' out dark yellow — like a road sign. She had to do it over twice! I been up at the spa since early this mornin'."

I kissed her lightly on one cheek. "It's beautiful — just like the girl who's under it."

Piddie waved her hand. "You don't have to go on so! You're already in my will."

A wave of party guests surrounded Piddie.

"You'd better watch it, lady." A smooth male voice cooed in my ear.

Officer Rich Burns, ex-high school beau and family friend, stood behind me.

"Wow, you wore your dress uniform. Piddie's gonna love you for that."

He tugged at the tight collar. "It's hot as hell in it, too. But, I know how much your aunt adores a uniform, so I'm making a sacrifice."

I glanced behind him. "Where's Carol?"

"She and the twins are on the way. I brought the food over. The girls were fighting over what to wear when I left the house."

I shook my head. "You poor thing. You're outnumbered three to one. Just wait till they hit puberty and the hormones start raging."

"I'll just head on out to the Hill, grab a pole, and head to Mr. D's fishpond." Rich's blue eyes twinkled, then he frowned. "Oh, no...," he said.

A wiry gray-haired woman pulling a rolling cart was heading our way.

Zelda Bunch, local lunatic — one of the few that really needed to be locked up. "Officer Burns!" Zelda called out. "You haven't been around to investigate my stolen property yet!" She halted her cart and glared up at Rich.

Rich's tone was gentle. "No ma'am. I'm going to send someone out first thing Monday mornin', Miss Zelda. That's a promise."

She squinted and pursed her thin lips. "I'll be calling you by nine, if someone's not out by then." She rolled her cart off in the direction of the buffet tables.

"She still think aliens are stealing her stuff?"

Rich shook his head and smiled. "Nope. It's the FBI now. Claims she's missing clothes off her outside clothesline — a couple of blankets, I think. Last time, it was her underwear. She's convinced the FBI's watching her, stealing her belongings to drive her insane."

"Seems to be working."

He nodded. "We have a whole drawer at the station full of her complaints — the *Zelda Files*. Keeps life interesting having someone like her around."

I straightened a corner of his collar. "Sounds like she calls you a lot."

"Lately, it's escalated. Seems to happen in the summer. Probably just the kids out of school, bored and up to mischief. But, heaven help me, why anyone would want to steal Zelda's underwear is a mystery to me."

I laughed. "Maybe it's some kind of right of passage. Who knows? You and I used to slip into old man Jones' yard and steal pears off his trees, remember?"

"Yep. A life of crime....you and me. At least we could eat the pears, though." Rich patted me on the back. "Let me go call and check on my girls. I'll be back." He leaned down and pecked me lightly on the cheek.

A half-hour went by before Jake managed to shuffle Piddie, Evelyn, and the throng of well-wishers away from the doorway toward the front table. The buffet tables strained under the load of food as the last of the guests trickled inside.

Jake was the first to spot the stately thin blonde woman standing at the entrance to the fellowship hall. Dressed in a crisp mint green linen suit, she glanced around the room with an uncertain expression. A young long-haired man appeared beside her, supporting a large camcorder.

"Oh my...Gah," Jake muttered. "Sister-girl, check out the front door."

Jake's shock spread to me when I realized her identity. The attractive young woman was Karen Fletcher, alias Mary Elizabeth Kensington, my cousin from Atlanta. No one had seen Karen since her college graduation, at least not in the flesh. I'd often caught a brief glimpse of her on Georgia Metro Public Television and had a difficult time equating the finely-dressed woman with the clipped British accent with the North Florida cracker I'd known in childhood.

Evelyn was fussing with a wrinkle in the intricately-decorated linen tablecloth. A ripple of chatter moved through the hall. Silence fell as the guests realized the potential for a good melodrama. Evelyn's face paled when she finally glanced toward the door where her estranged daughter stood. Always the refined genteel Southern lady, she rushed to greet Karen.

"Miss…umm…Kensington. I'm so glad you could make it! I'm Evelyn Fletcher, Piddie Longman's daughter." Evelyn extended her hand. "And, this is your camera man, I assume."

Karen, a.k.a. Mary Elizabeth Kensington, smiled and shook her mother's hand. "Mrs. Fletcher. Thank you for inviting us. My producers thought this would fit in with a feature film we're preparing on aging in America. I'm sorry I didn't have adequate time to formally respond to your invitation."

"No matter. Come on up to the family table. We'll make a spot for you."

Evelyn presented her daughter to the crowded room as if she were introducing a complete stranger. "Everyone, some of y'all might know Mary Elizabeth Kensington from the Public Television Station up in Atlanta. I invited her to attend our little party. Let's all try to make her feel welcome!" Evelyn initiated the applause and the stunned crowd joined in.

Karen/Mary Elizabeth held up one hand to still the applause. "Thank you, thank you. Just pretend we're not here, now. We'll be filming off and on." She moved to the far end of the family table and began to speak with her cameraman, pointing to various areas of the room.

UP THE DEVIL'S BELLY

Elvina Houston, seated beside her lifelong friend at the family table, leaned over to whisper into Piddie's ear. "This oughta be interestin'. Now, with Zelda Bunch and your granddaughter here, and countin' the one Ginny Pridgett brought for dessert, we have a total of three fruitcakes at your party."

Hank Henderson leaned back contentedly in a folding metal chair and rubbed his distended belly. The country cooking would be one of the few things he'd miss about Chattahoochee. Truly one of life's grease-dipped pleasures; none of that low fat, low sodium crap his HMO doctor tried to pawn off for the sake of preserving his health. He allowed his gaze to roam the fellowship hall. The role of local esteemed legal council allowed him, when needed, to call up the little dirty secrets of the fine citizens of town. Unlike Mandy at the beauty salon, he kept his information confidential; reserved for the occasions he needed a little extra push to power a personal agenda.

Piddie Longman held his gaze for a moment. Stupid old bat. She had a way of looking at him — like she *knew*. He turned it over in his mind. How? How could she possibly be privy to information relating to his business endeavors? She'd been bluffing when she'd turned the screws on him over the rezoning for the Witherspoon mansion. Just blowing smoke outta her ass. Look at the tacky old bitch — got-damned hair like a cowpie sprouting flowers. Got-almighty!

How anyone could admire the tacky old broad was a mystery. Her cathead biscuits were the only things Hank found the least bit redeeming about Piddie Longman. They were as close to his mama's as he'd ever tasted.

Mama. His thoughts strayed to the dim, time-fogged memories of a kind dark-haired woman with the gentle voice. He couldn't remember a lot about her. He tried hard to recall her face, her touch. He was a little boy, not much more than four, when she died of cancer, leaving him with his father.

The muscles at his temples pulsed as he gritted his teeth. "Father," he mumbled under his breath. Pillar of the community. An asset to the town. Founding Father – blah, blah, blah. If the church-goin', Bible-thumpin' people of this hole in the road only knew what dear ole Dad did to his young son behind closed doors — the beatings, the humiliation, the pain. And later as he entered his teens, when he felt the gentle hormonal urgings teasing around the edges of his awareness — the forced sex. Cruel. Rough. Full of hate. His duty as a son: to provide a receptacle for his father's needs.

Hank's father provided carnal knowledge of the dark underbelly of certain men's cravings. Hank had used the blood and tear-earned wisdom to develop a profitable enterprise. Men like his father — men who lived to lord over helpless children — paid dearly for his masterpiece videotapes. Modern technology made advertising and distribution a breeze. Through the anonymous magic of the computer and the Internet, he hawked the masterful creations.

The economically-deprived children Hank employed served his purposes well. The chase was almost delicious. Small gifts. Words of kindness. The winning of trust. By the time his little cinema stars made it to the concealed studio off the garage, they were too well paid, too enamored of the scent of money, to offer resistance.

Hank grunted. If dear old Dad only knew how the estate money had been spent, he'd arise from his grave and demand a cut of the action. Hell, the old letch would probably want to take top billing in the next film. Especially if it was one of the sweet-faced, untainted children — like Tameka Clark. Hank smiled. His last caper before leaving rural north Florida promised to be the most succulent of all.

His father's face appeared unsummonned, in his mind's eye — one of the few times his torment had been outside of the dark, claustrophobic cave of his parents' brick house on Satsuma Road. Summer: a time most country boys spent idling away the sun-drenched hours. On his father's expensive bass boat. Long, deserted miles down the Apalachicola River, hidden from the main channel of the waterway by the low-hanging branches of willow trees anchored in the soggy muck of the bank. Hank closed his eyes to block the memories.

A soft voice startled him back to reality. "You all right, Mister Henderson?"

Hank studied Tameka's innocent face — creamy unblemished brown skin the color of coffee latte, her deep brown eyes full of compassion.

He wiped the sweat from his brow with the corner of a paper napkin. "I'm just fine, honey. Mighty sweet of you to ask as to my well-bein'. I reckon I just ate a little too much of this fine meal." He patted his rotund stomach. "I could stand a little of that iced tea you have there."

Tameka nodded and refilled the Styrofoam cup.

"Sit down and talk to me a bit." Hank patted the metal seat of the folding chair beside him.

"I can't. I'm workin' right now." Tameka's beaded braids clinked like soul music percussion when she moved her head.

"Well, now...work's something I been meanin' to speak with you about. C'mon, sit for just a second. No one will mind."

Tameka hesitated for a moment, then lowered herself onto the edge of the folding chair.

"There, now. Tell me something. You working full time over at the day spa for the summer?"

Tameka shook her head. "Just a few hours a day."

"Reason I'm inquirin' — I need someone to help me out with some light house cleaning. The girl I had is moving over to Tallahassee to live with her cousin so she can go to the community college. How 'bout you coming over with your brother and doin' the inside work while he's outside working the yards?"

74

Tameka shifted uneasily in her chair. "I don't know...my Grandma May-May..."

He rested a hand on her slender shoulder. "I'll come speak with Miz Maizie for you. I think she'll agree that a little more cash coming in during the summer will help out — what with her bein' too sick to provide for you and Moses. Y'all going to be needing money for new clothes and supplies for school in the fall, am I right?"

She ducked her head. "Yes, sir."

"Well..." Hank reached over and brushed her cheek lightly with one finger. "It's settled then. I'll stop in some time this next week and speak with your grandmother. You get on back to your work, now."

Tameka nodded shyly and grabbed the tea pitcher. She glanced across the room to where Moses was cleaning tables. Her brother watched solemnly as she made her way toward him. "What you doin' talkin' to Mr. Hank?"

"He wants me to come clean for him this summer. For cash money. He's gonna come talk to May-May."

Moses looked across the crowded room, intending to fire a warning glare in Hank's direction. The table was vacant.

"We'll see about that," he said through clenched teeth.

"That went swimmingly well, don't you agree?" Jake grinned as he wiped a dollop of banana pudding from the seat of a folding chair.

I nodded. The last guests had left, as well as the birthday girl and her entourage. Moses, Jon, and Tameka carried double handfuls of folding chairs to the storeroom while Jake, Holston, Stephanie, Mandy, and I cleaned and collapsed the serving tables.

Mandy wiped a table with a damp rag. "I kept waiting to see if the real Karen was going to come out, but her new personality didn't crack open one inch."

"Didn't seem to faze anyone, though. Piddie certainly had a blast, especially during the video production. I've never seen her so lively," I said.

Jake tilted his head. "Can you believe that one shot of her and Carlton with the '54 Chevy? I'll bet they were a hoot when they were young."

I smiled. "Piddie told me that was taken only a few months before he had his fatal heart attack."

Jake snapped the welded legs shut on the table we were folding. "Well, it was worth every bit of planning to see her so happy."

"I can only hope I have as many friends if I get to be her age," Mandy said.

Jake grinned wickedly. "You will, sugar plum. You'll have so much dirt on folks, they'll show up in self protection."

A waded napkin missed Jake's head by inches.

"Ain't a day passes, I don't talk to someone who's nursing a grudge. Life's too dang short to hold on to past hurts. You got to soften up your heart and let the healing happen. The more hurt opens you up, the more joy you can hold."

Piddie Davis Longman

CHAPTER SEVEN

The Hill: Hattie

THE LAST FEW MONTHS I lived in Tallahassee before answering the country's beckoning call home, I grew more and more agitated with the press of snarled traffic and ill-mannered people. The once-friendly howdy-neighbor southern city charm tarnished each year with the influx of college students and politicians. Every direction I turned, I faced crowds; in the restaurants, stores, and city streets. Rude blaring car stereos with basses strong enough to interrupt the heart's rhythm jarred me at the intersections. As folks became more wrapped in their own agendas, common courtesy flew out the back window like a discarded fast food bag.

When midlife hormonal fluctuations were added into my personal mix, I fully grasped the validity of road rage. The move to the slower, kinder pace of Chattahoochee and its two lane blue highways was timely. Otherwise, I'd have ended up behind bars for choking the life from some poor slob who probably deserved to be removed from the gene pool.

On the Hill, the world awakened at a pace equal to my own. While Holston and Sarah chirped happily to each other over breakfast, I clutched my morning cup of strong black coffee, making my way to my father's old wood-framed

77

rocking chair on the wide front porch. Over the rim of my cup, I watched the early morning frenzy at the birdfeeders Holston had erected beneath the spreading arms of a southern magnolia tree at the corner of the wrap-around porch.

I rocked in time with the guitar licks and easy harmony of an old Loggins and Messina tune drifting from the two overhead speakers Holston and Bobby had installed on either end of the porch. Instead of facing the angry mishmash of dawn commuters, school buses, and road construction crews that dotted the Tallahassee roadways, I now spent my early morning hours stretching slowly into the new day.

The loud drone of Bobby's truck echoed from the driveway. The faded denim-blue pick-up slid to a stop in the soft sand at the edge of the yard. The truck's bed was filled to capacity with pressure-treated lumber, bags of nails, and a tangled mass of power tools and wires.

"Mornin' glory!" Bobby called as he erupted from the cab and slammed the creaky door. He clumped onto the wooden porch and shook his head. "Jeezus, Hattie! I don't know how Holston stands to look at you first thing of a mornin'. You look like something the dogs dragged in."

"Don't start up with me, Bubba. I'm only on my first cup of coffee. Perhaps you've forgotten the house rule?"

Bobby dismissed me with a wave of his hand as he opened the screened door. "How could I? I spent the first eighteen years of my life dealing with you and Dad, the two family crabs. I'll just go inside and seek refuge with the happy folks."

"Ummph." I rolled my eyes. I enjoyed the easy chiding banter — far better than the sarcastic trap we'd fallen into before Mama's death.

Bobby paused halfway through the door. "You coming down to the fishpond later? We're laying the support foundation for the gazebo this mornin'."

"I guess. I hate to take Sarah out around the water with all the mosquitoes. That West Nile virus thing has me spooked."

"I hear ya'. Bud Johnson, down the road toward Sycamore, lost an old horse to that stuff a day or two ago. I got plenty of bug spray with me, if you decide to come down. Leigh even found this all natural citronella spray that's safe for kids and animals."

I pointed toward his pick-up. "When you gonna break down and buy yourself a new truck? That one looks like it's held together with baling wire."

Bobby's tanned face wrinkled as he grinned. "Hey, don't cut old Flossie down, now. She's been good to me. Besides, I got a new truck for work. After taking one look at all the computer crap underneath the hood of that new F-150, I'll keep my old truck, thank you. At least I can do my own tune-ups on her. I wouldn't even touch the new truck. There's five mile'a wire around the engine!"

"It's still a pretty vehicle. I noticed it had the new logo and title on the side. Very impressive."

Bobby ran his fingers through his thinning hair. In another couple of years, he'd have the same *wide part and high forehead* our father sported by his mid-fifties. "Yeah, my new official title is *law enforcement officer*. No matter. Folks around here will still call me a game warden…like this place will always be the Davis farm, and the Triple C will always be the Witherspoon mansion."

Bobby stepped inside, then poked his head back out. "Leigh and Tank will be out later on. She said don't worry 'bout lunch. She's made some sandwiches and some kinda pasta salad for all of us."

My child squealed with delight when she spotted her Uncle Bobby. I would have to wait until all the merriment died down before I slipped back into the kitchen for a second cup of coffee.

"I usually don't like pasta salad much, but that was good, hon." Bobby flopped on to his back on the quilt Leigh and I had spread for the picnic lunch.

Leigh smiled. "It was easy as pie. I got the recipe from Angelina Palazzolo. Course, she makes hers with homemade pasta." She picked up Tank. "C'mon Holston, let's take the kids down to see the frogs."

They carried the children down the newly cleared pathway leading to the edge of the water.

Bobby released a large breath. "I'll be getting the steps in by the end of the week."

I punched him playfully on the arm. "You know, you don't have to finish this project overnight, Bobby."

"Hey...this is a vacation for me. I haven't actually built anything with my hands in years, other than the planter's pottin' bench I made for Leigh a while back. Besides, I felt like I needed some time off from work. I just get to the point sometimes where I'm dog-tired of dealing with stupid people...and, God as my witness, there're a boat load of 'em out there."

We watched our spouses and children. Spackle chased the frogs from the water's edge, and the kids dove through the grass in giggling pursuit.

I studied my brother's profile. The intense Florida sunshine had tanned his skin to the hue of aged leather. Fine wrinkles around his eyes and mouth gave him a chiseled, rugged, handsome-cowboy look.

"Hattie, I been meanin' to talk to you 'bout somethin'."

"Hmm?"

"How would you feel 'bout Leigh and me buildin' a house out here on the Hill?"

He turned to watch my reaction.

A few years back, I would've cringed at the thought of being cooped up in the same room with my older brother, even for a couple of hours. Now, the notion of being close to him gave me the same sense of security I'd treasured when our parents were alive.

I shrugged. "You want to live out here? I thought you liked it in town."

Bobby plucked a long blade of Bahia grass and stuck it between his teeth.

"I never liked livin' in town. That was Joan's idea. She had to be right up under her mama's skirt." His eyes roamed across the pond to his family. "I've always wanted a log cabin in the woods. And now, with Leigh and Josh. I just want my son to be able to grow up like we did, Hattie. Out here with loads of room, fresh air to breathe. I want to teach him about the trees, the land, the animals...like Daddy taught us."

Bobby turned to study me full face. His blue eyes squinted in the bright sun. "I know I haven't been the best brother in the world, Hattie."

I reached over and rested my hand on his shoulder. "There *have* been times I felt you didn't like me very much."

He shook his head. "It wasn't you. It was me. After Joan left the way she did, I was mad at the world. There you were — free as a bird, traveling all over the country — and I was here. It's like I was stuck for a long time. I was such a bastard. To everyone, not just you and your friends. I started drinkin' pretty heavy, almost got myself fired from my job...and, you know how much that means to me. I worried Mama sick, there for awhile."

Bobby's expression softened with love as he gazed down the embankment toward his wife and son. "Then, along came Leigh. She was my salvation. Shook me off, cleaned me up. I stopped crawling in the bottle to get away from myself and the world. First time I laid eyes on that woman, somethin' inside of me just opened up. It all came pouring out...the hate, the anger...all the junk that was keeping me down."

I shook his shoulder playfully. "Hey, can I believe my ears? Bobby Davis sitting here talking to me about his feelings? Lord help!"

He smirked. "Don't be a smartass."

"Sorry."

He pointed a finger toward the pond. "You can blame Leigh for all that emotional junk. She can dig down and pull stuff outa me. Nothin' gets past that woman."

"I think it'd be fan-freakin'-tastic to have you guys out here. But, you really don't have to ask my permission. It's your land too, after all."

"I know. I just thought it'd be the right thing to do."

I stretched my legs out in front of me. "You picked out a spot yet?"

Bobby grinned. His even white teeth flashed like quicksilver against his tanned face. "Yeah. I thought I'd clear a lane right off the main drive as you first come in...set the cabin in the deep woods on the top of the hill. I'd make it where you and Holston, and John and Margie, wouldn't feel crowded in. You wouldn't be able to see the cabin from either of your houses. I don't need to cut a lot of trees, either. Just enough to keep the snakes away from the house."

"Mama Tillie and Mr. D. would be happy as two pigs in a poke about us settling down with our families on the land."

Bobby slapped his hands on his thighs. "Well! Alrighty then! Wanna go tell the troops?"

We started down the embankment toward the pond.

I slipped my arm across his broad shoulders. "When will you start to build?"

"I'd like to go ahead and get started in a couple of weeks as soon as I can pull the permits. I'll have D.J. Hartman come out with his equipment, soon as he can get to it, and clear the road and homesite. He can do that pretty much without any help from me. For now, I'll concentrate on finishing the gazebo and decking."

Most building projects in the country aren't completed by one person. Bobby was perfectly content to work alone, but he was often assisted by a number of well-intentioned, if not talented, helpers. Holston, John, Margie, Leigh, and I pitched in as our schedules allowed. Shug and Jake visited the worksite periodically until the main portion of the covered gazebo was completed. Then, Jake arranged for the delivery of a truck full of river boulders, native ferns, and the PVC pipes and pump assembly for the waterfall. With Jake directing from his perch on a folding chair, Shug, Bobby, Leigh, Holston, and I positioned and repositioned the cascade of rocks from the edge of the gazebo to the pond. Once they were in place, Bobby constructed the final water-level deck with built-in benches and fishing pole holders. In less than three weeks, the gazebo was finished. After Bobby ran the underground wiring from an existing power pole, two ceiling fans and the deck lighting were the last items he installed.

"You know what this means, of course," Bobby said as he and I surveyed the work site.

I nodded. "Party?"

"I'm thinkin'…maybe a family and friend/helpers fish fry. We have plenty of catfish filets in the freezer, and I can bring my propane cooker from town. We could eat out on the picnic tables next to the pool. It'd be like old times on the Davis homestead."

I watched a small blue heron angle for minnows. "I can't think of a better way to celebrate the completion of the gazebo, and…the start of your log cabin."

My brother's broad smile stretched across his face, or, as Aunt Piddie would put it, *he grinned like a goat eatin' briars.*

"None of us have any reason to go gettin' all high 'n' mighty over anything we do. We don't do one thing on this earth alone, 'cept maybe some lowly body function. When we're born, there's at least one other person there. On the other end of our time, if we're lucky, we have someone keepin' watch over us when we pass over to the other side. No one ever does a single solitary thing without the help of others somewheres along the line. That's a thing best remembered if you feel like going and gettin' up on your high horse."

    Piddie Davis Longman

CHAPTER EIGHT

Triple C Day Spa and Salon

WANDA ORNSTEIN DUMPED a stack of soiled hairbrushes and combs into her sink and scrubbed briskly with a small, stiff-bristled hand brush. Soap bubbles scudded into the air around the workstation like miniature good fairies intent on escape. She wiped the countertops with a disinfectant-soaked sponge and polished the upholstery of the client chair. She was down on her knees with a toothbrush scouring the chair's electric lift base when Stephanie walked through the salon carrying a towering stack of freshly laundered and folded sheets.

"I've finally found someone who cleans as much as I do," Stephanie said.

"I just can't stand it," Wanda said. "One thing about this business — hair everywhere! I just don't want a patron to look down and freak out." She wiped her hands on the ragged towel hanging around her neck. "Why are you stocking laundry? I thought that was Tameka's job."

"She's mopping the wet treatment room right now, and I'm almost out of clean sheets. Besides, with her here only four hours a day, I'd rather have her help me with the cleaning duties. I can always put in a load of sheets to wash between clients."

Wanda frowned. "I don't know how I feel about her working over there with Hank Henderson, but I suppose it wasn't my decision to make."

Stephanie bent over to retrieve a pillow case that had toppled from the pile. "I know what you mean. I really wish we could afford to have her and Moses here full time."

"Hmmm...well...with the economy like it is, we're doin' good to have *us* here full time."

Stephanie tilted her head. "You got a bad feelin' about Hank, or something?"

"Nothin' I can put a finger on. He's nice enough when he comes in for a cut. Tips better than most folks." Wanda dismissed her doubts with a wave of her hand. "I guess I'm just being overprotective of those two kids. I love 'em like they were my own."

"How come you never had any kids?"

Wanda shrugged. "Mystery to me. Married to three men, and not one of 'em...well, maybe it was me. Who knows?"

"I think you'd make a great mom."

Wanda smiled. "Thank you. That's the best compliment anyone's paid me in a long time."

"Well, let me get back to work. It ain't gonna do itself," Stephanie said. "Why don't you just ask Tameka how things are going over at Hank's when you're doing her hair? She'd talk to you, I'm sure," she called over her shoulder.

Wanda rested her hands on Tameka's shoulders. "I have an idea for a different style." She pulled the hair away from Tameka's delicate oval face. "Why don't we bring it back off your forehead? We'll run a series of large braids back to here…then we'll pull it all back in a thick ponytail with a braided wrap to hold it together. What'd'ya think?"

Tameka's deep brown eyes sparkled. "That sounds real nice, Miz Wanda."

Wanda gently worked a wide-tooth comb through a section. "You hair sure is gettin' long. I tell you, with your pretty hair and face, you could be a model, child."

Tameka smiled shyly at the compliment. "That's what Mr. Hank says."

Wanda seized the opportunity to work in questions about Tameka's new employer. "He does, does he? Hmm. He treating you nice over there?"

"Yes'um. He pays real good, and the work ain't hard."

Wanda paused and studied Tameka's reflection in the workstation mirror. "Any…problems at all?"

"Not really." Tameka lowered her gaze and studied her hands.

"You don't sound so sure."

Tameka shrugged her thin shoulders. "I just think Mr. Hank's always watchin' me…like he's afraid I'm gonna steal somethin'. I'd never do that!"

"Of course not! What makes you feel like he doesn't trust you?"

She bit her lower lip. "Well…it's not like I think it's just me he don't trust. He has these cameras all over his house. They follow you around the rooms. He's even got 'em in the bathrooms!"

Wanda stopped working with the long braid she held in her hands. "That's a bit…unusual."

"Moses says he thinks Mr. Hank's just *pear-nawed*."

Wanda pursed her lips to suppress a smile at the child's pronunciation.

"Why's that?"

"Cause Mr. Hank has lots of guns in his house."

"That's not so odd. Everyone around here hunts."

Tameka shook her head. "No'um. Moses says they's not the huntin' kind. They's handguns. He has these locked cases full of 'em, and he's always sittin' around cleanin' and shinin' 'em. Sometimes, he talks to hisself."

A cold stab of fear ran through Wanda. "You don't bother with his guns, now."

"No'um. He made that clear my first day. I was never to go near his collection 'cept to dust the cases."

Wanda slid a blue pottery bead onto the end of a braid. "He doesn't leave them lying out then, that's good."

"I saw one in the drawer by his bed."

Wanda spun the chair around so that she was facing Tameka. "Sweetie, don't you *ever* mess with that gun, you hear? It's probably loaded. I couldn't stand it if you got hurt!"

Tameka pressed back into the chair, her almond-shaped eyes opened wide. "No'um. May-May told Moses and me never to touch a gun. Guns are for killin', and that's against God's rules."

Wanda turned the chair back to face the mirror. "Well now, I trust you and your brother to listen to your grandma."

"How is Grandma Maizie gettin' on?" Wanda asked after a few minutes had passed.

Fear mixed with sadness flashed briefly across the young girl's face. "She's not feelin' so good. Her hands pain her a lot. I rub 'em for her at night. And, sometimes she says she can't walk so good cause she can't feel where her feet's goin'."

Wanda studied her young patron in the mirror. "You know to call me if you need anyone, right?"

"Yes'um." The child's trusting expression tugged at Wanda.

She steered the conversation toward more pleasant topics. As Wanda's expert hands worked magic on the child's long hair, Tameka chattered about her teachers, classmates, and favorite school subjects. Wanda hummed as she developed the intricate hairstyle that would've cost a paying patron at least sixty dollars.

Jon *Shug* Presley was heating a plate of leftover lasagna when Wanda came into the spa's kitchen. "Umm! That smells great!"

"Want me to heat you up some while I'm at it? It's my spinach and zucchini lasagna recipe — really good," Shug said in singsong.

Wanda shrugged. "Since all I have at home is dried-up balogna, I'll take you up on it."

"Great. I hate to eat alone." Jon rustled in the cabinet and found two red-checkered placemats with matching cotton napkins.

"No need to go to all that trouble for just me. A paper napkin and plastic plate's fine."

Shug propped his hands on his hips. "That's the trouble with modern society. Everyone's so tuned in to rush, rush, rush! It's just throw away, throw away! I like to eat off *real* plates with *real* silverware and actually sit down to the table. Jake would be perfectly happy to eat right out of the container, standing over the sink! Too many years stuffin' down fast food has almost ruined the man."

Wanda held up both hands in surrender. "Hey, I'm not opposed to sitting down to a meal. I don't get to do it very often, that's all. Why bother — when I eat alone nine times out of ten."

Shug patted the wooden seat of a kitchen chair. "Just sit yourself down, and I'll serve you, then."

She plopped down. "Where's Jake this evening?"

Jon poured two glasses of red wine and set them on the table. "The Twin City golf tournament starts tomorrow, and the *who's-its* are havin' a *how-dee-do* party at the clubhouse later on this evening. He's finishing up the floral displays for the serving tables."

"That's right. How could I forget? That means poor Stephanie will be busy as a bee in a tar bucket next week with all the golf widows coming in for massage and spa treatments. I'm sure we'll pick up in the hair salon, too." Wanda sighed. "It's not that I mind the business, but some of those high society types are such a pain in the patootie."

Jon stuck a lasagna-laden plate into the microwave. "I heard that. I used to hate seeing them as patients when I worked on the floor at Tallahassee Memorial...always so demanding and unappreciative when you did what they asked." Jon smiled. "There were a few exceptions, though. I once had this old fella who looked like he was poor as a church mouse. Never breathed a word about the fact that his family owned half of the land north of Meridian Road — that's the high-falutin' side of Tallahassee. He was nice and cordial as you'd ever ask for. Only his ermine-dipped wife gave him away. I'll swear, he almost seemed sad to leave the hospital!" He delivered the plates to the table and sat down.

Wanda took a bite of the warm lasagna. "This is delicious! You ought to open a restaurant. Everything I've ever tasted of yours has been off the scale."

"Thanks." Jon sipped his wine. "I'd cook more often if I had the time."

"Shug?"

"Hmm?"

"I need your help with something."

Jon said around a mouthful, "Name it."

"I'm worried about Miz Maizie, Moses and Tameka's grandmama. She's diabetic." Wanda shook her head sadly. "She's all those kids have. Their mother is

89

god-knows-where — crack addict, from what I've heard — and Tameka says that Miz Maizie's not doin' so well."

"Diabetes is a mean disease. Properly monitored, a person can live a long, successful life. Left undiagnosed, or not carefully controlled, it can destroy the vision, kidneys, compromise circulation...eventually lead to death."

"Could I persuade you to come with me to check on Miz Maizie?"

Jon shrugged. "I'm not a doctor, Wanda. I can't diagnose or treat her, by law."

Wanda nodded. "I know. I just….well, if you could go with me for a social visit. I'll make some food to take over. I've got a little cookbook with recipes for folks with diabetes somewhere at the house. One of my friends when I lived down south was a caterer, and she worked a taste-and-educate function for one of the hospitals. She gave me one of the recipe books. Maybe we can stop in and you can just take a peek at her."

Jon nodded. "As long as I don't go in an official nurse capacity, I don't have any objections."

Wanda smiled. "Good. I'll talk to Moses tomorrow when he comes in for work —to see what day would be best. I do appreciate this, Shug. I'll owe you one."

"Friends don't keep tabs, Wanda'loo. If you'd corner Jake and give him a trim, it'd be repayment enough. His hair's longer, and far shabbier, than Elvis'!"

Wanda laid her head back and a huge belly laugh echoed through the room. "Maybe you could take a picture and enter him in next year's calendar dog contest! Give little Elvis some competition."

Jon smirked. "You're so funny, you should've been queer."

"You shore can't judge a person by what they got. Material possessions don't amount to a hill a'beans in the by-in-by. I've yet to see a hearse a'pullin' a U-Haul full of money. A person who'll sit in the kitchen and pass the time of day and share what little they've got – now that there's quality, and the good Lord sees it, too."

Piddie Davis Longman

CHAPTER NINE

Happytown

LIKE MANY SMALL SOUTHERN TOWNS, Chattahoochee remained, for the most part, racially segregated. The majority of black citizens maintained residences in the southeastern side of town, an area known to locals as *Happytown*. Grandma Maizie's small wooden frame house claimed a small lot on Wire Road. Deeply shrouded by one ancient live oak tree and a row of overgrown shrubs, it was one of the few shotgun houses left from the 40's. The term *shotgun house* had been coined to describe a long, narrow, cheaply-constructed house that you could *shoot a shotgun through the front door and it'd go clean through and out the back door without hittin' a thing*.

Unlike many of the neighboring dwellings, Miz Maizie's house sported fresh paint, new windows, and a new roof, compliments of a recent charity clean and fix-up program sponsored by the local churches. The front cement walkway, though cracked, was cleanly swept of sand and leaves.

Shug Presley parked the 4Runner in the shaded dirt driveway and studied the house intently. "Wow! Aren't many of these left. At least, not in this good a condition. People are just recently starting to realize their historical value. They're the one true example of African-American architecture in this country."

Wanda raised her eyebrows. "I didn't know you were such a history buff."

"It's a hobby. I read a lot on the Internet. My mom loved history, so she always bought me books, particularly about the South." Shug glanced back at the house. "This style was a reflection of the intimacy of African-American familial ties of the time period. I'll bet there was a row of these here at one time — they were usually built close together."

"Hmmm...I've seen a few down in Key West and Miami. They're probably all over the state. I've never paid much attention."

Jon killed the engine. "Most folks don't. Bet you didn't know that Elvis was born in a shot gun house."

"Your dog?"

Jon chuckled. "No, the *human* Elvis. People associate him with the Graceland mansion, but his beginnings were very humble."

He pulled the keys from the ignition. "Need some help with the food?"

"If you can grab your bread basket, I can get the rest."

They climbed the concrete block steps and stood on the small painted wooden plank front porch. An old metal kitchen chair and an electric box fan stood on one side of the door.

"Miz Maizie?" Shug called as he rapped on the screened door.

The sound of Maizie's shuffled walk echoed down the long dark hallway. "I'm a'comin'! Jess a minute!" A short bowed black woman in a flower-print housedress appeared at the door. "Whew! The old gray mare shore ain't what she used to be! Y'all come on in."

Jon studied the old woman with a nurse's trained eye. In her youth, Maizie would have been a formidable force. Now, in her early seventies, she had been dealt a cruel blow by nature and hardship. Her frame slumped forward, curling with the effects of osteoporosis. Jon noted the slight tremor of her hand as she reached out to shake his, then Wanda's hand. Maizie's swollen feet were packed into soft bedroom slippers with holes cut out to accommodate bunions on both of her big toes.

Jon and Wanda were ushered into a cozy sitting room. Though the few pieces of furniture were old, the chintz covers and handmade curtains gave the tiny room a cheerful, homey ambience. A window fan and a 19-inch television, complete with a rabbit ear antenna, were the only visible concessions to the current century. Jon recalled the words of his mother: *It's no crime to be poor – Jesus was no rich man. But, you keep yourself and your home clean. There's no excuse for slovenly ways.*

"Y'all make you'selves comfortable, hear? I made some fresh teacakes and iced tea for us." Maizie shuffled slowly from the living room down the hall to the kitchen at the far end of the house.

Wanda's gaze was drawn to one wall filled with family pictures. Many were faded black and white prints, the subjects standing rigid with soulful, solemn expressions.

She could see the strong family resemblance to Maizie, Moses, and Tameka.

"Oh! Let me help you with that!" Wanda called when she saw Maizie struggling to negotiate the hallway carrying a food and drink-laden tray. The old woman smiled appreciatively when Wanda retrieved the tray and set it on the coffeetable.

Wanda closed her eyes and smiled. "These teacakes smell wonderful! My aunt used to make them for us when we were kids. We visited her here every summer from Michigan. She had a house off Morgan Avenue. I haven't had one of them in, oh, thirty years or so."

Maizie brushed a sprig of wiry white hair from her temple. "I can't eat 'em on account of my blood sugar, but I *love* to cook 'em. Likes the way my kitchen smells when they're bakin'. Moses and Tameka love 'em to death, so I keep in practice."

Wanda bit into one of the soft teacakes, still warm from the oven. The blended flavors of fresh butter and vanilla teased her tastebuds. "These are incredible! I don't care how many times I've tried to make them, they never come out like this. I'd beg you for your recipe."

Maizie waved her hand. "Law, I don't use no recipe. I throws in a handful a'this and a pinch a'that. Any cook worth a hoot does it by feel."

Wanda brushed the crumbs from the corners of her mouth. "Suppose that's why I'm not a good cook, then."

Maizie sat down and propped her feet on an upholstered ottoman. "Don't fret none. You can learn. Anybody can, if they've a mind to."

"We brought you something for dinner," Shug said. "And, no matter what she says about being lousy at it, Wanda cooked it all and did a great job of it. All I contributed was the bread. That's my passion, though I usually bake bread in the cool weather."

"All the recipes I used are special for diabetics, even the mandarin orange dessert," Wanda said.

Maizie blew out a breath. "I'm surely obliged to you for it, I'll tell you. I can hardly hold out anymore to stand over the stove and cook a full meal."

"Your legs bother you?" Shug asked.

She reached down and tugged at the elastic stocking on her left leg. "I shouldn't complain, I suppose. I knows some folks my age can't even walk a'tall. I gets along okay. Good Lawd never said it was gonna be easy."

Shug nodded. "We sure love having Moses and Tameka at the Day spa. They're good kids. Hard workers, too."

Maizie smiled. "I'm mighty proud of both them kids. I reckon I've done better with them than I did with their mama. She was a wild gal from the get-go."

Wanda sipped her iced tea. "You ever hear from her?"

The old woman's eyes clouded with concern. "Last I knew of, Dorie was down around Miami somewheres. I 'spect a call any day sayin' she's turned up dead. She got on the dope, and it's been a monkey on her back."

Wanda reached over and patted Maizie's arthritic hand. "Well, her kids surely turned out well, thanks to you."

Maizie dabbed the sweat from her face with a handkerchief. "I've tried to bring 'em up right. Miz Lucille Jackson picks us up every Sunday for church, and the kids walk to the sanctuary once a week for youth events, when they aren't havin' to work." Maizie smiled. "You two are just like I had pictured in my mind. The young'uns are always talkin' 'bout you. Described you to a 'T'."

"What'd they say?" Jon asked.

"Well…Moses says you, Mr. Jon, remind him of a fella he saw a couple of years back, when the church took a bunch of 'em to the circus over in Tallahassee."

Wanda chuckled. "A clown?"

Maizie waved her hand. "No, no. One of them fellas who walk on those sticks. I guess 'cause you're so tall, with your long legs, and all."

"How 'bout me?" Wanda asked.

"Tameka said you were what she always wished her mama to be — kind, pretty —just maybe, with a bit darker skin." Maizie smiled. "She thinks the world of you, Miz Wanda."

Wanda swallowed around the lump that had formed in her throat. "That's…nice." The notion of motherhood stirred in a spot buried deep in a place she'd stuffed it long ago.

"I'll bet you miss them bein' round a lot this summer, with them working at the spa and Mr. Henderson's," Shug said.

"Yes suh. I do at that. They do love workin' at the mansion. Tameka says she wants to be a hairdresser when she grows up, and Moses, he's learnin' new stuff 'bout plants every day. The boy reads everything he can lay his hands on."

Wanda seized the opportunity to ask about the kids' other summer job. "Are they doing okay with Hank Henderson?"

The old woman shifted in her chair, wincing with the effort. "They don't neither one talk much 'bout Mr. Hank. I know Moses don't like him much. He was mighty firm 'bout not lettin' Tameka clean for him." Maizie shook her head. "Law, it's hard to know what to do. Mr. Hank, he pays mighty good. He came over here special to speak to me — ask my permission for Tameka to work for him. He even offered to do some legal services for next to nothin'.'"

Wanda leaned forward. "Legal services?"

"Yeah. I didn't have a will made out. Been meanin' to. Just been tryin' to get up the money. I don't have much in the way of worldly goods. Just this house and one old insurance policy that's just enough to lay me out when I pass. But, I wanted to make sure the kids got whatever's left...and, that my wishes were clear as to who takes them on, once I'm gone."

Jon asked, "And Hank is doing the papers for you?"

She nodded. "He's drawin' them up for twenty dollars. Says he likes to help folks in need."

Wanda shot a worried glance Jon's way. "That's...umm...nice of him."

"He's not such a bad man, I reckon. Moses don't like him much, for some reason. I figure he's just a growin' boy resentin' someone tellin' him what to do. You know, 'round 'bout his age, boys get a bit biggety. They's tryin' to find the way to bein' a man. James, my son, was much the same at Moses' age."

Wanda's eyebrow shot up. "You have a son?"

"Uh-huh." Maizie stood slowly, shuffled over to the picture gallery wall, and removed a 5 x 7 framed color photograph of a man with his wife and two young sons. "That's my James," she said proudly as she handed the picture over to Wanda and Jon. "He lives up in Montgomery, Alabama, with his wife, Alicia, and his two boys, Alfred and Antwoin. This picture's a couple of years old. My grandson's are eight and ten now — good boys."

"I never heard Moses or Tameka mention having an uncle," Wanda said.

Maizie shook her head. "James stays busy. We don't see much of him or the family. He sends money when he can. I don't reckon we'd get by without my boy's help." Maizie slapped her hands on her knees. "No need a'talkin' 'bout hardships, now. Good Lawd provides for his chil'ren. I want to hear all 'bout both of y'all and the spa. I'm gonna get by there one day and see where my grand youngun's are workin'."

"Maybe, if you want...I could come get you some mornin'," Wanda said. "I specialize in African-American hairstyles."

Maizie brushed absently at the stray gray hairs curling at her temple. "Oh, I could never afford none of that."

Wanda tilted her head. "Actually, I was thinkin' of a trade."

"What could I have that you'd need, now?"

Wanda grinned. "Cookin' lessons."

Maizie returned the smile. "Well, now...we might just be able to work us a swap, after all."

After chatting for almost an hour, Jon and Wanda left the modest shotgun house on Wire Road. Miz Maizie issued an open invitation for them to return any time.

"Well...?" Wanda asked as they turned onto the pavement.

"Her skin is a bit ashen, and the swelling in her feet is worrisome. Best bet — try to get to know her better. Prompt her to follow up with her doctor — even drive her there if you can."

"In other words, get involved."

Jon glanced at her. "Wanda'loo, honey, seein' the way you've taken to those kids, you're already involved."

Wanda stared out the passenger side window. "Yeah, suppose I am." She turned to face him. "And, what 'bout that deal with Hank doing her will for next to nothing?"

"Maybe he's just being charitable."

Wanda shook her head. "I don't know. When I think 'bout that man, the hair stands up on the back of my neck. I don't know him very well, just what I hear 'round town. But, he just doesn't seem like the charitable type. He has some agenda. I'm sure of it!"

"Like my mama used to say, *it'll come out in the wash*."

"Shug?"

"Hmm?"

"Can I ask you something kinda personal?"

Jon glanced away from the road for a second to study Wanda. "If it's about my hair — the answer is, yes. It's my natural color. I can't help it if it looks like Lady Queer-all's Boot Black!"

Wanda chuckled. "That wasn't my question, though I *had* wondered. Gee…I don't know how to put this…"

"Spit it out, Wanda'loo."

She shifted in her seat to face him. "You and Jake are the only two gay people I've ever gotten to know well."

He smirked. "This isn't gonna be some kinky sex question, is it? I just *hate* those. People always asking — *what do two men do together?* — like it's any of their business what another person does in the privacy of his own home!"

She shook her head. "No, that's not it. I'd never ask, at least not when I'm stone cold sober. I was reading this article the other day 'bout how ten percent of the population's gay. So...why aren't there more around here? I mean, we see a lot of people in the salon."

Jon shrugged. "That's why they call us *fairies*, I reckon." He reached over and tousled Wanda's red hair playfully. "We're all around you, but you can't see us!"

She patted him on the shoulder. "That's not exactly the answer I was looking for."

"Hon, if you're wanting me to point folks out, I won't do that for you. That's not my place."

Wanda frowned. "But, why all the secrecy? Why do they feel they have to hide?"

"I find it hard to believe you asked me that. Think about it, sister. Why would they open themselves up to pain and public ridicule, or worse?"

They rode in silence for a few moments.

"Shug, I'm sorry for what happened to Jake."

"You didn't do it, Wanda."

She sighed. "I'm just as guilty as any other straight person who pokes fun and hates for no good reason. Before I met you and Jake, I wasn't exactly Mother Teresa."

"And you are now?"

"Of course."

Jake reached over and patted her hand. "Well, hon. If getting to know me and Jake turned you into a saint, then I'm proud to the very core of my being."

Wanda boxed him on the shoulder.

"Not to change the subject, but are you going out to the Hill for the big gazebo-warmin' fish fry?" Jon asked.

"Surely. I've got to work till four on Saturday. After that, Piddie's marked off the appointment book so all of us can go. I'm gonna whip up a quick three-bean salad — somethin' I can make the night before and keep in the refrigerator. How 'bout you and Jake?"

He nodded. "We'll go, of course. We can all ride out together, if you want. There's plenty of room for five people in here."

"That'll work. I'll bring a change of clothes and stick the salad in the fridge at the spa. I'll talk to Steph and Mandy, too. I'm sure they'd like to carpool."

Jon slipped the 4Runner into a parking place beside the Triple C. "Jake's bringing a little gazebo-warmin' gift from us — two huge Boston ferns and the hanging hooks to go with them."

"I don't know what I'm gonna do yet. I'll think of something. Evelyn's making a flag she's designed. I caught her working on it the other day."

"Oh! I almost forgot to tell you!" Jon's face lit up. "You'll never guess in a *grillion* years who was in Evelyn's shop the other day…just browsin' around like *who shot Sam*!"

Wanda rolled her eyes. "I positively suck at guessing games. Who?"

Jon puffed his chest out. "Just the First Lady of Florida herself — in the flesh!"

Wanda's mouth hung open. "No way."

"Uh-huh. She was so nice…and that wonderful accent of hers! She ordered two gowns from Evelyn's new formal line — what she calls her *evening elf-wear*."

"You're kidding!"

Jon drew across his chest with one finger. "Cross my heart and hope to die."

"What was she doing over here?"

"She's one of the dignitaries, or guests of honor — whatever — for the upcoming Twin City golf tournament. She and some of her friends were over here for a kick-off luncheon."

Wanda huffed. "How about that!"

Jon opened the door and uncoiled his long legs. "Between the expansion of the gardens and the growing popularity of Evelyn's designer duds, Jake's convinced the Triple C's gonna end up in *Southern Living Magazine* some day."

"Be sure to let me know. I'll have to buy a new outfit."

"One good thing about living in such a small town – if I forget something I've done or said, and that happens more and more the older I get – there's always someone there to remember it for me. Sure as I'm sittin' here, that's true, and especially as long as Elvina Houston draws a breath."

Piddie Davis Longman

CHAPTER TEN

The Hill

IN THE SOUTH, food is the tie that binds. Any occasion can be parlayed into a reason to eat. Shaded by an old pecan tree, two seven-foot-long picnic tables, made by my father several years before he died, were draped with red-checkered cloths. Two smaller folding tables held red plastic plates, matching napkins and cups, utensils, condiments, an ice bucket, and three gallon-sized containers of tea. Two glass bowls held sprigs of freshly cut spearmint and lemon wedges.

Bobby's deep-fryer fish cooker stood ready on the cement patio by the pool.

"I need a brown paper grocery bag, some flour, and a big bowl to mix the beer batter in!" Bobby called from the kitchen door.

Leigh grabbed the bag and bowl from the pantry. "You already have everything else out there?"

"Yep. I got Holston beatin' the eggs. I'm teaching him how to make daddy's beer batter. I'm gonna make a Florida Cracker outta that Yankee, yet!" He slammed the screened door behind him as he left.

Leigh shook her head. "Men are just overgrown little boys. Bobby doesn't like to cook unless there's an element of danger involved. What makes it manlier to cook fish outside over a propane flame is a mystery to me."

I added a generous glob of mayonnaise to the shredded cabbage and carrot cole slaw. "Beats me. My daddy was the same way. He lived for the weekend when he could fire up the grill — ours was charcoal. I guess the danger came from splashing on the lighter fluid and watchin' the coals erupt into a towering pillar of fire."

"We doin' the fries inside?" Leigh pointed to the deep iron Dutch oven filled with cooking oil on the stove.

"Yeah. That way, everything's hot at one time. Bobby'll fry the catfish and hushpuppies outside." Remembering past family fish fries, I smiled. "The same system always worked for my parents. Mom'd stay in the house making the potato salad and cole slaw and the menfolk would be out frying the fish. Dad would give her a signal to start the fries when he finished the fish and was starting on the hushpuppies."

The crew from the spa arrived in Jon's 4Runner simultaneously with Evelyn, Joe, and Piddie following in the Lincoln. Leigh and I grabbed the babies and left the kitchen to greet them. While Joe and Jon helped Aunt Piddie settle into her wheelchair, Evelyn, Wanda, Stephanie, and Mandy unloaded the food. Jake carried Elvis in one arm.

"Party's arrived, Sister-girl!" Jake said as he kissed me on the cheek.

I tousled the Pomeranian's silky hair. "Why don't you let Elvis run around and be a real dog? Spackle gets along great with him."

Jake glanced over his shoulder. "Jon'll pitch a hissy-fit if Elvis gets a speck of dirt on him. But...I'm with you. Elvis deserves a break from being the dog-centerfold God." He placed the Pomeranian on the grass. Elvis cowered timidly by Jake's feet for a few moments until Spackle's playful bouncing enticed him away.

UP THE DEVIL'S BELLY

"Jake!" Jon yelled. "It'll take me *hours* to get him clean!"

Jake swatted the air with his cane. "I'll bathe him when we get home. He deserves to have a little fun, too." Jake grabbed my arm. "I made some cocktail sauce. You never put enough horseradish in yours for my likin'."

"I need my sinuses opened up, anyway."

Jake smirked. "You'll never admit mine's better than yours, will you?"

"Not in a month of Sundays. That hellish stuff you make'll put hair on your chest."

One of his eyebrows shot up. "Perhaps, Sister-girl, if you eat enough to sprout hairs on your chest, you'll quit sproutin' them out of your chin."

I boxed him on the arm. "You're just downright mean, sometimes. You know?"

Jake curled his arm around my shoulders. "You love me madly, in spite of it all. To make up for my insult to your culinary skills, let me tell you, — I brought one of my homemade red velvet cakes."

"You're forgiven."

Jake's twin dimples showed when he smiled. "You are *so* easy."

"Goo-gah!" Sarah shouted when she spotted Aunt Piddie. The baby held out her stubby little arms and bounced up and down.

"Hand her here." Piddie settled Sarah into her lap and motioned for Joe to push the wheelchair over to the shade of the pecan tree.

"I'll take Josh for you," Evelyn offered.

"That'd be a big help, Evelyn. He's into everything." Leigh handed her son over with a grunt.

"Whew! He's gettin' heavy. I'll just stay out here with Mama and the babies. If y'all need me in the kitchen, just call."

Leigh and I exchanged glances. I knew she was thinking the same thing. Could it be, with her new passion for clothing design, my cousin had finally given up on cooking? Local sales of indigestion relief medication would plummet.

104

Margie and John walked up the lane carrying their offerings: a five-layered coconut cake and a cooler filled with homemade vanilla pecan ice cream. When the catfish were cooked and piled high in tinfoil-lined pans, Bobby whistled the signal for me to cook the fries.

Like many of my parents' cookouts on the Hill, the timing was perfect. I drained the last of the golden brown fries and moved the hot grease to the back burner to cool, just as my brother completed his cooking outside.

Bobby stuck his head in the kitchen door. "You done in here?"

"Comin' right out," I called.

Leigh and I carried the hot french-fried potatoes and chilled cole slaw and a heaping bowl of potato salad to the food table. Along with the towering platters filled with beer-battered fried fish and hushpuppies, the table held three types of salad, sliced deep-red homegrown tomatoes, bread and butter pickles, and the two cakes.

"Who's gonna say the blessing?" Joe asked.

Piddie scowled. "Don't even start up, Evelyn. Nobody here wants to eat cold fish."

Evelyn sighed. "Oh, Mama."

"I'll say it," Bobby offered.

We bowed our heads.

"Lord, thank you for our good fortune, for the food we are about to partake, for the help of all our friends and family. Please watch over us as we go through this day. Take care of those who've passed on ahead of us. In the name of our Lord, Amen."

"Amen," we echoed.

Aunt Piddie's loud peal of laughter startled everyone.

"Mama?" Evelyn rushed over to the wheelchair. "You okay?"

"Whew! Lord-amighty! Of course I'm okay. Why is it…ever time I do somethin' out of turn, someone thinks I've got that *Old-timer's* disease? I ain't lost my mind. Not yet, anyways. Somethin' just popped into my head…clear as a bell…just like it was yesterday! You 'member the time we were out here for a fish fry a few years back? Margie and John, y'all were here. I remember it well. It was a big to-do. Some kinda church thing. Tillie was runnin' 'round like a chicken with her head cut off — fetchin' stuff, makin' sure everyone had what they needed. You know, the hostess is always the last one to set down after everyone else is situated. Well, your daddy, Mr. D, was sittin' down already with a big plate of food, and he realized he didn't have anything to drink. He started to yell for your mama to bring him some iced tea. '*Tillie*', he bellered like an old cow, '*bring me some tea!*' Well, Tillie didn't hear him the first time, I guess. He kept callin' it out over and over. When your mama turned around, and I saw the look in her eyes, I knew trouble was brewin'. She'd just taken all she could take, I reckon. She walked over real slow and deliberate, grabbed up a full gallon pitcher of sweet tea, and tumped the whole dang thing over his head!"

Everyone laughed, some of us nodding in remembrance.

"We were all quiet as church mice for a minute or two waitin' for him to pitch a full-fledged conniption fit. He just sat there, tea drippin' off the end of his nose, T-shirt wet to the bone. After a while, he started to laugh. Then he said, '*I reckon I got what I asked for.*' We all joined in laughin' then, since he was takin' it so good."

Piddie wiped the joy-tears from her eyes. "He 'scused hisself, went inside to wash up and change clothes. He came back outside, sat down like nothin' ever happened, and we all finished eatin'. I reckon it was one of the funniest things I've ever witnessed."

We settled the babies into highchairs with plates of food. Spackle took a position at the base of Sarah's seat, awaiting the inevitable globs of food that would fly his way. Elvis sat at Jon's feet, patiently watching for a handout. Even Shammie lowered herself to attend the family function. I pinched off a few soft pieces of fish and put her with her plate in the fenced-off pool yard away from the greedy canines. Conversations ebbed and flowed around the table, mixed with compliments to the various cooks.

"Great cocktail sauce, whoever made it!" Joe called out.

Jake shot a *nah-nah-nah-boo-boo* look in my direction. I rolled my eyes in return.

"Who made this funny-lookin' mixed-up salad with the little crunchy stuff?" Mandy asked.

Evelyn pointed to her husband. "Joe did. He's taking up cookin' as a hobby since I've had my business to run."

"It's called 'Fu Mi Salad'. Easy recipe. I'll give it to anyone who wants a copy."

Mandy looked pensive for a moment, as if she was considering whether or not to bring up a sore subject. "By the way, Evelyn…have you heard when the film Karen made of Piddie's party's gonna be aired?"

Everyone turned to watch for Evelyn's reaction. "Actually, Karen's assistant called me this mornin'. He said it'll probably air in early October. They'll be sending me a notice of the exact date. I didn't talk directly to Karen…to Mary Elizabeth."

"Well," Piddie said, "I can't wait to see how we all look on TV. Mandy was all worried the camera wouldn't pick up the shade of my hair."

Mandy chuckled. "Some things are just better in person, Miz Piddie. I don't think I'll *ever* match that exact shade of yellow again!"

Piddie patted her hair. "It was a sight to behold, I'll tell you."

"Speaking of always being a sight to behold, where's Elvina today? I thought you said you invited her." Jake's brow furrowed.

Piddie shook her head. "She's off somewheres in Alabama at a funeral. Help me, that woman goes to more layin'-outs than Carters has little pills. I've promised to fill her in on any good gossip we come up with while she's gone."

By the time we made it to the cake and ice cream, everyone was filled to capacity, lolling on the long benches like fat pigs lazy in the summer sunshine. Bobby and Leigh positioned a circle of folding chairs under the shade of the pecan tree, and we reminisced as we digested and picked our teeth.

Holston left to answer the phone. When he returned, his expression revealed the serious nature of the call.

I stood and met him halfway. "Honey, what's wrong? Who was on the phone?"

"Claire. Her mother passed away yesterday morning."

I hugged him. "I'm so sorry. I know you really thought a lot of her."

"I'd like to attend the funeral."

I nodded. "Of course."

Holston leaned over and kissed me. "Thank you for understanding. I love you, Hattie Davis Lewis."

"Back at you. When will you leave?"

Holston sighed. "I'm going to go call the airlines. If I can, I'd like to get a flight out first thing in the morning."

"Okay. Go do what you gotta do."

Holston walked back inside the farmhouse.

"Everything okay?" Mandy asked when I returned to the circle.

"His ex-mother-in-law passed away, up in New York."

"That's too bad. It's never easy getting that kind of news. Is he all right?" Evelyn asked.

108

I nodded. "Yeah. He's going to try to fly out tomorrow to attend her funeral."

"He's never talked much 'bout his first wife," Piddie said. "I kinda got the idea she was a bit of a pill to swallow. But, I've often heard him comment on her mama. She sounds like she was a fine lady."

"Do you need for us to go on home so you can help him pack?" Stephanie asked.

I shook my head. "No, Holston wouldn't want y'all to do that. He's so used to taking off on a moment's notice — he has to go up every now and then to meet with his editor, you know. He keeps a travel bag ready to go. It won't take him long to pack. Then, he'll join us."

As the conversation resumed, a nostalgic wave washed over me. I recalled the numerous times over the years when I had sat under the old tree surrounded by a circle of family and friends. The faces changed. People were added. Some were taken away. The love remained the same.

"Hey," Jake said, "why don't we go see the gazebo? That *is* the whole reason for this cookout, after all."

We formed a procession with Jon's SUV, Bobby's pick-up, the town car, and Margie and John's ATV bringing up the rear.

"I grabbed your guitar," Bobby said as he settled behind the wheel. Leigh and I were crammed hip to hip on the pick-up's bench seat beside him with the babies in our laps.

"I haven't played in years."

Bobby winked. "You'll remember the basic chords. It'll come back to you."

"Glad you have confidence in me, bro." I gestured over my shoulder. "By the way, what's under that old green tarp in the back of the truck?"

"Our gazebo-warming gift," Leigh answered.

We pulled the vehicles into a line in the freshly-graded drive circling a stand of stately pines. Since the ground was soft, Bobby and Jon carried Piddie to the gazebo, then settled her into her wheelchair. From the back of his truck, Bobby unloaded two new white ash rocking chairs and two old porch rockers he and Leigh had stripped and refinished.

"Here you go!" Bobby said as he placed the rockers on the floor of the screened room.

Jake and Jon followed with two of the fullest, most lush Boston ferns I'd ever seen.

"I'll pop out and feed them, Sister-girl. You've been known to kill delicate plants from ten paces away." Jake used a battery-powered screwdriver to install two wrought iron hooks for the hanging ferns.

Evelyn presented a 3 x 5 foot appliquéd flag. Joe tapped two small nails above the door facing the pond and hung the colorful banner. The scene in the center of the cloth depicted our farmhouse on the Hill surrounded by trees, framed by the outline of two interlocking hearts.

"Stephanie, Mandy, and I weren't sure what to give you, so we went together and bought these little wooden side tables," Wanda said.

John and Margie sat a large cardboard box by the door. "This is a ceiling fan — the kind that can stand the elements out-of-doors. We'll come down and hang it later on."

"It's beginnin' to look like home." Jake motioned for Jon to bring the folding chairs from the back of the 4Runner.

Holston joined us shortly. After everyone had *ohh-d* and *ahh-d* over the waterfall and design of the gazebo and the series of decks, we settled into the rockers and chairs.

Bobby went out to his truck and brought back our guitars.

Jake moaned. "We're not goin' to sing *Kum-Ba-Yah*, are we?"

"Only if you're a pain in the butt," Bobby said.

"I'll be good, I promise." Jake traced an imaginary halo above his head and smiled angelically.

Bobby smirked. "I should've thrown you in the fishpond years ago, when I had the chance."

Jake dabbed dramatically at the corners of his eyes. "I just *hate* it when we fight."

After a few missed licks and twanged strings, I got the hang of traversing the guitar's fretboard. I had put the instrument down several years back to spare my over-worked hands and forearms. Now that I no longer banged a computer keypad for the state all day long and had trimmed my massage therapy practice to part time, I could afford to use my hands to play.

The dusky early evening in the gazebo on the hill by my father's pond was one of the rare times to save in memory forever; relished like the sweet, first taste of a summer peach when I closed my eyes and let the syrup dribble down my chin. All of us sitting around in a circle, lantern light painting fancy shadows on our faces, swaying and singing. Half the time, we *lah-la-lahed* and laughed when we couldn't remember all the words. Old songs —folk, gospel, country. Blowin'-in-the-wind, lost-my-baby-and-my-best-dog standards.

Hands clapped and feet stomped in time as Bobby's guitar cut out the tune and I struggled to follow his lead. The new generation at our feet raised their young voices in wordless song to match ours. Two dogs, one mutt and one pedigree, yipped out of tune.

Piddie summed it up. "I reckon if I died right here, right now, I'd die happy."

"Elvina got herself one of them fancy food processors here a while back. She'd chop up the devil hisself if he fell in it! She makes up this salsa dip for the football parties. It'll put hair on your chest, then rip it right back off. Eat too much, and you'll have to take a fan to the privy with you to keep from settin' the woods on fire."

Piddie Davis Longman

Elvina Houston's Fires-of-Hell Salsa

2 14 ½ ounce cans diced tomatoes (drain the water out and save)
1 bunch of green onions, chopped up
4-5 fresh jalapeno peppers, chopped up. Use less if you're a wiener.
¼ cup lemon juice
3 cloves garlic, minced
1 bunch of fresh cilantro, chopped
salt and pepper to taste
2-3 dashes hot pepper sauce (optional)

Put the two cans of tomatoes in and process a few seconds. Add everything else and let that thing rip! Don't let it go on too long, or the whole thing will blend down too far. You want it a little chunky. Here's the thing – if you want the salsa to be on the mild side, scoop the little seeds and white stuff innards out of the peppers. That's the part that makes the heat. You can leave off the hot pepper sauce, too, if your stomach can't take it. If the salsa is too thick, add a little bit of the tomato water you drained out to start with. Serve it up with tortilla chips and lots of something to wash it down with.

CHAPTER ELEVEN

The Hill: Hattie

SINCE HIS FLIGHT to New York was scheduled to depart Tallahassee Regional Airport at 8:20 AM, Holston prepared to leave the farmhouse by 6:30.

"I'll be home as soon as I can after the funeral. I may try to meet with my editor while I'm up there. It'll save me a trip later." He kissed Sarah and me goodbye. I watched his car ease down the lane until it turned onto Highway 269 and disappeared.

"I guess you'll have to settle for having breakfast with your crab-cake mother, hmm?" I tickled my daughter underneath her chubby chin.

Sarah giggled and blew spit bubbles. If they could somehow bottle the delighted innocent happiness of a baby, I'd buy a lifetime stock of the magic elixir. Shammie sauntered into the kitchen and whirled around my feet until I opened a pouch of kitty tender turkey cutlets with gravy and dispatched her to the feeding bowl.

"Why don't you and I have breakfast on the porch?" I asked. Before we moved outside, I placed a small pan filled with water on the stove to heat for steeping teabags. No Southern Belle worth her salt *ever* allowed the home to be without a freshly-brewed gallon of tea.

I settled Sarah into her highchair with a bowl of Cheerios and milk and watched her alternately eat and wear her morning meal. My healthy start consisted of a day-old cinnamon bun from the Madhatter's Sweet Shop and a cup of strong coffee. The way I had it figured, the meal covered two of the important food groups: sugar and caffeine. In the distance, I spotted Margie walking up the lane carrying the daily paper under one arm. She waved when she saw us and turned toward her house.

UP THE DEVIL'S BELLY

The birdfeeders were unusually vacant for first thing in the morning. I crammed the last bite of roll in my mouth, wiped the crusty sugar from the corners of my lips, and rose to refill both hanging feeders with seed from a five-gallon can at the corner of the porch. A little birdie sentinel must have been perched nearby. As soon as I returned to the rocker, the magnolia branches were thick with birds taking turns dipping, diving, chirping, and looking the aviary equivalent of shoppers at a discount department store blue light sale.

Spackle did his part to help make after-breakfast cleanup easy. He captured the spilt milk and clots of soggy cereal that made their way to the wooden planked porch floor.

"Now, missy...," I said to Sarah as I extracted her from the chair, "you and I have to go feed the fish."

The early morning mists swirled over the water of the fishpond. I parked the ATV at the top of the hill next to the gazebo and gathered Sarah in my arms. Bobby and Holston had moved the barrel of commercial fish food from its old spot on the earthen dam to the edge of the lower deck near the water.

"Come and get it!" I yelled, banging the side of the rusted drum with a pipe.

The musky scent of fish teased my nose as the surface of the pond began to ripple. I removed the heavy cement-lined lid, scooped an old coffee can full of the round pellets, and swung the can in an arch through the air. The moment the floating pellets hit the water, the catfish rushed to feed. Sarah giggled and clapped her hands. The fish scooped pellets into their gaping black-whiskered mouths before flipping and diving underneath. In a few minutes, every piece of food had disappeared, and the water smoothed into a mirror of the surrounding trees. Though I'd watched this spectacle hundreds of times growing up, it still fascinated me.

Sarah and I rocked in the screened gazebo, enjoying the solitude of the deep woods. Understandable, why this had been my father's favorite spot to unwind at the end of a workday. Distant noises carried in the early morning air. The roar of the locomotive engines switching boxcars three miles away at River Junction Crossing sounded deceptively close-by, as if I could walk to the rise of the hill and see them jockeying back and forth. From the direction of the farmhouse, I heard Spackle's distinctive high-pitched bark.

I gathered Sarah in my arms. "We'd better get on back, Sarah Chuntian Lewis. Sounds like we might have unannounced company."

Halfway through the overgrown field beyond the edge of the woods, the rear of the farmhouse came into view. Alarmed by the thin line of dark smoke streaming from the roof, I gunned the ATV's accelerator. I screeched to a halt in the front yard and rushed with Sarah balanced on one hip to the front door. My worst fears were confirmed; the kitchen was on fire!

"Oh, my God!"

I had seen enough movies about fire to know that I shouldn't enter a burning building. I glanced toward the pool house, then sprinted across the yard and fumbled for the hidden key ring.

"C'mon! C'mon, dammit!" The lock finally clicked, and I scurried to the extension phone we had recently installed under the dressing room shelter.

"911...what is the nature of your emergency?"

"Fire! My kitchen's on fire!" My mind was a turmoil of thoughts.

"Your address, please."

"Umm....umm...133 Davis Road off Highway 269 south of Chattahoochee. Please hurry!"

I dropped the receiver, trying desperately to tame my panicked mind. "Fire extinguishers! In the shop!" I placed Sarah carefully into a small fenced play yard by the swing set. "Stay here, honey."

I ran to my father's wooden workshop behind the farmhouse and located the two large extinguishers behind the door and lugged them outside, one by one.

"Too heavy! I can't carry them. The ATV! Get the ATV!" a voice in my head prompted.

I ran to the front yard, wheeled the vehicle into position, hoisted the extinguishers onto the wire rack on the rear, then screeched back to the front yard. In the distance, I saw Margie and John running up the driveway.

I was struggling with the pin on one of the extinguishers when my neighbors reached the house. "Margie told me she saw smoke! Did you call the fire department?" John called out.

"Yeah! On their way!"

John ran toward the pool. When I saw him head toward the pump with a long coil of hose, I remembered Bobby saying something about always having the backwash action of the pool pump as a means of putting out a fire. Margie and I had the fire extinguishers ready and dragged them toward the kitchen door.

"Wait!" John called. He opened the screened door and felt the wooden door for heat.

"Should we wait for the fire trucks?" I asked.

John shook his head. "It'll take them a few minutes to get all the way out here from town. Let's at least see if it's anything we can start on. If it's too bad, we'll get right back out! The door's cool. Let me go in first with one of the extinguishers, then y'all follow with the other one and the water hose." He opened the door and a gush of black smoke boiled from the opening. "Stay down low!"

John began to express the chemical foam. The smoke cleared slightly. "I can see the flames. They're comin' from the stove end of the kitchen!" He waved. Margie and I flanked John. I sprayed the walls with water as they used the extinguishers on the stove and space above the exhaust hood.

116

Sirens sounded in the distance. In a few minutes, the professional firefighters burst into the smoke-filled room and helped us outside. As the three of us coughed to clear our soot-filled lungs, the crew successfully drenched the remaining flames.

"I know exactly what caused the fire," I said, in answer to the chief's question. "I put a small pot on the stove. I was boiling water to make some tea." I stared numbly at the smoldering remains of my mother's country kitchen.

Chief Hall cleared his throat. "Ma'am?"

"Oh…sorry. Anyway, I guess I forgot it. My daughter and I went to the pond to feed the fish." Tears gathered at the corners of my eyes. "How stupid of me!"

He squinted his eyes. "This was a pretty intense fire, Hattie. Looks more like a grease fire."

"Oh my God." The realization hit me full in the face. "The oil we used to cook the French fries for the cookout yesterday…it was on the back element of the stove where I left it to cool. Like I've done a million times before." I shook my head in disbelief. "There was a large Dutch oven full of oil. I guess I accidentally turned the wrong knob." I closed my eyes. "I am responsible for torching my mother's kitchen…my kitchen!"

Chief Hall rested his hand on my shoulder. "Hattie, this kind of thing happens. Why, my wife and I have left pots of oil sittin' on the stove to cool off, just like you did. The important thing is — you and your daughter are all right. Heck, it's almost like Mr. D. built this house with a kitchen fire in mind."

I wiped my tears with the backside of one soot-stained hand. "What do you mean?"

"I remember my daddy helpin' Mr. D. on this house years ago. Your daddy built this farmhouse a section at the time…as he and your mama had the money. There used to be an old wooden house on this site. As I recall, your daddy built the kitchen first, right before you were born. Then, he added the living room and master bedroom, I believe. I think the back two bedrooms were the last he did. Anyway, it effectively stopped the fire from spreading fast. The cement block walls between the kitchen and the other sections were double thickness, on account of the way he constructed the rooms. We're checking over the rest of the house. Looks like the professional cleaners will have to deal with some minor smoke damage in the living room, but the doors separating the bedroom sections were closed off. Overall, you're pretty fortunate. Any other house, you would have had a lot more damage, maybe even lost the entire structure."

Spackle licked my fingers, as if to say he felt sorry for me. My heart sank.

"Oh, no."

"What's wrong?"

I ran my hands through my hair. "Shammie. My cat. I can't remember…was she in the kitchen when I left?"

"Jerry?" Chief Hall called to one of his firefighters. "Is it safe for Mrs. Lewis to go in and look for her cat?"

The firefighter coiling a hose nodded. "Yes sir, boss. Floor's pretty slippery, but the roof's stable. Only one place right over the stove's burned all the way through."

"You go on and hunt for your cat," Margie called over to me from the swingset. "John and I will watch over Sarah."

The sight of the charred kitchen made the bile rise in my throat. Blackened water and foam stood in sludgy pools on the melted flooring. I took a deep breath. First things first.

"Shammie? Kitty…kitty," I called in a soft voice.

She'd be cowering somewhere, if she was alive. A disgruntled yowl sounded from the underside of my favorite recliner. Fortunately, the chair was on the side of the room that had escaped the formidable heat and smoke.

I flipped the footrest up and leaned down to peer beneath the ragged underbelly of the chair. A sooty, frightened feline face blinked back at me. Shammie wormed her way from under the upholstery and studied me with large yellow eyes oozing with disdain.

"YOW-ULLLL!" she cursed.

"I know, I know." I scooped her into my arms and sobbed into her soiled fur.

I stepped from the remains of my kitchen, soot covering my face, clothes, and hair, my face bent toward the scruffy cat cradled in my arms. By this time, the neighbors from as far away as two miles had arrived.

The news of the fire's location brought the family screaming from town. As soon as they phoned Bobby and Leigh, Evelyn and Piddie broke the posted speed limit hurtling toward the Hill in the Lincoln. Joe had already left for the Sunday Men's Breakfast at the Baptist Church, but immediately followed in his truck as soon as word of the fire reached him. Jon and Jake skidded to a halt in the 4Runner. My family and friends surrounded me like a mother octopus.

Jake pushed a damp hank of hair from my eyes. "Sister-girl, you can stay at the mansion. I'm sure Holston would want you to do that tonight."

"We got the extra room, Hattie. Why don't you stay with us?" Evelyn offered.

"I'll whip up some cathead biscuits for you, sugar," Piddie said.

I sank onto one of the swing set seats. "Lord help me. How am I going to tell Holston?"

"Everything will be okay, Hattie," Bobby said. "I know lots of builders around here. We'll have the kitchen good as new in no time."

Jake plopped down on the seat next to me. "I can help you redecorate. Look at the bright side — you wanted to update the appliances and fixtures anyway."

My soot-dusted neighbors stood to leave. "We're gonna go on home and get cleaned up now, Hattie. Margie and I will watch over the place for you. Don't you worry about that."

Evelyn rested her hand on my shoulder. "Why don't you and I go gather up some of your and Sarah's clothes and essentials and pack a bag to take to town. You both need some rest. It's been an excitin' morning for you. We'll all think more on this tomorrow after a good breakfast…after the shock's worn off."

"I'll take Spackle and Shammie back with me. We can keep them at the mansion for now," Jake said.

I felt numb, tired, and sick at heart.

"Sister-girl," Jake said as he circled me in his arms, "it's probably best if you wait and call Holston in the morning. He'll be at the funeral today, and you'll be a little calmer by then, hmm?"

Before she left the house for the Triple C, Evelyn made the coffee, strong — just the way I needed it. To my amazement, I had slept soundly the night before. Sarah, her normal morning self, didn't seem to notice, or mind, that her surroundings had changed. She sat in an old wooden highchair Joe had rescued from the attic; a leftover from visits from the grandchildren when they were young.

"Goo-gah!" Sarah babbled to Aunt Piddie.

"Yeah, my little chinaberry, I'm your Goo-gah!"

Piddie and Sarah continued the conversation in mixed English and baby-eze. Joe, draped in an apron, was browning a pan of thick-cut country bacon. "Over easy, Hattie?"

"Hmm?"

He grinned. "Your eggs. How do you like 'em?"

"Oh, Joe, don't go to any trouble on account of me being here."

120

He waved the spatula in the air. "No trouble. You need to eat, and I like to cook. Started up when Evelyn needed to spend so much time at the workshop. I'm thinking of taking some classes next semester. I can handle the simple stuff, but I kinda think I'd like to try my hand at gourmet cooking."

I sipped the strong black coffee. "In that case, eggs sunny-side up."

Joe whistled as he broke two eggs onto the hot griddle. Finally, Evelyn's professionally-outfitted kitchen had a true chef at its helm.

At noon, I reluctantly dialed Holston's cell phone number. His deep voice brought fresh tears to my eyes. After we talked for a few minutes about the funeral and his ex-wife's family, I broached the subject of the fire. "Honey...do you love me?"

"Madly."

"You sure?"

He chuckled. "Of course I do, Hattie. Please tell me you're not feeling insecure about me being up here around Claire. Believe me, it's not an issue."

"No, I'm okay with all of that." I hesitated. "You remember when I told you I thought I might like to buy a new stove?"

"Yes."

"...and a new refrigerator — one with the ice and water dispenser on the front?"

"Yes."

"And, umm, how Jake wanted to redecorate and update the kitchen a bit?"

"Yes."

"Well... it seems as if we're going to get to do all of that."

There was a brief moment of silence on the other end of the line. "For some reason, I feel a little uneasy. Should I, Hattie?"

I swallowed around the golf ball-sized lump that had formed in my throat. "I burned down the kitchen yesterday."

A sharp intake of breath sounded. "Everyone's okay?"

"We're all fine. The only thing that's hurt is my pride."

Holston chuckled softly. "You been taking cooking lessons from Evelyn, hon?"

I laughed hard; a deep, gurgling belly guffaw. My entire physique dissolved into a hiccuping, snorting fit. Tears rolled down my cheeks as pent-up fear and tension left my body.

"Hattie....Hattie....HATTIE?"

"Yes, Holston," I managed when I was able to speak.

"I'll come home first thing tomorrow," Holston said. "Where are you now?"

"At Joe and Evelyn's, but I figure we can stay at the mansion while the kitchen's being rebuilt. Jake has the animals there, already."

He sighed. "I'll come straight to the mansion when I get back. We can ride out to the Hill together, later...to look things over."

"Holston?"

"Yes?"

"Sorry I was such a big dope."

"I'll think of a suitable punishment for you when I get home," he said in a low, sexy voice.

"It don't much matter what side of the tracks you come up on. Bad circumstances can be overcome, with a little doin'. Where you think they find diamonds? In the rough, that's where."

Piddie Davis Longman

CHAPTER TWELVE

Moses Clark

TWO DIRT AND RAIN-SPLATTERED TRASH BAGS leaned against the side of the tool shed in the rear of Hank Henderson's yard.

"That dang Aflonso!" Moses muttered under his breath. "He was supposed to take those to the dump two days ago." Antagonism toward the older boy bubbled like a festering peat bog.

Moses halted the lawnmower at the edge of the grass and grabbed the yard cart. The first bag was heavy with soggy leaves and twigs. When he loaded the second bag, he heard an odd metallic clank as it settled on the cart. Moses looked around to assure no one was watching and opened the twist-tie at the top of the bag. Rooting under the top layer of leaves, he uncovered a small cloth sack containing two men's Rolex watches, five diamond rings in assorted sizes, and a tangle of gold neck chains. Digging further, his hand felt the hard edges of a slim, plastic-covered box. He tugged it to the surface — a laptop computer.

"Man!" He plunged his left hand deep into the muck. Something sharp pierced the soft flesh of his palm, and he jerked away from the bag. "Dang!"

Blood dripped from a gash in the center of his palm. He grabbed the filthy sweat rag from his back pocket and wrapped it around his hand to staunch the bleeding.

Using his right hand and the free fingers of his injured left hand, he twisted the bag shut and replaced the tie. A thought struck him: Alfonso would sense that someone had tampered with the bags. Moses emptied the yard cart, careful to replace the trash bags in their original position against the tool shed.

Since the garage door was closed, he couldn't tell if Mr. Hank had left while he was mowing the back yard. Being careful to avoid making noise, Moses slipped into the house through the unlocked side door. A search for first aide supplies in the hall bathroom proved futile. Except for a spare roll of toilet tissue and a set of clean towels, the cabinets were barren. He'd find Tameka. She knew where everything was in the house.

Moses proceeded to the master bedroom. The blinds were drawn against the midday sun, giving the dark room a gloomy, closed-off feel. Moses' eyes adjusted to the dim light.

"There's that side table where Tameka said he keeps the gun," Moses said to himself. Reckon it wouldn't do any harm to look at it. He slid the drawer open stealthily and removed the SigSauer .45. The handgun felt cool and deadly in his palm. He turned it over to study it from all sides. Resting his finger on the trigger, he gently pulled. The double-action safety prohibited easy movement of the trigger. Only a strong, deliberate pressure could fire the handgun. After the initial discharge, the gun would remain cocked and ready to fire with the faintest of touches.

Moses heard a stealthy movement in the hall behind him. He carefully relaxed his index finger and the hammer eased into rest position.

"Moses!" Tameka's scolding whisper broke the silence. "What you doin' back here in Mr. Hank's room?" Her eyes widened with alarm when she spotted the handgun in her brother's hand. "Put that back!"

She rushed over and grabbed the .45 from his palm, eased it into its proper place next to the telephone book, and closed the drawer. "We would lose our jobs if he caught us touchin' one of his guns! What you tryin' to do?"

Moses fought the urge to laugh at her, standing there tight-lipped, hands propped on her hips all grown-up acting. "I was lookin' for you." He held out his loosely bandaged left hand. "I cut myself. I thought you'd know where Mr. Hank keeps the Band-Aids and stuff."

Seated in the oxblood-red leather chair of the desk in his study, Hank Henderson balanced his latest acquisition in the palm of his right hand. He had splurged on the handgun: the latest Kimber's .45 ACP Ultracarry. With a caliber known for stopping a fight with a single hit 95% of the time, the gun was the most effective man-stopper he knew of, short of a bazooka. The precision piece sported a slick, cool gunmetal blue finish. Even more reassuring was the knowledge that it was loaded with Remington's Hot +P golden sabers. The salesman had assured him he would *see light through the hole* if he shot someone coming, uninvited, into his bedroom at night.

The cherished collection currently contained thirty handguns; all clean and oiled with an obsessive regularity. Though he preferred a weapon with a visible external hammer, he owned two Glocks, complements of his jerk-off cousin's evidence room clear-out special.

Strangely enough, his omnipotent father had spurred his passion for weapons acquisition. The love of firepower was the only interest they had shared. Hank greatly admired the family heirloom dueling pistols, still resting in their original tooled leather case. One of his favorite pieces was the Colt single-action .45, made in Colt's custom shop; his father's last $1,500.00 deal two weeks before his death.

Hank smiled. No doubt, the Kimber .45 would bump one of his SigSauer's back into the locked gun case. The weapon would stay close to him like a clingy new lover —far less trouble than any female he'd ever encountered. He stood and slipped the handgun into a new Wilson Combat Pager Pal, a cleverly-designed concealed holster that slid under the rim of his pants with a fake pager over his belt in the front. His paunch worked to his advantage. The holster fit snugly against his body, made even more invisible by the baggy excess of material necessary to span his waist.

Hank grunted. He supposed he'd have to endure the company of the annoying group of wannabe commandos his cousin called buddies. The firing range south of town where the local yahoos practiced their limited skills was dull as dirt compared to the walk-through course the paramilitary group maintained near Greensboro — hidden deep in a two hundred acre private woodland area.

He grudgingly endured the secret code password, fatigue-clad nonsense the group embraced in order to hone his reflexes on a series of pop-up life-sized dummies. A few of the members frowned on his refusal to trudge through the three-mile series of military-style obstacle courses. He overcame their grumbling reticence by quadrupling his monthly membership fee. Money opened more doors than brute force and diplomacy put together.

Hank heard the faint click of the side door. "These got-damned black kids just think they can waltz into my house at will! I'll be so glad when I can leave here. Just one more month…that should be plenty of time. Tameka!" he called.

No response came from the opposite end of the house. He carefully removed the Kimber .45 from its holster, placed it in the gun case, and secured the lock. After he figured out who'd entered his house without so much as a perfunctory knock, he'd return the handgun to its rightful position.

At the entrance to his bedroom he paused, straining to hear the muffled conversation. "What are you two kids up to back here?" he asked in a firm voice as he slipped into the room behind Tameka and Moses.

Tameka spun around, startled. "Mr. Hank! Umm…Moses cut his hand."

Hank stepped forward. "Let me see."

"I was lookin' for Tameka to find me a Band-Aid," Moses said.

Though he had a gut instinct there was more to it than they were letting on, Hank motioned the children toward his private bathroom. "C'mon in here, Moses. I have a first aid kit."

Hank donned the pair of rubber gloves that came with the kit. "I don't believe in handling blood. You can't be too safe, these days. Let's see how bad it is…and, whether you'll need to go around to the clinic for some stitches."

Moses winced and turned his head to one side as Hank removed the bloodstained rag from the wound. The two-inch superficial cut had almost stopped bleeding.

"Well…it's not that bad, see?" Hank attempted a comforting tone. "Just a surface scratch."

He washed Moses' hand with mild soap under running water, applied a thin glaze of antibacterial ointment, and applied an oversized adhesive bandage to protect the wound. "What'd you cut this on, son?"

Moses mind raced, casting around for a believable lie. "I was takin' the leaf bag off the back of the mower and it stuck. I put my hand up underneath to jiggle it loose. I reckon I caught it on somethin'."

Hank frowned. "Good thing that mower shuts off when you let go of the handle. Otherwise, you'd have cut your fingers off on the blade. You should never stick your hands inside the working part of the mower! There're a lot of sharp edges."

Moses nodded. "Yes'sir, Mr. Hank."

Hank sighed. Everyone was looking for a reason to file a lawsuit, nowadays. He'd best play it safe. "I suppose I'd better take you on around to the clinic for a tetanus shot. Whatever you cut yourself on could've been rusted."

Moses groaned. "Those tetanus shots hurt like the dickens! Do I have to get one?"

"It's a sight better than getting lock jaw and dying," Hank said.

"Moses had to get one of 'em last year. He stepped on a nail one time when he was goin' barefoot last summer," Tameka said.

Hank's mood brightened. "Well, then! That's good news for you. A tetanus shot's good for ten years. If you're sure you had one recently, you're protected."

Hank stood and peeled off the gloves, discarding them in the small metal trashcan near the sink. "Why don't you store the lawnmower, for now. Tameka, finish up your chores, and I'll run you both on home to your grandmother's. We don't want this cut to get dirty and infected, now do we?"

"I'm not through with the back yard, Mr. Hank."

He forced a smile. "No matter. It doesn't show from the road, anyway. You can finish it when you come next time. Won't hurt a thing 'til then."

Moses nodded and left to store the yard tools. Hank returned to his study for the new .45.

"Mr. Hank?" a soft voice called behind him.

He turned to see Tameka, head bowed shyly. "Thank you for taking care of Moses' hand."

He smiled. "Well, now. That's what I'm here for, isn't it?"

Fate had just provided another opportunity for him to display kindness and generosity to his next little video star.

*"When I get up to Heaven, I'll have a few questions for the
feller in charge. Like, why is it good folks suffer from cancer
and the like, and the bad ones just live right on and on? If it
was up to me, the mean and cruel would be the ones gettin' all
the bad ailments. You rape someone, your tally-wacker just falls
right off – like an overripe fig. That'd slow down meanness,
I do believe. Then, we could spend all our money on buildin'
schools and parks, rather than prisons."*

  Piddie Davis Longman

CHAPTER THIRTEEN

Triple C Day Spa and Salon

FOR THE FIRST TIME IN A WEEK, the waiting room at the Triple
C Day Spa and Salon was barren. The sole patron, Ladonna O'Donnell,
and Mandy were sequestered in the hair salon dreaming up possible new
up-do's for the imminent Miss Madhatter beauty contest, a recent addition
to the Madhatter's Festival.

The Twin City golf tournament had come and gone, leaving an exhausted
staff in its wake. The town's citizens could now breathe easier and prepare for
the upcoming football season. Delighted Seminole fans anticipated Florida State's
kick-off game against Duke University. University of Florida Gators, fans as
rabidly faithful as the Seminoles, geared up for their season as well. Both teams
had lost several starting players to graduation the previous year and speculation
sizzled as to which Florida team, if any, stood a ghost of a chance to snag the
National Championship title. Though the two factions were polarized against

each other, they joined in despising the other Florida football powerhouse, the University of Miami Hurricanes.

Jake deposited a fresh flower arrangement in front of Piddie's station at the reception desk. She looked up from the appointment book. "What's got you grinnin' like a goat eatin' briars?"

"It's almost here, Pid." He picked at a stray sprig of maidenhair fern.

"Don't I know it! I got to get me a new roster and study up on my Seminoles. There're so many new fellers, I don't know all their names and where they're supposed to play."

"Jon has a friend who works in the athletic department at FSU. I'll see if he can get us one of those media guides." Jake's face curled into a pout. "Hattie doesn't want to go to the first home game with me. She's still a bit peevish about the fire. Usually, by this time, I can get her all fired up about football season. She's just all depressed." He propped his chin on his hands and frowned.

"Well, now…a shock like that does take a lot outta a person. She's been busy as a stump-tailed cow in fly season, meetin' builders and pickin' out the fixin's for the redo on the kitchen. I hear it's goin' along pretty fast, with all of Bobby's buddies helpin' out."

"Yeah. I was out to the Hill yesterday. They already have the flooring and the burned-out wall behind the stove ripped out, and the cleaners have removed the soot from the walls in the living room. I finally talked Hattie into going ahead and replacing the carpet in the living room and putting a wood floor in there and the kitchen." Jake rolled his eyes. "I don't know what I've gotten myself in for, helping her redecorate. She's slow as Christmas when it comes to making a decision."

Piddie shook her finger. "It's a woman's *pero-gitty* to change her mind, after all. You let her be. She'll figure it all out. Even a blind hog finds an acorn, ever' now and then."

"I guess." Jake pointed to the wall behind him. "I noticed you got your new artwork up. Looks fantastic."

Piddie grinned. "I just love havin' it here where I can rest my eyes on it durin' the day. All the whirling colors! I had the time of my life at my birthday party, thanks to you and all my friends and family. I never laughed so hard in all my life as I did at that video Hattie and Holston put together. You never realize how funny-lookin' you are till you see yourself on the big screen!" She pivoted to study the abstract artwork. "I was shore surprised when little Ruth gave me the paintin'. She's somethin', ain't she?"

Jake nodded. "Her mama told me that she's gonna have a show at Lemoyne Art Gallery in Tallahassee, end of October."

"Is that so? She was plain precious. Told me the paintin' was called…oh, I can't remember that Chinese word to save my life. It was the word for *heaven*, her mama told me. I reckon the young'un wanted to give me a sneak peak of things to come."

Jake shook his head. "Hope not…I mean, I want you to *as*cend instead of *de*scend…just not anytime soon."

"Lordy-be, Jake. I'm over 98 now. It's bound to happen some day. I'll be sure to come back and visit y'all if I figure out a way."

Jake steered the conversation away from death. "You gonna hang your plaque here too?"

Piddie shook her head. The mass of sprayed curls trembled. "I had Joe hang it in my bedroom at Evelyn's. That tickled me pink, too. I reckon if I don't make it all the way to a *hundret* to get my letter from the Prez-e-dent, that plaque from the Chairman of the Chattahoochee Downtown Merchant's Association will do me just fine!"

Jake leaned over the desk and whispered, "I got an idea."

UP THE DEVIL'S BELLY

"It ain't gonna end one of us up in jail, is it?"

Jake shook his head. "Why don't you plan on going with me to the first FSU home game?"

Piddie clutched her chest. "Me? What about Jon?"

Jake smirked and swatted the air with one thin hand. "He'd rather watch paint dry than sit through a football game. C'mon Pid, you'd love it! We could stop by and pick up a bucket of chicken. I'll pack a cooler with drinks, make some potato salad. I can get a parking pass for the handicapped section right up close to the stadium, and there're elevators to help us get up to the top."

"I 'preciate you thinkin' of me, sugar, but, I promised Elvina I'd watch the games with her this year. She done went out and bought a big screen TV, special for football season. The best part — she's got her some new hearin' aids. I used to couldn't talk to her on the phone with out yellin' like I was in the next county. Law, it got to where I couldn't stand to watch TV with her. The sound was turned up so loud, my eardrums almost caught a'fire!"

Jake laughed. "I oughta just come watch the game with y'all."

"That'd be a hoot. Elvina's decided she's gonna root for the dang Florida Gators when our Seminoles play them this year. She's crossin' over to the other side just to peeve me. It might be good to have you there to tip the balance." Piddie leaned over and whispered in a low tone. "Elvina's discovered them hard lemonade drinks. After a few, you forget who you're rootin' for, anyway...but, don't you dare tell her I told you so. She'd pitch a fit and fall in it!"

"Lips sealed, throw away the key." Jake pressed his lips together between his index finger and thumb, then flung his hand into the air.

She pointed to the flower arrangement on the corner of her desk. "Jolene sure did a good job with this LadyHat arrangement. I think she was rightly cleaver to come up with the idea of usin' hats as flower pots." Piddie patted the daisies and baby's breath bouquet.

"She said you gave her a bunch of your old hats."

Piddie nodded. "I'm gettin' rid of stuff I don't use. I gave a passel of 'em away when I moved in with Evelyn. I don't wear my hats much anymore, not since Mandy got the hang of gettin' my hair piled up just right. I'd hate to press it down and spoil the fruits of her labor."

"It's a shame, really, that women don't wear hats much anymore. I think they look so sexy and sophisticated…ah, well." He tilted his head. "You know, Piddie, you don't look like you feel too good."

Piddie let out a big sigh. "I ain't felt worth a plug nickel this mornin'. I went to bed with the chickens, and I reckon I slept okay. I feel a mite sick to my stomach, off and on…even though I can't imagine why, with Joe doin' the cookin' now. Here lately, my get up and go has got up and went."

He turned toward the elevator door. "Jon's still upstairs. He hasn't left to see patients yet. Let's get him to check your blood pressure and just make sure you're okay."

"I don't want to be a *bothermint.*"

Jake shrugged. "It's no bother, Piddie. I'll ask him to check in with you on his way out."

Holston appeared at the door leading to the kitchen, holding Sarah in his arms. "Piddie, would one of you mind watching Sarah for a few minutes? I'm on a conference call, and she's talking up a storm."

Piddie held her pudgy arms up and waved her hands. "Come here, little chinaberry. Goo-gah will take you."

Sarah nestled happily into Piddie's soft lap.

"I won't be much longer," Holston said as he turned to leave.

Piddie patted Jake on the hand. "Go on 'bout your business, now. Don't you worry 'bout me. Sarah and I got some book work to do."

"Okay. I'll get Shug to check on you. Toodles!" He shuffled toward the elevator.

Settled in the stylist chair, Ladonna O'Donnell tugged at a wispy sausage-shaped curl trailing down her left cheek. "I don't know that I like all this scruffy little stray stuff, Mandy. Can't you up-sweep my whole head of hair?"

"Won't work, hon," Mandy said, talking around the two hairpins she held in her pressed lips. "The new growth 'round your face's too short. Besides, it'd make you look too severe if I pulled it all back. The fringe softens your facial features."

"All right. I suppose you know what you're doin'. I'll hush. You're the boss."

Mandy smiled. "I love it when someone says that to me!"

The sound of crying emanated from the direction of the reception room.

"That sounds like Sarah," Mandy said. "She must be teethin'. She's been a little peevish here lately."

When the wailing failed to stop, Mandy glanced toward the salon door. "I better go check on her. Piddie's probably on the phone and got her hands full. Be right back."

Ladonna studied her reflection in a hand mirror, trying on seductive smiles. "Sure, take your time. I ain't got nowheres else to be, this mornin'."

"Piddie?" Mandy called as she walked to the front desk. The sound of crying grew louder and more urgent. When she reached the antique reception desk, she saw Sarah sitting on Piddie's lap, fat tears rolling down her reddened cheeks. From Piddie's slumped posture, Mandy knew immediately. Something was terribly wrong.

Mandy took Sarah into her arms and gently shook Piddie by the shoulder. "Miz Piddie? Miz Piddie?"

Piddie's head lolled to one side. Her face was ghostly pale with a faint blue tinge.

"Oh, my God! Evelyn?! Holston?! Ladonna?! Somebody!"

Ladonna, still wearing her plastic drape, was the first to arrive. "What's'a matter?"

"Dial 911!" Mandy ordered as she loosened the top buttons of Piddie's dress. "Somethin's bad wrong with her!"

Evelyn and Holston rushed into the room. Jon and Jake heard the commotion from the balcony of the second floor. Jon took the steps on the winding staircase in two's while Jake shuffled to the elevators.

Jon felt for a pulse, leaning over Piddie to listen for breath sounds. "She's not breathing and there's no pulse! Holston, help me get her onto the floor."

The two men eased Piddie as quickly as they could manage onto the Oriental rug. Jon tilted her head to open her airway and, once again, checked for any sign that she was breathing on her own. "Anyone besides me know CPR?" he asked.

Mandy handed the baby off to Evelyn and crouched beside him. "I do. Where you want me?"

"I'll do the compressions. Go ahead and give her two breaths."

Mandy pinched Piddie's nose together, pressed her mouth to the older woman's, and gave two even breaths. Jon positioned his palms and began chest compressions. Evelyn, Ladonna, and Holston watched helplessly from a short distance.

"I'm going outside to wave down the ambulance," Jake said.

For what seemed like an eternity, Jon and Mandy administered CPR, switching places after a couple of minutes. Jon checked again for any signs of life, then switched positions with Mandy. Finally, the wail of sirens echoed from the street. Jake motioned the paramedics into the room.

UP THE DEVIL'S BELLY

Jon and Mandy continued CPR until the paramedics signaled them to stop. Marney Sullivan, EMT, opened Piddie's housedress and positioned the two adhesive pads of the defibrillator on her upper right chest and lower left abdomen. Once activated, the machine assessed her condition, charged, and delivered an electrical jolt.

Piddie's eyes fluttered slightly, and she took a few shallow breaths. Terence Odom, the second paramedic, administered oxygen as Marney relayed information on pulse and blood pressure. The paramedics inserted an IV and continued to work until they felt they had Piddie stabilized. Her friends and family trailed the gurney to the front entrance and watched wordlessly as Piddie was loaded into the gaping maw of the ambulance.

Jake turned to Evelyn. "You going with her to the hospital?"

"I'll get my keys. Will someone call Joe?" she asked as she handed Sarah to Holston.

"Certainly. You go on over to Tallahassee. We'll take care of calling anyone who needs to know. You sure you're okay to drive?"

Evelyn nodded and rushed from the room.

"My God," Mandy whispered. She leaned over and picked up a small silk daisy that had fallen from Piddie's hair. "What'll we do?"

"Hold down the fort." Jake smiled weakly. "That's what Piddie would have us do…and, pray."

Piddie's heart continued to beat weakly until the ambulance arrived at the emergency entrance at the rear of Tallahassee Memorial Hospital. She felt a gentle warmth — saw a glow above her. She felt herself lifting off and looked down at the worn out, sad, old woman's body on the gurney. Joy flooded her spirit. She hadn't felt this good since her twenties. As she watched her physical body being wheeled through the double doors, she felt her soul open up, release.

"Lord almighty! If I'd'a known goin' to my glory was gonna feel this good, I'd'a quit fightin' it long ago!" She felt the words leave her consciousness, having no mouth to speak.

Piddie became part of the morning breeze, whirled with the colors of the sky. She turned toward Home. Then, she hesitated. Home was right there — where it would be for all eternity.

"Maybe I'll just enjoy this whole floatin' thing for awhile. It's gonna be stirred up down there like a kicked-over fire ant hill. I'll wait a bit before I take care of a few things."

At 10:25 AM, after several unsuccessful attempts at resuscitation, Liddyanne "Piddie" Davis Longman was pronounced dead by the attending emergency room physician.

"When we leave this old world, and we all will some day, we'll find out what's on the other side. I've heard there's no pain or sorrow. That sounds mighty appealin'."

Piddie Davis Longman

CHAPTER FOURTEEN

The Madhatter's Sweet Shop and Massage Parlor

I KNEW IMMEDIATELY from the ghostly, stricken expression on Jake's face; something terrible had happened while I was cloistered in the massage therapy room with my first morning client.

"Sister-girl." Jake hugged me, sobbing.

"Wha...?"

"Piddie...it's Piddie..."

I grabbed a tissue and offered it to him. He blew his nose loudly and heaved a huge sigh. "We think Piddie's had a heart attack. The ambulance just left for Tallahassee. Evelyn's following in the Lincoln." He rested one hand on my shoulder. "I called your other clients. Jolene can take over the shop. I'm willing and ready to go over to the hospital with you." His face sagged with sorrow and worry. "I just feel so helpless being here doing nothing."

A switch inside of my psyche flips on when disaster hits. Once I move past the initial shock and disbelief, the *General in Charge of Emergency Operations* steps in, blows a whistle to staunch the scream of emotional gibberish, and orders my body to action.

"Okay. Let me get Mrs. Harris dismissed. I'll clean the room real fast, and ....Holston and Sarah...."

"They went back to the Hill. He was in his office when it happened, and he wanted to take Sarah home so they could both calm down. You want me to call him and let him know we're heading on over?"

I shook my head. "No. He'll know to sit tight until he hears from me. We'll call from the cellphone as soon as we're on the Interstate."

Jolene leaned her head into the sweet shop. "Y'all go on ahead. I'll see to Ethel Harris and straighten up the therapy room. I can always call Julie down at the Homeplace if things get too wild for me to handle here."

"Thanks tons, Jolene. We'll call you as soon as we know anything." I grabbed my purse, and we exited by the rear delivery door.

"I'll drive," I said as I bumped the keyless entry button.

Jake crossed himself and slid into the passenger's seat.

I rolled my eyes. "Don't worry. I'll be careful. I'd just rather it be me who gets the speeding ticket, especially since Betty's on my insurance policy."

I had made the same balls-to-the-wall drive from Chattahoochee to Tallahassee Memorial's emergency room twice in the past four years — following Jake's assault and Piddie's first visit.

No matter how far the speedometer needle tipped to the right, the asphalt felt as if it had turned into a soupy quagmire. I pushed the SUV to the limits of my driving abilities. The parking gods smiled down upon us, saving a spot near the ambulance bay.

I stood behind Billy-Bob Redneck and his extended interbred family at the registration desk, fidgeting with frustration.

"Sister-girl, look…," Jake said softly. He pointed toward the crowded waiting room.

Evelyn sat amidst the sea of human pain and suffering. Her expression was blank. She stared into space with no recognition of the bedlam churning around her.

I picked my way through the crowd and knelt at her feet. "Evelyn?" I asked in a soft voice.

Slowly, she lifted her head and studied first me, then Jake, as if we were total strangers who'd come to tell her the Lincoln was double-parked.

I rested my hands on her knees. "Ev?"

Recognition and a flicker of pain registered in her eyes. "Hattie?" She looked up. "Jake?"

I asked in a soft voice, "Ev, where's Piddie?"

Evelyn sighed as if the weight of impending sorrow had planted a heavy hand on her shoulders, keeping her bolted to her seat. "Mama's gone Home."

My brows knit together. "Home? She just got here! Jake said she'd had a heart attack. How could she possibly have gone home?"

Jake reached down and touched my arm gently. "Sister-girl, I think what Evelyn may be trying to say is…" His voice cracked as he struggled for the words. "Piddie's passed on."

Evelyn lowered her head. Her shoulders shook slightly as she sobbed.

"I'll go call and make sure Joe's on his way," Jake said.

Elvina Houston

Elvina Houston shuffled into her cramped kitchen for her morning cup of green tea. She had given up coffee a couple of years back after reading an article on the benefits of the exotic brew. Millions of Chinese couldn't be wrong, after all. If her gene pool dictated longevity, she might as well make the best of it. Elvina would never admit her true age to a soul, the exception being her personal physician in Tallahassee. She plied him with enough home-baked goods to hopefully seal his lips. Only Piddie Longman knew that Elvina trailed her by a mere nine years.

Elvina shook her head in disbelief. "I can't rightly fathom that I'm gonna turn ninety soon. If I'd'a known I was gonna live this long, I'd'a taken more lovers."

She settled into her favorite worn recliner. Two bright red cardinals and three chickadees battled for position on the bi-level birdfeeder by the picture window.

"Been dull as dirt around here lately," she said out loud. She and Piddie would have to resort to dredging up past scandals to spice the daily morning conversation.

Elvina heard the muffled jangle of the phone and finally located the headset under several layers of old newspapers.

"Hello? Hello?" Silence answered. "Dang kids!"

The familiar whine and a scratch at the sliding glass door announced the arrival of Buster, an old tomcat she'd reluctantly befriended. "Did you get you some last night, Buster?" she asked as she cracked the door.

Buster narrowed his large yellow eyes. "Yowl!"

"Don't grump at me! I can't help it if you lay out all night and come draggin' in all beat up and wore out." Elvina poured a dish of cream and filled Buster's catfood bowl.

The phone rang in the other room. Though she'd purchased the portable phone so that it could be her constant companion, she was forever leaving it somewhere other than where she was. Shuffling as quickly as she could, she caught it following the third ring. Once again, the line was devoid of sound. Elvina held the phone in her hand and studied it, as if it might suddenly yield a clue to the crank caller.

The third call found Elvina sitting on the toilet. "Dang it! It's almost like someone knows I'm indisposed." She grumbled. "Hang on!" she called out.

As she rounded the corner to the den, the ringing stopped. "If you'd let it ring more'n three times, I could get to it!" she said. "I'm an old woman, not a racehorse." She shook her finger in the direction of the silent headset.

The significance of the three calls hit her. For years, she and Piddie Longman had used the signal to alert each other. It meant: *I've arrived safely. Don't worry about me.* Piddie insisted that Elvina triple-ring her every time she drove alone to her doctor's appointments in Tallahassee. Any time they were separated, the signal served to comfort the one left behind. Elvina smiled, remembering that Piddie had even signaled her from Vancouver before she boarded the cruise ship for Alaska.

Elvina checked the time on the antique mantle clock. Ten forty-five. She propped her hands on her hips. "Where you reckon that old biddy's off to this time of a mornin'?" She took a sip of her tea and flinched. Stone cold.

"Well," she said to Buster, "I might as well get dressed and go on around to the Triple C. Mandy's got me down for 11:45. I reckon I'll find out where that nosey-butt friend of mine's off to."

Triple C Day Spa and Salon

The river rock parking lot at the Triple C Day Spa and Salon was vacant. After positioning the gold Delta 88 in the shade of a magnolia tree, Elvina eschewed the formal front entrance and pushed through the unlocked delivery door. The kitchen was oddly quiet. Unwashed coffee cups tattooed muddy rings on the Formica countertops. Her mouth curled into a scowl as she investigated Holston's study area. The computer screen was black. The lingering scent of cologne remained. She poked her head into Evelyn's workroom. The sewing machines were silent. Clumps of material were thrown haphazardly around the room.

Elvina stepped briskly through the kitchen toward the business end of the spa. The scene in the reception room stopped her cold in her tracks. The typically tidy desk was in disorder. One appointment book lay upside down and half-opened on the floor, surrounded by a clutter of spilled business cards and envelopes. Piddie's wheelchair was shoved against one wall.

"Evelyn?" she called. "Mandy? Somebody?"

She stood with her hands on her hips for a second, and then whirled around to head in the direction of the hair salon. At the entrance door to the formal waiting area, she ran face to face into Mandy.

"Whew!" Mandy grabbed her chest. "You scared the dickens out of me!"

Elvina propped her hands on her hips. "What the blue blazes is going on here this mornin'?"

Tears formed at the corners of Mandy's eyes. "Oh, Elvina…" She sobbed into her palms.

"Now…what's the matter? You can tell me." Elvina draped her arms around the younger woman's shoulders and guided her gently to one of the over-stuffed parlor chairs.

"I don't know how to tell you this…" Mandy paused and studied the old woman's face. "Piddie had a heart attack this morning. They took her by ambulance to Tallahassee."

The cell phone in Elvina's purse trilled, making her jump. She dug around; finally located it near the bottom of her bag, but it was silent after the third ring. "There." She smiled as she returned the phone to her purse. "Nothin' to worry about, Mandy."

Mandy blew her nose and sniffed. "Who was that? I didn't hear you say anything."

Elvina patted the side of her bag like she was praising an obedient lap dog. "That was Piddie's three-ring signal tellin' me she's safe. She already did it at the house earlier, but I reckon she wanted to make sure I got her message."

Mandy dabbed her eyes, careful not to ruin her mascara. "Why didn't she just talk to you and tell you herself?"

Elvina waved her hand. "That'ud steal the suspense out of it! Piddie Longman loves drama. She was just lettin' me know that she'd arrived at her destination safe and sound and not to worry about her."

Mandy managed a weak smile.

"Now, brush yourself off and come on in here and attend to my hair before I snatch it out by the roots. I'll bet you a blue-nosed bottlefly that Piddie Longman'll be back here *real* soon."

Hank Henderson

Hank Henderson smeared the condensed steam from the center of the vanity mirror and leaned forward to inspect his reflection in the mirror.

"Shavin's a pain in the ass," he said.

Hank smiled as he pictured his new life in his mind's eye: slung up on a chaise lounge, oiled to a high gloss, barking drink orders to a nubile brown-skinned waiter hungry for a tip. The ex-Florida Cracker turned millionaire tropical transplant. Chick magnet. Grantor of small favors in return for larger ones.

The new house would be grand; an estate fringed with sprawling banana trees and bird of paradise fronds, well-paid security guards patrolling the periphery in bouncing jeeps. Perhaps he would start a legitimate business of some sort — nothing that would interfere with the lucrative Internet pornography enterprise, of course.

Hank's mouth morphed into a greasy smile. The third world children would be dirt poor and ripe for the picking. He wouldn't need to play the elaborate games he'd played here. Officials could be bought and paid for, and money was no issue.

Something frosty-cold brushed across his bare shoulders, sending his skin into rows of prickly gooseflesh. He jerked his head around. Behind him, the master bedroom was dark, the shades pulled against the morning light.

"Rabbit must've run over my grave," he mumbled.

Hank brushed his face with a thick curd of shaving cream, picked up the safety razor, and began to carefully carve long strips. Thoughts of his immediate plans made him smile again. The universe was providing the opportunity he needed to further his agenda with Tameka Clark. Today was Grandma Maizie's 75th birthday. A complete meal was being prepared to his specifications by Julie at the Homeplace restaurant. He would deliver the food at noon: Styrofoam containers of fresh vegetables, creamed potatoes, and a pot roast, topped off by a birthday sponge cake dripping with strawberries. If the way to the heart was through the stomach, he'd take the path provided.

Hank stopped the razor in midswipe. An eerie feeling of being watched crept over him. He shook his head. "Impossible! No one could get by the alarm and video surveillance in this house."

The mist on the mirror cleared. Hank glanced down to reload the shaving brush. When he looked up, the image of Piddie Longman, her glowing beehive hairdo stuffed with daisies, was reflected in the mirror beside his face.

Hank whirled around. The shaving brush clattered onto the tile, splattering clots of shaving cream across the wall and floor. The insistent ticking of his father's oak wall clock was the only sound in the vacant bedroom.

"Got-damned old woman!" He retrieved the brush and dabbed at his face. "I gotta get out of this town soon, or I'm gonna end up at the 'hooch in a private suite of rooms with padded walls and no sharp utensils."

"Here's how I see my life. When I was young, I was like a new river — rushing headlong over rocks and stumps, and carving out the banks on either side with my passin'. Later, I became like an old river — meandering this way and that, buildin' up sandbars along the side that slowed me down even more. Now, here in the twilight of my life, I'm like one of them little eddies at the side of the great water — content to swirl around in circles at a snail's pace and watch the rest of the world pass on by."

Piddie Davis Longman

CHAPTER FIFTEEN

Joe and Evelyn's

EVELYN PAUSED OUTSIDE of the door leading to her mother's living quarters. Joe had planned and helped to construct the addition to the main house containing a twelve by fourteen bedroom, small sitting room, and handicapped accessible bathroom. Evelyn squeezed her swollen eyes shut to staunch a fresh barrage of hot tears, sighed, and opened the door.

Piddie's scent permeated the sitting room; an airy combination of flower-fresh talcum powder and rosewater. Evelyn walked slowly through the cozy parlor, pausing to notice the opened scandal magazine, *The National Informant*, on the coffee table next to her mother's love-worn Bible. Piddie's most recent personal journal, a military-green spiral notebook, was tucked beneath a dog-eared TV guide. The portable phone headset rested on its side on a short wicker table close to the lift-assist chair. Evelyn rescued a silk daisy from the floor beside the television cabinet.

146

"Oh, Mama…," she whispered, "you dropped one of your little" stood rooted to the floor for a few moments.

"Come on, Evelyn Longman Fletcher, this ain't gonna get done l , ... one squared her shoulders like a guilty schoolgirl heading into the principal's office to defend her wayward actions.

When Evelyn entered the bedroom, she noticed the tidiness of her mother's private domain. The pastel handmade crazy quilt was pulled military tight, neatly tucked under two pillows. A droopy, solemn-faced teddy bear, a recent hospital get-well gift from Elvina, lay propped against one pillow. A low oak bureau topped with a hand-woven lace doily held an array of framed family pictures, a carved music box jewelry case, and a silver-plated comb, brush, and mirror set.

Evelyn opened the sliding mirrored closet door and sank onto one side of the bed.

"Mama, how am I gonna get through this?" Evelyn addressed her own reflection. "I thought all along…you'd be here a few more years. How could you just up and leave me so all of a sudden?"

She waged her finger in the air. "And this thing about you wanting to be cremated and scattered behind the Triple C! Why, that's the most outlandish thing I've ever heard tell of. I just about fell out when Hattie told me what you wanted us to do!"

Evelyn stood and began to pace back and forth. "I don't think I can bear the thought of it, Mama! Burning you up like that!" She whirled around to face her reflection, gearing up for a full-fledged have-it-out argument. "And… why didn't you tell me that's what you wanted to do? Give me some time to talk some sense into you? What am I supposed to do now? I can't very well go against your last wishes, now can I?"

"And," she brushed across the row of hanging clothes with one hand, "I don't

...ave a smattering of an idea of what you'd like to be laid out in."

Evelyn walked idly over to the bureau and picked up the intricately-carved silver hand mirror. She busied herself with a sprig of stray hair for a moment. "I want to do right by you, Mama. I really do. I'm just…I'm having trouble with how to go about it. Maybe you could send me a sign — just between you and me."

No mighty trumpets blared. No angelic voices broke the silence. Evelyn sighed wearily and turned back to face the task at hand — choosing her mother's laying-out ensemble. Her gaze rested on the bedside stand where she noticed a solitary cassette tape labeled with her mother's precise, fancy script: *Listen to this, Evelyn.*

"Where's that cassette recorder of Holston's?" She opened and closed the drawers of the bureau and found nothing except rows of carefully folded gowns, socks, and underwear. The single drawer of the bedside table held the recorder/player and several tapes, all carefully labeled with Piddie's handwriting.

With shaking fingers, she inserted the tape on side A and came close to jumping when her mother's distinctive Southern drawl sounded from the speaker. "Hello? Hello? Testing one, two, three! Hah! I know how this thing works, I just always wanted to say that." Piddie's musical laughter filled the room.

"Well, Evelyn, honey…I reckon if you're listenin' to this recordin', I'm either in the hospital, or I've passed on to my reward. Either way, there're some things I need to say to you. So…, if you ain't sittin' down, I suppose you'd better. I know how easily overcome you can be."

Always the obedient daughter, Evelyn settled onto the bed.

"All righty then. Here goes nothin'. Evelyn, you've been a good daughter. I know it ain't been easy for you, sharin' your weddin' home with your old mama here these last few years…but, I want you to know, it was greatly appreciated.

148

"I know you've heard me say how your father Carlton, God rest his soul, and I wanted to have a passel of young'uns. I don't want you to ever feel like you were looked down on 'cause you were the only one the Good Lord chose to give us. You were a'plenty. And, we both loved you till our hearts nearly-bout busted out of our chests."

A single tear rolled down Evelyn's cheek. A deep ache started in the center of her soul.

"Don't you cry now. I know you're tunin' up to start. You've always worn your feelin's on your sleeve, bless your heart."

Evelyn quickly wiped the moisture away from her cheeks.

"I ain't tellin' you to bottle it up, neither. Just try to calm down so you can hear what I'm tellin' you. There'll be plenty of time for grievin' — that's what the layin'-out and funeral's for. If you hold it inside, it'll turn your soul black and blue.

"Now, I done told Hattie what I wanted done with me. I'd'a told you, but you'd of pitched a royal snit-fit, and honestly, honey, I just wasn't up for it. This old bad heart just sucked the energy out'a me.

"This is what I want you to do. I 'spect you to honor my last wishes. I want you to lay me out for the visitation at the Triple C. I've passed it by Jake, and he sees no reason for anyone to object. Then, I want to be cremated and my ashes sprinkled over a nice sunny spot fit for a daisy patch."

She heard her mother pause for breath.

"Put a little sittin' bench there, if you'd like. It'll give you a place to come visit when you've a mind to — I'll be right there with you. I promise. It'll be a place I don't mind comin' back to. Don't you dare close me up in no dang coffin for all eternity! You know I'm *claude-o-phobic*. I'll haunt you till the end of your days if you close me up in one of them awful boxes. Just rent one for the layin'-

out, and you can turn it back in. I gave Hattie some instructions, too, on havin' a headstone made to put up home in Alabama next to your daddy."

A brief silence followed before Piddie spoke again.

"I want you to spread the word to everyone. Tell Elvina. It'll give her somethin' to focus on. It's okay by me if you wear your dreary mournin' clothes to the layin'-out, but I want bright colors and singin' at the sprinklin' service. I've lived a long, happy life, and I want you all to praise God and celebrate for me. I'll be somewheres listenin' in."

Evelyn sighed. "All right, Mama."

"Now…that's all the hard part I gotta say. Next is…I'm so proud of you, I could just about bust! You've finally found the one true thing you've been called to do — sewin' and makin' folks look pretty. Even the governor's wife! I still ain't over that! I'll suwannee!"

Piddie stopped briefly to clear her throat.

"Keep up with that. It's your God-given talent. As to the cookin' — even though you have improved a sight, I'd let Joe take that task on. He's havin' a big time doin' it, and it'll give him a hobby for when he retires from coachin' those nuts up at the 'hooch. It's important that a person keeps on livin' and learnin'. Otherwise, what's the use of stayin' around takin' up space and gettin' in ever'body's way? Joe Fletcher is a good man, Evelyn. If you never done nothin' right again in your natural born life, you could rest easy that you chose your partner well. I love Joe like a son.

"Well, sugar…I'm kindly windin' down. I've made some other tapes for a few folks. Please, if you will, make sure they get into the right hands after the service. I'll be obliged for it.

"Oh, I almost forgot…I want to be laid out in that pretty yellow dress you made for me for my birthday party. Ask Mandy to do up my hair like I had it then. Maybe she can get some real daisies from Jake for my hair. I'd like that. Since it's only for a few hours, they should hold out without wiltin'. Be sure to tell Mandy to be careful with the color. It's the pale yellow I like. She'll remember."

Her mother's voice grew soft.

"I love you, Evelyn. You're everything I ever wanted in a daughter. Don't worry. I'll be holdin' you and Joe a place over on the other side...if the Good Lord's willin' for me to be there my own self."

The hiss of dead air filled the room. Evelyn hit the stop button. She looked up. "Thank you, Mama," she whispered.

"How a person grows up, how the family treats a little youngun – that's awful important. Makes all the difference in the world. The older you get, the more you realize that your roots are what's holding you up, not tying you down."

     Piddie Davis Longman

CHAPTER SIXTEEN

Hattie

A S PIDDIE'S ESTATE EXECUTOR, the responsibility for carrying out her last wishes rested with me. For the first time in my life, I was pushed into making final arrangements: speaking with the funeral director, choosing the casket for the visitation, meeting with the minister, and asking Mandy to style Piddie's hair one last time. Initially, Evelyn was passionately opposed to cremation. Just when I thought I'd have to dig in for a drawn-out confrontation, she mysteriously changed her attitude, graciously allowing me to attend to the details.

The notion of death as a business was difficult to grasp. I wandered through the casket viewing room like a first-time car buyer, aghast at the quoted prices running the gauntlet from modest to extravagant. Piddie's voice whispered in my head. "Ain't you glad we're just rentin' one of these boxes instead of buyin' it, gal?"

I suppressed a giggle and felt a momentary blush of warmth on my shoulders, as if an unseen entity had rested an arm around me in comfort and camaraderie.

"There are two ways we can proceed," Joseph Burns, the funeral director, said. "You may choose to rent one of our ceremonial caskets for the visitation. However, if I may suggest, we do have a complete selection of specially-designed cremation caskets. The deceased will rest in the casket for the viewing, then we will provide transportation to the crematorium we contract with in Tallahassee. Since it is designed to be combustible, the cremation casket is less expensive than a conventional one." Joseph paused. "I say this only to offer you a choice, Miz Hattie. I'll be pleased to arrange whatever you think best."

I nodded.

"Because your aunt requested a public viewing, it will be necessary for me to prepare her body. We will return her cremated remains to you within two to three days of the viewing."

I was leaning heavily toward the choice of a pale rose-colored casket embellished with painted flowers when I tripped on a wrinkle in the carpet and almost fell headfirst into an emerald green casket lined in pastel green silk.

"Mr. Burns? I think she'd like this one. Evelyn's sending up the yellow outfit Piddie wore for her birthday party, and I just believe it'll look good next to this shade of green."

"Fine, Miz Hattie." Joseph motioned toward a side door. "If you'll step into my office, we'll go over the itemized statement of expenses the state law requires me to cover with you."

I checked the contact list: Dragonfly Florist, Morningside AME church, and Hank (ugh!) Henderson's law office. The tiny brass bell on the front glass door of the Dragonfly Florist shop announced my arrival.

Jake looked up from the clipboard he held. His face was painted with a mixture of confusion and sadness. "Oh...hi, Sister-girl," he said absently.

"At the risk of sounding totally lame, how are you feeling this morning?"

Jake frowned. "Dismal. Washed out. Like I have a hangover from an all-nighter."

He pushed his hair back with one hand. "I can't believe she's really gone. How can that much life and energy be snuffed out just like that?" He hugged the clipboard to his chest. "What are we gonna do without Piddie?"

I sighed deeply. "That, I can't answer."

For the third time in the last few years, I had lost a loved one, and grief was proving to be the one thing practice did not make perfect. "I can't shake the feeling that she's still hanging out with me...all around...watching, commenting on the preparations for her wake and funeral service."

Jake's left eyebrow arched upward.

"Why are you looking at me so funny?'

Jake rested one hand on my shoulder. "It's not you...for once. The shipment of flowers I ordered before Piddie died came in this morning. My usual order — nothing additional. When the van arrived, I got ten extra containers of daisies."

The hair prickled on the back of my neck. Jake looked at me for a moment, then we said in unison, "Piddie!"

"She practically threw me into the casket she wanted." I said. "Why should I be amazed that she'd make arrangements for you to have plenty of her favorite flowers on hand?"

"She hated carnations. Said they reminded her too much of a cemetery plot." Jake pulled thoughtfully on his chin. "You know, since I don't have to make a drape for the top of the casket, I could flank it on either side with a stand of daisies and leatherleaf fern —even scatter a few arrangements through the parlor at the mansion. Piddie told me not too long ago, she didn't like the look of a casket smothered in a cape of flowers."

"She'd love whatever you come up with, I'm sure. Well...that takes care of that. Save the bill for me, and I'll write you a check out of the estate account."

Jake waved his hand. "This one's on me, Sister-girl. I'll do it up right."

"That's really sweet of you, Jakey. But, that's a lot of flowers."

He shrugged. "Even if I could charge you, I wouldn't. I just got off the phone with my supplier. I wasn't billed for the daisies, and he insisted that he didn't send anything over the normal order and won't accept payment for them. The man thinks I am a total lunatic, I'm sure of it."

"That...is weird. Let me run. I have to stop by Hank Henderson's office this morning."

Jake wrinkled his nose as if he had bumped into a pool of fetid air. "You poor dear."

"Necessary evil. He has Pid's updated will."

"I suppose you and the family'll have to endure him long enough for the reading."

I tipped my head and smiled. "Actually, sweet love, you'll get to be there, too."

"Whatever for?"

"Hank gave me a list of benefactors to contact, and you're on it."

Jake lay the clipboard down. "Imagine that. What do you reckon Piddie's been up to?"

"Stirring things up, as usual. I have a good inkling that death won't stop the likes of Piddie Longman."

Jake's blue eyes sparkled. "Hmm. Wanna meet me later at the Homeplace for a French dip sandwich?"

"I'm not really hungry, to tell you the truth, but I could stand a tall glass of iced tea." I checked the time on my watch. "How 'bout around one? That'll give me time to stop by Hank's office and then talk with Reverend Jackson at Morningside AME."

"He's preachin' Piddie's service?"

"Get this. Piddie pulled him aside several weeks ago and told him exactly what she wanted for her funeral...down to the music. I think it'll be unlike anything this town's ever seen."

"Just like Piddie, herself." Jake smiled sadly. "Okay. I'll meet you down the street at 1:00. Jolene will be back to cover the shop by then."

"Go on a cry if you need to, when I'm dead and gone. But, cry for yourself – to rinse your soul clean of sadness. Don't shed one tear for me. No sir! I'm gone to glory."

Piddie Davis Longman

CHAPTER SEVENTEEN

Triple C Day Spa and Salon

THE DAY OF PIDDIE DAVIS LONGMAN'S wake dawned dreary and overcast with the promise of rain. Though the heavy low-hanging clouds kept the blazing August sun at bay, the air was sluggish with humidity. The weather matched the somber mood of the attending friends and family.

The slated plantation blinds were half opened, allowing the meager gray natural light to filter into the front parlor of the Witherspoon mansion. Jake's floral artistry filled the cavernous room. Pale yellow pots of daisies, fern, and wispy baby's breath were scattered throughout the parlor. The casket was flanked by two massive Boston ferns on white wicker stands and matching floral arrangements of daisies, white roses, fern, and slender barren branches coated with white paint and clear glitter. The opposite end of the parlor was filled with the floral tributes that had arrived in time for the wake. Most were of the typical funeral spray variety. One stood out; a red and gold asymmetrical oriental design wired from family friends, Dr. Paul and Sushan Wong of Beijing, China. The room appeared cheerful and uplifting in an odd way, and I knew instantly that Aunt Piddie would approve.

Following tradition, the members of the immediate family were the initial visitors to the Triple C's formal parlor. Bobby, Leigh, Holston, and I stepped through the front entranceway, followed closely by Piddie's grandson, Byron, his wife, Linda, and two great-grandsons. Joe supported Evelyn with one arm wrapped around her waist.

"I'll go with you if you want to see her," Holston said softly.

In that instant, I decided to break a lifelong taboo. I slid my hand into my husband's, and we walked toward the coffin. I gasped involuntarily.

"You okay, hon?"

I nodded. Piddie's physical earthly form, though devoid of animation, appeared peaceful and angelic, as if it glowed with an internal light. An extra-long head cushion supported her hairdo; layer upon layer of soft yellow curls dotted with fresh daisy blossoms. Her hands were folded over a weathered white Bible. A plain gold wedding band was her only jewelry.

My aunt's expression was one of peace; the many small worry-line wrinkles smoothed by Joseph Burns' practiced hands. The corners of her lips turned slightly upward, as if she was privy to some important and vastly amusing cosmic joke. My thoughts drifted back to when Bobby and I were children. Piddie would pretend to be asleep, and then suddenly jump up and scare the dickens out of us. We'd squeal with a blend of mock terror and delight.

Seeing her body resting amidst the flowers in the dark green casket she *helped* to choose, I felt my spirits lift slightly from the oppressive gloom. Somewhere deep inside, I knew. Piddie was safe — in a peaceful, happy place. My challenge would lie in releasing my selfish need for her physical presence. The grief I felt was for me, not for her.

For the next three hours, multitudes of people of mixed races and economic levels came to pay last respects. Folks who would normally pass each other on

Washington Street with a polite nod joined in their unified praise of a woman who had possessed the ability to look past the earthly covering of a person, clean through to the essence of spirit.

As soon as Piddie's passing became known, the community had folded my family in a warm cocoon. They provided food by the armloads, planned childcare for Sarah and Josh, and ran small errands we didn't have the energy to do ourselves. Grief had thrown us into pure survival mode. Without neighbors prompting us to eat and sleep, we would've just as soon stared numbly into space. The chronological age of the deceased loved one didn't matter. Whether attired for an infant or an aged person close to a century in years, grief wore the same heavy gray cloak.

Dressed in a crisply pressed tailored black suit, Joseph Burns stood by the entrance to the hair salon. His calm, discreet presence was reminiscent of an English butler — aware of every nuance and ready to attend to the needs of the visitors.

"Mr. Burns?"

He snapped to attention, his face painted with genuine warmth and concern. "Yes, Miz Hattie?"

"I…I…just wanted to say…thank you. Piddie…she looks beautiful."

Joseph extended his hand and rested it lightly on my shoulder. "I'd like to think I treat all of my clients with the same respect, but I have to admit…when it came to Miz Piddie…well, she was like my own family. There're a lot of folks who feel the same way. Piddie Longman's done a lot for this town."

We stood side by side watching the ebb and flow of mourning-clad visitors filing by the casket.

Joseph turned to face me. "She helped me make up my mind about becoming a funeral director, you know."

"Is that right?"

He nodded. "I was interested in the field, but I worried about what my friends would think of me."

"It's a very noble profession, Joseph."

"Yes. But, when you're a teenager, confessing that you want to go into the field...well, some of my peers were a bit...unsupportive." He smiled slightly. "Not your aunt. She saw me looking all gloomy one day after school — she was there to meet with some committee for the Fall Festival, part of the Parent/Teacher Association. I can remember it like it was just yesterday. Isn't that incredible? Anyway, she grabbed me by the arm and managed to get me to talk to her about my future plans after graduation."

Joseph looked toward the casket. "She said, *Joseph Burns, you ain't livin' for nobody else 'cept yourself and the Good Lawd...and two things are for certain in this life — death and taxes. I'd whole lot rather see you becomin' a funeralist than one of them IRS fellers. Besides, if you set up shop here in town, who knows? Maybe, one day, you'll get to fix me up for my layin'-out. I can't think of a better fella to do it, neither!*"

"Imagine that." I glanced toward the front entrance. Elvina Houston stumbled slightly as she stepped into the front parlor. "Excuse me, Joseph. Let me go see if Elvina needs my help."

He reached out and grasped my hand. "Certainly. Miz Hattie, please call me if you or your family need anything, will you?"

"Thanks, Joseph." I met Elvina near the door and hugged her, offering my arm for support.

"Walk with me to see her, will you, Hattie? I feel like my feet are stuck in cement."

The crowd parted respectfully as the two of us made our way to the opposite end of the room.

Elvina held a lace-embroidered handkerchief to her face. "Ain't she beautiful, Hattie?" Her head fell forward as she sobbed aloud. I circled one arm around her shoulders and stood silently by her side as she wept. "What am I gonna do without her? We've been friends for goin' on forty years. That's longer than most folks stay married!"

"She loved you very much, Elvina."

Elvina sniffed and dabbed the corners of her eyes. "We had some spittin' contests in there, too. Wasn't all peaches'n'cream. But, we never stayed mad at each other too long. One of us'd pick up the phone pretty soon, and we'd be right back to ourselves."

"She was lucky to have you for her best friend."

She shook her head. "Nope, it was me who was the lucky one. When I first moved to town after my husband died, I didn't know a soul. Piddie saw me up at the grocery store — that was when the IGA was in the small store 'bout two blocks down from where it is now. She came right up and introduced herself and commenced to fillin' me in on this town and all the goin's on. We've been fast friends since that day. Not a mornin' went by I didn't think of her and ring her up."

I squeezed her bony shoulders. "Elvina, I feel like Piddie's close by…watchin' over all of us. We'll all have to help each other get through this."

"I reckon so. My old heart feels so heavy right now, it's a wonder it's keepin' on beatin'." Elvina studied the calm face of her friend.

"Hattie?"

"Hmm?"

"I brought somethin' I want to put with her. I know she's gonna be cremated, and all. It's a gesture I want to make."

"Of course, Elvina."

She dug in her black patent leather purse and extracted a small cellular phone. "I was gonna give this to her for her birthday in a couple of months." Elvina reached over and gently placed the phone next to Piddie. "I know it's silly....but, it's like...well, she was never too far from a telephone...and..."

"You don't have to explain to me, Elvina. I'm positive Piddie's lookin' down right now, smilin' at you."

She tilted her head. "She called me, you know...after she died. I figured out the time of day, and she passed away a few minutes before it happened."

"What?"

Elvina lifted her chin proudly. "Piddie gave me the triple-ring signal to let me know she was safe and sound. She had arrived at her destination."

Since I had no clue how to respond, I nodded.

Elvina scanned the crowd. "Where're Evelyn and Joe?"

"They're sittin' in the kitchen. I believe one of the church ladies was getting Evelyn some coffee and a bite to eat. She didn't have any breakfast and was feeling a bit faint."

Elvina patted my hand. "I'll go and speak to them, now. Thank you, Hattie... for helpin' me. You're as good as gold, just like Piddie always maintained."

I watched my aunt's best friend move slowly through the crowd toward the kitchen, stopping along the way to console and be consoled.

After circling the block twice in search of a proper parking place, Hank Henderson edged the Mercedes into a small clearing between two pine trees at the rear of the day spa property. The sedan would capture a few pine needles, but it would be safe from an ill-mannered hillbilly driver intent on chipping the paint. Every nick, each deviation from perfection, would pound a nail into its resale value.

162

RHETT DEVANE

As Chattahoochee's sole legal counsel, Hank had grudgingly attended many wakes and funerals. He didn't give a rip about the people, for the most part. It just looked good to put in an appearance.

The first funeral he'd been dragged to was his mother's – an event he barely recalled. He had been five, and the memories had dimmed over time. Hank was certain it was the last time he'd felt much of anything resembling sorrow.

At his father's last hurrah, he had played the bereaved, dutiful son. Fresh out of FSU law school, he'd been called home from Tallahassee after the old man suffered a massive stroke. His father had clung to life for two days before the devil swept up to claim his spawn.

Hank used the button on the keyless remote to set the car alarm and then walked up the steep incline toward the corner of Morgan Avenue and Bonita Street where mourners by the carload jockeyed for position outside of the Witherspoon mansion. He smiled. This particular wake would be well worth dragging his tailored black silk suit from the back of the closet — just to be sure the nosey old bat was truly dead. He had to see it to believe it. She'd always reminded him of a trick birthday candle; one of those annoying party favors that popped back to life a few seconds after you'd blown your guts out to extinguish the flame.

The room was packed when he stepped through the main entrance. Hank worked his way into the crowded parlor, stopping to speak with a handful of guests, acknowledging others with a slight nod. He waited patiently for the area in front of the casket to clear and stepped forward. Even in death, Piddie Longman's peaceful countenance mocked him.

Tacky old bitch. It would be a pleasure not to see her anymore. He studied Piddie for a moment. If he never saw another daisy as long as he lived, it'd be too soon. You'd think her daughter would have made the funeral director

163

calm down the old woman's makeup and outrageous hairdo for her final appearance in public.

Hank glanced up and looked directly into the frowning glare of Hattie Davis Lewis. Even from across the room, her resentment for his intrusion into her family's somber occasion was obvious. As he watched, Elvina Houston shuffled into position beside Hattie and reinforced the visual warning. Could it be possible? Had the old biddy broken her promise to him? What did those two know?

Hank's stomach lurched, the acid mercilessly pealing away its protective lining. His motto had always been: never stay long enough to be asked to leave. After pausing to speak briefly to the Mayor Jimmy T. Johnson, he slipped through the clots of mourners and escaped into the open air.

"Comes a point in your life that you either got to whiz or get off the pot. Stop blamin' your parents, your partner, or the circumstances you was born into. A person has to stand up for his own self, in the end. The Good Lord doesn't put in a call to your friends and relatives when it's time to look back over your life. He turns to you."

Piddie Davis Longman

CHAPTER EIGHTEEN

Hattie

IN CONTRAST to the sultry stickiness of the weather during the wake, the morning of Aunt Piddie's funeral was clear and cool. Dry northern air nudged the jet stream southward into the panhandle of Florida, bringing unseasonable fall-like temperatures. By the time of the midafternoon service, the thermometer on the front porch registered a comfortable 78°. Piddie had special-ordered the weather.

Spackle yipped, hopped, and chased his tail with fall-induced glee when I emerged onto the porch for my first cup of coffee. Shammie had celebrated her feelings at five AM, honoring Holston and me with a running fit that had included our heads as part of its path. A fresh breeze rippled the leaves of the magnolia tree at the end of the porch, coaxing me to feel light-hearted for a moment before I had to go inside to prepare for my aunt's funeral.

As requested, we dressed in light-colored clothing. I chose a short sleeved linen smock in a pale shade of lavender, and Holston wore casual kakhi pants with a blue and white pinstriped shirt. Sarah sported an *Elfwear Designs* yellow sundress embroidered with flowers and butterflies.

I felt odd attending a funeral in garden party attire, but quickly relaxed as I watched members of the community arrive at the Triple C. Elvina Houston had successfully spread the word on required dress. As the crowd assembled in the garden surrounding the side of the mansion, I saw no evidence of traditional mourning attire. The ladies of the Morningside AME choir wore the most colorful dresses; bright, eye-popping tropical floral and geometric prints reminiscent of the islands. Scanning the crowd, I understood Piddie's request. The vivid colors lifted my sagging spirits and invited me to smile — to feel the joy of a long life lived well.

"I hope Mama's happy...wherever she is...," Evelyn groused as she took a chair next to Holston and me. "This just beats all I've ever seen for a funeral!"

"GOOO-GAHHH!!!" Sarah squealed. We looked at my daughter. She was waving her stubby arms in the air, jabbering nonsense syllables.

"That nearly breaks my heart in two," Joe said. "She's going to miss Piddie as bad as we are."

Oblivious to the adults surrounding her, Sarah giggled and chattered to a point just in front of her.

Jake and Jon sat in the white wooden folding chairs directly behind us. "Has anyone heard from Karen-slash-Mary Elizabeth?" Jake whispered in my ear.

I shook my head.

Jake motioned toward the mansion. "There's a huge prayer plant from her. I just delivered it to the front parlor."

I turned slightly to answer him over my shoulder. "I doubt she shows. That would be openly admitting she's related."

"Hmm..." Jake looked thoughtful as his eyes scanned the crowd. "Piddie would be pleased. There're almost as many folks here as at her birthday party."

The Reverend Thurston Jackson took his place behind a plain wooden podium positioned to the left of a patch of freshly-turned earth. Moses Clark had carefully prepared the ground the day before, digging deep to aerate the soil, then mixing in mulch from the compost pile at the edge of the wood thicket. The bronze-finish urn holding Piddie's remains rested on a low table at the edge of the plot.

The Reverend's off-white linen suit and yellow shirt and tie made him look more like a Bahamian tour director than a Southern preacher preparing to deliver a eulogy.

"Let us pray," he requested, his voice deep and melodic.

The large crowd quieted.

"Dear Lord…we come into your presence today to honor the life of Piddie Davis Longman. We ask that you fellowship with us as we bid our earthly farewell to our departed sister in Christ…and as we go forward through our lives…knowing that she is in your glorious presence, protected by your loving grace. We ask that you sit amongst us today…extending your comforting arms…for *blessed are they that mourn, for they shall be comforted.* We ask these things in your holy name, Amen."

Amen echoed throughout the crowd.

The Reverend slowly scanned the gathering that enveloped him in a circle, taking a moment to dramatically rest his eyes on each of Piddie's closest friends and family members. He lifted his gaze toward the clear blue sky. "Isn't this a fine mornin' to bid farewell to our Sister Piddie Longman?"

The audience murmured. A few people nodded.

Reverend Jackson stepped from behind the podium and began to weave between the rows of seated guests, speaking as he went.

"Some…times. Sometimes…I am asked to preach for a person I didn't know very well. I have to speak to family and friends to learn who that person was in this life."

He stood still for a moment. "That was not the case for Miz Piddie. You see…I *know* the woman well! I tell you that…I…know her…and…" He paused for effect. "God knows her….then…and now!"

"Amen!" echoed through the crowd.

"I could ask…you!" He pointed to Elvina. "Or…you!" He spun around to gesture to the entire group. "And, you would tell me some story — some wonderful story of how Piddie graced your life!"

The Reverend dipped his head slightly and smiled. "Not more than a couple of Sundays ago, Miz Piddie attended services at our church with her good friend, my wife Lucille. Piddie pulled me aside after the service and instructed me on her wishes for her final ceremony. *I want it happy, now!* She told me… *I want singin' and clappin'…cause I'm goin' to my glow-ree, and I need to be…*" He hopped up and down in place, "*lifted up!*"

"Amen! Amen!" the crowd chanted.

He cupped his hands together and lifted them over his head. "*Carried high on the love and best wishes of my family and friends!*"

"And…," he continued in a softer voice, "*I will be reborn in a new body…and I will watch over all of you…and wait to greet you on the other side.*"

"That…is what Piddie Longman wanted me to say to you today…"

The Reverend Jackson scanned the crowd. "There was something Miz Piddie Longman could do that I, a man of the cloth, purveyor of the Word of God, can *not* do. Try as I may, I still look out on this sea of faces before me and…I'm sorry to say…I see color. The color of a person's skin."

He held one hand up. "Miz Piddie was one of the few bless-ed people I've ever met who did not see color. Ever' one of you..." He swept his hand through the air. "...know this to be true."

"Piddie Longman had a way..." His rich voice faltered briefly as he choked on emotion. "She could look right through to a person's heart of hearts."

The Reverend gestured toward Elvina Houston. "Miz Elvina told me one time...and I know this to be the gospel truth...the reason Miz Piddie kept up with all the goin's on in this town...was because she cared so deeply about all of us. Miz Elvina, you remember what she said?"

Elvina nodded and dabbed her eyes with a handkerchief.

"She said that *God! — God told us to love our neighbors like ourselves, and she had to know what was goin' on with them to love 'em better!* Can't we all learn that lesson?"

"Amen! Amen! Yessuh!" echoed in ripples through the crowd.

"Now, one thing Miz Piddie made clear to me..." He smiled slightly. "...was that I was not to stand in front of you and preach a long-winded sermon on her behalf. She wanted us all to remember her in stories we could tell each other. And, she wanted her ashes to be scattered in this garden so that we could stop in and visit her ever' now and then. So..." He raised his hands. "Let us dust her remains on the Mother Earth to nourish the flowers that will grow here in the spring during the rebirth of nature."

The Reverend motioned for the choir members to join him. They formed a circle surrounding the plot of turned soil. "She wanted us to sing one of her favorite hymns, *O Happy Day.*"

A tall, portly black woman in a vivid scarlet dress hummed a single note to set the key. She sang the verses one by one, echoed by the choir around her.

Oh happy day...Oh happy day...when Jesus washed...all my sins away....

Reverend Thurston Jackson lifted the cremation urn toward the sky and motioned for Evelyn and Joe to come forward. Evelyn removed the lid and carefully bent forward to dust the ashes of her mother across the dirt. The Reverend handed her a shiny new rake, and she and Joe worked together to till the chalky remains into the rich soil.

Lucille Jackson encircled Evelyn and Joe with her arms and drew them into the circle. The pitch of the old hymn changed slightly, and the choir members began to clap in time. At the Reverend's urging, the audience stood and joined in song, until the garden was awash in the song of thanksgiving.

Sarah Chuntian Lewis, held high in her father's arms, clapped her small hands and sang *Goo-gah* over and over.

I stared at my daughter, my mouth agape. "Holston?"

My husband stopped clapping and looked down at me. "Yes, hon?"

"Did you stick that daisy in the top of Sarah's sundress?"

He looked at our daughter. "No, did you?"

I smiled. Joy and awe washed over me as I slipped back into the rhythm of the song.

"I ain't leavin' much of value behind. Never was one, much, for jewels or finery. I've been rich in ways you can't buy from a store. Way I see it — the more you own, the more owns you."

Piddie Davis Longman

CHAPTER NINETEEN

Law office of Hank Henderson

ONE WEEK LATER, those of us who had been summoned for the official reading of Piddie's will were seated around a large oval table in Hank Henderson's office.

The space was tastefully decorated with wood-framed watercolor originals scattered on the beige walls and several lush tropical plants standing in terra cotta pots near a linen-draped bay window. The two pieces of furniture, the conference table and glass front armoire, were constructed of highly-polished oak. A thick maroon carpet cushioned the floor and helped to dispel the echo of voices in the cavernous room.

Elvina Houston and Jake Witherspoon were the only members of the gathering who weren't blood ties. Evelyn and Joe, Bobby and Leigh, and Holston and I represented the extended Davis/Longman lineage.

Hank Henderson walked briskly into the room. "Sorry for the delay, folks." His brisk manner and slight smirk belied the fact that he was here in an official capacity to dispense with our family matters as quickly as possible.

"I'm providing a copy of Mrs. Longman's will for each of you, so there's less chance of confusion," he said as he dealt stacks of stapled papers around the table.

UP THE DEVIL'S BELLY

"I usually read the will. However, Mrs. Longman wished to have you view a statement my secretary taped in my office at the time the written document was finalized." He paused. "This was recorded about two weeks ago."

Hank opened the doors of the oak armoire, revealing a 32-inch television monitor. "Can I get anything for anyone before I start the tape?"

Everyone shook their heads and sat forward slightly in anticipation.

He jabbed the power button. "Alright then, here goes."

Aunt Piddie's face popped onto the screen. Evelyn gasped.

"Am I on?" Piddie asked the off-camera video operator. "I feel like Marilyn *Mon-row* up on the big screen!" She laughed heartily.

"Whew! Okay...down to business now. I thought this might be a more personable way to let you all know how I've set things up in my will...and, how I came about my decisions so there won't be any stepped-on feelin's. This won't take too long. I ain't got that much to divvy up.

"First of all, to my life-long friend, Elvina Houston...I'm leavin' you my position of employment at the Triple C. Now, I know that sounds kinda weird, like maybe it ain't mine to give...but, Elvina, you're the logical one to replace me there. You know ever'body and ever'thing what goes on, and it'll be a smooth transition...almost like I wasn't gone a'tall!"

Piddie leaned forward. "I done spoke to Jake and Mandy and the rest of them 'bout it...off and on. They shrugged it off 'cause they reckoned I'd never die. That dee-nial, it's a wonderful thing, ain't it?" She waved her hand through the air.

"Elvina, I'm leavin' you my favorite old gold watch that Carlton give me for our fortieth weddin' anniversary. Evelyn, you'll make sure Elvina gets it, won't you? Now, Elvina, I know how you don't hold no stock in wearin' a time piece... but, you gonna have to have one now, with workin' and all. Besides, you can

172

think of me when you look at it!" Elvina smiled slightly. Naturally, she was the logical choice to take over the front desk duties at the spa. She'd be right there, keeping her fingers on the pulse of the community.

"Also, I'm leavin' you my recipe box. It's got all my favorites in it, along with little notes on where they came from. Now, Evelyn, honey, don't go getting all pouty-lipped over this. Elvina is as much a cook as I am. Half the recipes I stole from her anyways."

Elvina and Evelyn exchanged glances.

"Alrighty, then," Piddie continued. "Jake, I'm leavin' you my little house on Morgan Avenue."

Jake's jaw dropped open.

"Shut your mouth, now. You'll draw flies, son." Piddie said.

Jake smiled sheepishly and cleared his throat.

"The reason for this, all of you...you all got houses of your own. You'd just end up sellin' it or lettin' it sit and get run down. A house needs to be loved and tended to —just like a person does. That's why Jake is perfect for the job. I hope you love it, Jake, like I did. That little house was my haven of peace for many years after Carlton passed. The yard needs some work. I don't reckon those old azaleas have been cut back in two, maybe three, years. You have my little frame house with my blessin', son."

Jake sat quietly — one of the few times he lacked for words.

"Hattie? Bobby? I've given the bank directions on settin' up schoolin' funds for your babies. It ain't a bunch of money, but it'll help out some. Those younguns been a blessin' to me in my old age. Go see Miz Josie up on the teller line, and she'll give you the details. I'm mighty happy both of you kids have settled down and are gonna live on the Davis homestead. Your Mama and Daddy would be proud of that."

Bobby and I exchanged glances.

"Now…as to you, Evelyn, and you, Joe…you get the rest to do what you see fit. What money there is, I'd really like to see two things done with it. First, make sure Karen and Byron and the two great grandyounguns get a share. Then, and I mean this thing with all my heart…I want y'all to take a chunk of it and take that cruise you been promisin' each other you'd go on one day. You postponed it on account of my failin' health, and I thank you for thinkin' of my needs over your own…but, I can't rest 'till I know you're off on some tropical island dancin' under the moon. Evelyn, make you a pretty new ball gown, and y'all go kick up your heels, you hear? And, the rings and bracelets you and Joe's give me over the years, turn them in for the money, too. Only one I want you to keep is the band your daddy give to me. Rest of them needs to be turned back into cash for you to use how you see fit."

Piddie took a deep breath. Her energy was obviously waning.

"I don't know if Evelyn's told you all yet, knowin' how she forgets stuff when she's all overcome — I know she hasn't give it another thought if she's found them. I made some tape recordin's — one for each of you. They're in my bedroom in the bedside stand. They're a bit more personal than what's on this here video. Evelyn, will you make sure they get to who I've intended them for?"

Evelyn nodded.

Piddie paused. Her cornflower blue eyes watered. "I love all of you. And, I'm takin' that love with me. The best way you can honor me, if that's what you've a mind to do, is to go on about your lives in the here and now. We'll all be together in the by and by. I know it! In the meantime, carry on like I was right there proddin' you on."

Piddie pursed her lips and blew a kiss to the camera. The screen went blank.

Hank hopped up, pushed the stop button on the video recorder, and handed

174

the ejected tape over to Evelyn. "Any questions on the legal details, you know where to find me," he said as he turned to leave the conference room.

Evelyn stood and put her hands on her hips. "Well!" She snorted. "I'm sure glad Mama recorded her last wishes and we didn't have to hear them outta the likes of him!"

Hank slammed his hand down on the reception desk, sending a stack of pink-slip memos fluttering on to the carpet. "Cancel my appointments for the rest of the day and tomorrow!'" he barked. "I'm leavin' for the coast for a few days."

"But, sir…I think…," his secretary said.

Hank glared at Maxie. "I didn't hire you to think! Just do as I say!" He snatched his briefcase into his left hand and pushed through the front door.

The Mercedes responded to his anger-driven acceleration, flinging flecks of loose gravel in its wake.

"Anything could be on those tapes," he muttered as he blew through the stop sign at the end of Franklin Street. "That's all I need — a whole got-damned family of meddling cretins watching every move I make!"

"

Elvina has a sayin'—no act of kindness goes unnoticed. Well, I'm here to tell you that no act of meanness goes unnoticed, neither! Not if I get any say in it!"

   Piddie Davis Longman

CHAPTER TWENTY

Hattie

IN THE FIFTEEN MINUTES it took to drive three miles from the Hill into town, stop at the post office, and make a bank deposit, Sarah fell sound asleep in the car seat. When I parked Betty in the shade by the Triple C, her dark brown eyes popped open and she waved her stubby arms gleefully.

"Hey, kiddo." I cooed as I lifted her from the seat. "I will love it to death if you're half as happy as a teenager as you are now."

"Goo-gah?" she said loudly.

My heart sank. "Yeah, honey. We're going to where Goo-gah used to work." I sighed deeply to dispel the grief bubble lodged in my throat.

Holston pushed back from his computer armoire when we entered the private study. "There're my two girls!" He grinned. "Mandy able to fit you in for an estimate this morning?"

"Very funny." I propped my free hand on my hip. "Maybe you and Jake should start a stand-up routine. You could share jokes about me and my vastly amusing hair."

He spread his arms. "C'mon, honey. I'd still love you if you shaved your head bald and painted it bright blue."

176

I rolled my eyes. "Good answer. You just saved yourself from being cut off for a week."

His dark eyes twinkled. "As Piddie used to say...*my mama didn't raise no fool.*"

I motioned toward the hair salon. "Is the entire gang here today?"

"All except Melody and Evelyn. Melody's taking the day off, and Evelyn's gone to Tallahassee to pick up some material for some creation she's designing for Christmas. She explained it all to me in great, exhausting detail. I'm afraid I wasn't paying close attention." Holston cocked his head to one side. "She seems to use me to bounce ideas off...now that her mother's not around."

I handed our daughter over. "Just nod a lot. You'll get by. I'll be in the hair salon if Sarah's any trouble."

Holston settled Sarah into the kiddie corral beside his desk. "She'll be all right. Go get yourself all prettied up. Oh, remember...I'll be leaving here around three this afternoon. I'm having dinner with Sam Rosenthal from Magnolia Printing Company."

I shook my head. "I'll bum dinner off Jake and Jon. Does this mean that Sam's company got the contract?"

"They're putting in a bid on the second printing of Jake's abduction story. I don't have a lot of pull as to where the contract lands, but I'd sure like to see Sam's company get it."

"Yeah, keep it local. That would be good." I kissed him on the cheek. "Maybe if I get a new hairstyle, I'll feel a little more...you know..."

Holston brushed my chin. "It's okay to be sad, Hattie. No one's really all peppy right now. Don't be so hard on yourself."

Elvina waved as I passed the reception desk. "Mornin', Hattie! Mandy's all ready for you. Just go on back."

UP THE DEVIL'S BELLY

How strange to see Elvina Houston perched behind the antique mahogany desk, officious and self-important.

Mandy and Wanda were huddled over the latest hairdo magazine when I walked into the salon. "Hattie!" Mandy waved me over. "Wanda's found the perfect new style for you." She patted the seat of her stylist chair. "Sit yourself down, hon."

Mandy smoothed the Velcro strip of the plastic drape into place and began to pick at my hair. "Looks like you been trimmin' it up yourself again, hmm?"

"It started to drive me nuts."

Mandy propped her hands on her hips in mock disgust. "I'm gonna break down and buy you a pair of sheers for Christmas, Hattie Lewis. I suwanee, looks like you been using a hedge trimmer on this head of hair."

I shrugged. "That's why I'm here."

Wanda sat on her stylist chair and swiveled to face us. "I think it's great when folks cut their own hair. Makes me look that much more like a magician when I save the day. Besides, Mandy, you have to admit…Hattie's not near as bad as the last time Ladonna O'Donnell picked up a pair of scissors."

"Lordy-be! Don't you know it! Took me three months to straighten out that mess. Said she was tryin' to layer it in the back. Ended up lookin' like she'd had a spittin' match with a Weedeater!"

Wanda and I laughed.

Mandy assumed her professional voice. "Now, hon, here's what I had in mind. Shorter on the sides…a few fringe bangs around your face. Then, we'll make it a little longer in the back with the lower layer doin' that little up-flip that's so popular right now. Like that girl on the Mornin' Show on channel six…what's her name?"

"Carmelita Cullens," Elvina said. She plopped down on one of the director's chairs and rested the portable phone headset on her lap. "That'll

178

look good on you, Hattie. With your heart-shaped face, and all."

"Listen to you, Elvina. Not here two weeks and already you're talkin' the talk." Mandy grinned.

Elvina smiled sweetly and batted her eyelashes. "I'm just doin' the best I can…workin' with what I got."

"Let's get you shampooed." Mandy leaned the seat back and positioned my head over the wash basin. The tension eased as the warm water coursed through my hair. Mandy's expert hands gently massaged my scalp as she worked the hair into a frothy lather.

"Don't this smell nice? It's sunkissed pear. I could smell it all livelong day and not get tired of it."

"I prefer the island mist one," Wanda said. "Reminds me of suntan lotion smell."

The seat back popped into the upright position. Mandy used a fluffy towel to remove the excess moisture, and then began to gently tease the tangles into submission with a large-toothed comb. "Your hair is fine, fine, fine," she said. "Oh, My Gawd! I don't bee-lieve it!"

I studied her shocked expression in the mirror. "What?"

"Look-y here! Hattie Davis Lewis finally has a gray hair! I found one!"

"There are several, thank you. I *am* over forty, after all."

"Just you wait till you find gray in your short hairs like I got," Elvina said. "That's when you know age is creepin' up on you."

Mandy grimaced. "That's way more information than I need, Elvina."

Elvina huffed. "I gotta toughen you girls up some." The phone in her lap trilled. She hopped up and headed toward the appointment books on the reception desk chattering cheerfully into the headset.

"Evelyn told us the work was comin' right along on the farmhouse," Mandy said. "You pretty close to finishin' up?"

UP THE DEVIL'S BELLY

I nodded slightly. "It's been amazing. I know folks over in Tallahassee who have taken over a year to build a room. I guess it must be easier getting the permits over here in Gadsden County. Bobby's had crews of builders out there practically around the clock. The house is almost ready to move back into. That's where I was earlier this morning. I left Jake and Jon hanging the window treatments in the kitchen. The new appliances are due to be delivered in a couple of days."

"I know you'll be glad to be back home...not that any of us have minded y'all campin' out here for awhile," Mandy said.

"How 'bout Bobby and Leigh's log cabin?" Wanda asked.

"They're pouring the foundation this week. Ran into a hitch on one side, though. Something about finding pipe clay."

"I know *all* about pipe clay," Mandy said. "When I built my little house, they found a patch of it. Cost a few hundred dollars extra to sink a support thing-y on one side. Didn't make much sense to me, but the workers told me that kinda dirt won't hold up to the weight of a house." She held a hank of hair above my head and lopped it off. "We'll have to throw a kitchen and log cabin warmin' when y'all get all settled in out there on the Hill."

"That's one thing I've noticed about this group. Never at a loss for a reason to celebrate," Wanda said.

I asked, "How're things working out with Elvina at the front desk?"

"Well..." Mandy sighed. "Elvina's at a bit of a disadvantage, I suppose — heaven knows, fillin' Piddie's shoes — but, she's actually doing pretty fair. There have been a few minor glitches." Mandy measured a section of hair and briskly snipped.

Wanda laughed. "The funniest was when she put Angelina Palazzolo down on Stephanie's column for a full body exfoliation. She was supposed to be on Mandy's book for a cut and set."

Mandy nodded. "We didn't discover the mistake till five minutes before she was due to walk in. By that time, I was already booked with another client. Piddie would've called it an *O.S. Moment.*"

Having an *O.S. moment* had been my aunt's delicate way of saying *oh shit.* I smiled as I dabbed at a trickle of water that had dripped down my right temple. "What'd you do?"

"Elvina didn't even miss a beat," Mandy said. "When Angelina walked in, Elvina took her by the hand and told her she'd planned a little surprise for her. Told her she'd been worried 'bout her looking so stressed here lately…and how she'd arranged to pay for a full body skin treatment with Stephanie, then she could have her hair done right after. *I know you'd never do this for yourself, Angie,* she told her, *so I'm treating you — as a gift!*"

Mandy stopped to compare the two sides of my hair to assure herself they were even. "Angelina was so surprised and pleased, she had the body treatment, then paid to have her hair done afterwards in the spot Elvina found for her on my book. Angelina walked out of here lookin' like she'd just found religion!"

Wanda slapped her hands on her thighs. "She said her skin felt smoother than a newborn baby's behind. That it was the best thing ever. And, she scheduled next week with Steph for a full hour massage!"

Elvina hustled into the salon. "Wanda, that was Hank Henderson's secretary, Maxine. He's stoppin' in for a trim at one before some meeting he has to attend."

Wanda rolled her eyes. "A person should be so lucky."

"That reminds me," Elvina said. "Hattie, have you listened to your tape Piddie made you, yet?"

"No."

"Evelyn brought the one Piddie made for all of us here, yesterday, but we haven't had a chance to listen to ours, either," Mandy said.

Elvina leaned forward. Her eyes narrowed. "Piddie had a stern warnin' on mine 'bout that Hank Henderson."

"That right?" Wanda asked. "You better fill me in…since I'm the only one here who has to touch the man."

Elvina settled into a director's chair. "Piddie wasn't one to cuss much, mind you. If you got her good and riled up, she could heck and dern you up one side and down the other. She said three cuss words when she was talkin' 'bout Mr. Hank Henderson." Elvina shook her head. "She didn't say anything real specific — just that we should all keep an eye pealed in his direction. Piddie said she felt like he was up to no good."

"She's been suspicious of him for awhile," I said. "I should listen to my tape and see if she adds to what she said to you. I just… haven't felt up to it yet."

Elvina fiddled with a stray sprig of her hair. "Some parts of it made me sob like a baby." She smiled slightly. "Other parts, I laughed so hard I nearbout lost my mind. That Piddie…"

We fell silent for a moment, remembering.

"You know what's been kinda weird?" Mandy asked softly.

We looked at her.

Mandy continued, "stuff's been happening around here…"

"Like what?" I asked.

Mandy shook her head. "I feel stupid mentionin' it…but, I keep findin' daisies around the spa. There was one stuck in an empty shampoo bottle last week, and another was lying on the seat of dryer number three when I opened up this past Saturday. That ain't all. Steph said someone's been moving the clean sheets and towels over to the dryer. She swears she ain't doin' it herself… and none of us are."

"Maybe Tameka? Or Moses?" I asked.

Wanda shook her head. "Nope. Tameka's here only on the weekends, now that school's started up. She's missed a few times on account of her grandma feelin' bad. And Moses, he pretty much stays outside tending to the grounds."

Mandy chuckled. "And we know it's not Jake or Jon. For one thing, they're so busy, they're barely here…what with gettin' Piddie's little house down the road ready to move into. For another — Jake would toot his own horn if he did Steph's laundry for her —not that he would mind — he just loves the praise."

Elvina stood to leave. "Well, I'd love to stay back here whilin' away the time like I used to do before I was a workin' gal….but, I've figured a new system for the appointment books…to keep me from…accidentally messin' up."

"What would that be, Elvina? Brain transplant?" Mandy ducked her head and grinned.

Elvina spun around. "For your information, missy, I'm color-coordinatin' the books. I'm drawin' a colored box around each column so's I can quick-reference the professional to the intended service."

"Just listen to you," Wanda said.

Elvina ticked off her points on her extended fingers. "Blue is for massage therapy and full body treatments…cause blue's the color that comes into my mind when I get all relaxed. Red is for Melody's manicurist patrons. Yellow is for Mandy, on account of her always bein' so bubbly and fun — makes me think of yellow. And, orange is for Wanda cause it's nigh close to the color of her hair."

Mandy nodded. "That works for me, as long as it works for you."

"I feel organization comin' on." Elvina charged out of the salon.

"There we are." Mandy patted me on the shoulders. "I'll just use a round brush and polish the ends with a curling iron, and you'll be a new woman!"

I had been so caught up in the conversation; I'd failed to notice the growing mound of shorn hair on the tile at the base of the chair. I studied my reflection in the mirror. I looked like a wet disgruntled squirrel.

Mandy beamed. "Don't look so pent up, Hattie-sue. It's an easy hairdo for you to maintain at home. You're gonna love the attention it draws to you."

"As long as nobody calls animal control when they see me," I said.

Hank Henderson

A single daisy bloom was propped in the cup holder of Hank Henderson's Mercedes; the first thing he saw as he wedged his distended belly behind the steering wheel.

"Got-dammit! Got-dammit! Not again!"

He squeezed out of the driver's seat and snatched the flower from its perch. He then proceeded to pitch a full-blown hissy fit. His secretary, Maxie, and Officer Rich Burns, who had just stepped out of the police station headquarters next door, watched with their mouths agape. Hank stomped the daisy to a glossy pulp, cursing loudly. Maxine feared for her boss's sanity, and her job. Rich felt for the handcuffs affixed to his service belt, ready in the event restraint became necessary.

After a few minutes, Hank's stomping frenzy ceased. He stood with clenched fists, beads of perspiration dripping from his reddened face, staring at the ruined flower at his feet. The *daisy invasion*, as he now called it, had started two days after Piddie Longman's funeral. Every day, the infernal blossoms appeared in different locations: in his locked gun case, on his pillow, and once, dangling from the shower nozzle in the master bathroom. A review of the security tapes held no clue to the demented perpetrator.

"Mr. Hank?" Maxie asked in a soft voice. "You all right?"

Hank looked up to see Maxie and Rich studying him. "Umm...there was a wasp in my car. Dang near bit me on the hand." He smiled weakly. "I hate wasps."

Before either bystander could offer up a reasonable response, Hank hopped into the Mercedes, slammed the gearshift into reverse, and vacated his private parking space.

He accelerated sharply as he passed the Chattahoochee City Limit sign on Highway 269. A small neatly-wrapped package rested on the seat beside him; his excuse for dropping by unannounced at the Davis/Lewis farmhouse.

Hank willed his breathing to calm as he teased the finely-tuned German automobile well past the 45-mph speed limit. He mulled over the recent unfortunate developments in his financial dealings. Earlier in the day, his dip-shit cousin had phoned from Midview, frantic with worry.

"That got-damned half-breed cretin," he muttered. "I should have my ass kicked to Cuba and back for getting involved with him in the first place!"

Perhaps his cousin, Lamar Mason, had been a bit too zealous with his illegal clean-out of the Midview Police evidence storage room. Hank shook his head angrily. "If the fool would've thought for *just* a second — given that he even possesses a brain — he'd of been more selective…taken it slower, so that things wouldn't have been missed."

The problem lay in the fact that Lamar had completely cleared one twelve-by-twelve storage room. He brought in a table and six chairs, a foosball table, and a color television, transforming the former evidence room into a break space for his buddies. Naturally, they were quite happy with the new provisions. The old break area had consisted of three metal folding chairs and a stack of outdated magazines in one cramped corner by the rear entrance to the police station.

Recently, a few questions had popped up. *Where's all the stuff we had stored in here, Lamar? You move it to another room? Who authorized this?* The way Lamar told it, the vultures were circling the highway, and he was the fresh roadkill *du jour*.

185

UP THE DEVIL'S BELLY

Hank had spent close to an hour of precious time coaching the whining idiot, trying to calm him down and help him think of creative ways to avoid discovery. It had been like pushing a cement truck uphill. Hard to reason with someone with the IQ of an ice cube.

Hank's chest tightened with apprehension. He'd come close lately to manifesting a full-blown panic attack. The anti-anxiety drugs his Tallahassee physician prescribed helped somewhat. Now, to add to his growing lists of aggravations, he had to be aware of the watchful eyes of Piddie Longman's cohorts. How could he get his hands on the tapes she'd left behind? He felt sure she'd found a way to reach beyond the grave to be a thorn in his side, just as she'd been in life. The daily daisy encounter added to his sense of gloom.

Hank's plans for Tameka Clark weren't moving along at a fast clip, either. She was fast proving to be his greatest challenge. The other kids — the older ones — had been easy to bend, easy to coax with the promise of money or fame. Little Tameka was impervious to his charms. He had carried several meals over to her Grandma Maizie, even felt a brief twinge of premature remorse for his planned actions. The old woman was genuinely kind — almost made him put a halt to the entire thing.

If things didn't gel by September 12th, he'd have to put Tameka Clark in the loser's column. He was getting ready to blow this town. Instead of being delivered locally, the new Mercedes would arrive in Port of Miami on the 14th, and he'd be there waiting to make the arrangements for its deportation to his island hideaway. Soon, he would be miles distant from the town of Chattahoochee; far from the dragnet he sensed closing in from all sides. A Delta jet-prop would cushion him in its cramped bosom and spirit him away to a new life.

Hank pulled the Mercedes onto the lawn in front of the Davis farmhouse. When there was no answer to his ring, he walked around the house to the rear

186

carport. "Good. Hattie's SUV is here. She has to be nearby." He smiled. "Wouldn't it be perfect if she was down by Mr. D.'s fish pond? Down there in those deep woods...alone?"

He wheeled around and returned to his car.

Hattie

As I emptied the thirty-pound bag of commercial floating fish food into the steel drum by the lower-level deck, Spackle woofed twice, and I heard a car motor shut off. Glancing up the hill toward the gazebo, I spotted a Mercedes sedan parked beside Pearl. "C'mon, honey," I said, gathering Sarah into my arms, "looks like we have uninvited company."

Hank flashed his best neighborly *just-stoppin'-by-to-say-hi* smile. On him, the expression looked as natural as a quarterback in a lace slip. "Hi there, Miz Hattie! Mind if I come down?"

"Uh...I'll come up there. I'm finished feeding the fish." I frowned as I mounted the steps to the gazebo. Normally, seeing Hank Henderson would have elicited mild annoyance, but the discussion at the spa had painted an aura of suspicion around the man.

"What brings you all the way out here?" I asked when I crested the hill.

Hank presented a small gift-wrapped package. "Sarah's welcome home gift. I just got it back. Had it special ordered and engraved with her initials."

"Oh...well...that was nice of you. Would you like to sit down for a minute or two?"

"Only for a minute." He plopped into a rocking chair. "You can open it if you'd like."

Inside the box, an intricately engraved silver and gold baby spoon rested in silver embellished tissue paper. "This is beautiful! Thank you, Hank. You didn't have to go all out..."

"It's just a token — a keepsake. I still have the one my mother saved. It's a lot like that one."

"I'll be sure to put it in a safe place and keep it for her."

Hank looked out over the pond. "My father used to bring me out here. He thought a lot of your folks…liked to fish with your daddy every now and again." He released a heavy sigh. "Sure is a pretty spot. I always wished I'd grown up out here in the country on some acreage, but Father wouldn't have any part of it. He wanted to live in town."

"It's not too late, Hank. You could always watch out for a piece of property. And, it's still reasonably priced, at least until the south Florida developers sniff out how nice this part of the state is."

"Huh!" Hank chuffed. "I can't see myself living my whole life in north Florida."

"Where do you want to live, if not here? I mean, I know it's not my place to ask. You have your law practice here, and everyone knows you."

"Nope, can't see it. You might be happy settlin' for Chattahoochee small town life, but…not me. No sir-ee."

I shifted Sarah to the wooden floor with one of the toys we kept stored in the gazebo. Spackle moved into guard position between the baby and the over-blown attorney. "I don't see myself as *settling* for living here, Hank. It was a conscious choice. I happen to *like* it here…so does Holston, and he moved from New York."

Hank waved his hand in dismissal. He turned to study me with cold, hard eyes. I felt the hair rise on the nape of my neck. A low growl sounded from deep inside the dog's throat.

He turned back toward the pond. "Don't you ever worry 'bout being down here by yourself?"

I studied his profile. "No, not at all."

Sarah reached over and bopped him on the foot with a plastic baseball bat.

Hank frowned. "Kid's a regular little slugger, isn't she?"

"Sorry." No need for me to worry about my daughter's taste in men. She was showing great intuition in that respect.

"All I'm sayin' is — you better be careful coming down here all alone. There's a lot of meanness in this world. Woman could get caught off all by herself..."

"Why, Hank. That almost sounds like a threat."

His lips parted slightly. "Hattie, I wouldn't have a reason to threaten you, now would I?"

Margie's ATV slid up behind the two parked vehicles, sending a puff of orange dust into the air. "Yoo-Hoo!" she called out.

"In the gazebo, Margie! Come on in!"

Spackle greeted our neighbor with a wagging tail and a wet hand-lick.

Hank stood as Margie entered the screened room. "Miz Margie." He nodded.

"Well, Hank Henderson. You out conductin' your legal business this fine afternoon?"

"No, ma'am. Just a social call." Hank tipped his head in my direction. "Reckon I'll leave you two ladies now. I've dallied here long enough. Work's not gonna get itself done." He stepped to the screened door. "Pleasure to see you, Miz Margie. My regards to John."

"Likewise," Margie said.

After Hank's Mercedes disappeared down the cleared lane, Margie settled into the rocker beside me. "You all right, gal?"

"Yeah...although, I'm kinda glad you came along."

"Hank Henderson bothered you?"

I shuttered involuntarily. "Not really. Nothing I could put my finger on.

He's just…strange. Even worse than he was in school."

"Elvina Houston phoned me up — told me to check up on you and the baby. She said Wanda let it slip to him that you were out here by yourself. Hank was having his hair cut, and he said he'd have to stop in and visit you and the baby. Elvina — she pitched a liver-bustin' fit and fell in it! She called the farmhouse first, and then called us when there wasn't an answer. John was taking his afternoon nap, so I came on up the lane. Figured you were down here at the pond. Anyway, I saw Hank's car go by a bit ago. Didn't think much of it 'till Elvina called up in such a fizz. She was flat-out adamant that one of us check on you. I'm not tryin' to be a meddlin' neighbor, now."

I reached over and patted her on the arm. "I'd never think that of you. One more guardian angel's okay by me."

"Long as there's a loved one to tell your stories, you're never really dead. Remembering brings you back to life for a little while. Life stops still for no one. But, it will slow up for a few precious moments while we remember."

Piddie Davis Longman

CHAPTER TWENTY-ONE

IN SPITE OF THE SLIGHT LIFT I'd received from the new hairstyle and ensuing slew of compliments, I slipped into an abysmal case of the blues in the weeks following Piddie's funeral. Grief was not new. Both of my parents had died in the past few years. The process would unfold as it should, with time — honoring the spirit's wise ability to feel deeply and rise above the loss.

Aunt Piddie's maxim floated through my consciousness:

Life is full of good and bad. Things happen in clusters — both good and bad. When you're in a cluster, you just have to keep your head above the surface and tread water like the dickens 'till the cluster passes you by.

My newly-discovered soul mate/best friend had been ripped grievously from my life. Piddie had always been there — a steadying presence in the family. Because of the years spent escaping my small town upbringing, I had missed experiencing her humor and acute sense of humanity. No one could equal her talent for fashioning words to match her needs, regardless of correct pronunciation: *hysterectum* for hysterectomy, *the AID* for AIDS, and *karate arteries* for carotid arteries. How many more had I missed over the years? The sad truth hit me full in the face: by the time I had acknowledged an interest in

191

the older generation, they were making the final transition to another place, far from my questions.

For a month, I dragged through the daily routine of work, home, baby, and husband with nominal interest. Though it was comforting to be home again, I wasn't particularly excited when we moved back into the farmhouse. Holston could've paraded past in a Chippendale G-string, and I would've waved him away for blocking my view of the television. Food tasted bland. My fine hair was more limp than usual. Domination of the remote control lost its glitter. I was a flat-liner.

Holston plopped down on the couch next to me. "She's out like a light, finally. I don't know what had her so wound up. I have a sneaky feeling that our Sarah's going to be both a night owl as well as a morning person."

"Uh-huh." I stared at the documentary on rainforest frogs as if it was my last chance to understand life in the tropics.

Holston hit the mute button on the remote. "I called Jake today. He's arranged with Stephanie to take your Thursday and Friday clients. Sarah and I have a surprise for you."

I squinted at the silent screen. "What."

"Wouldn't be much of a surprise if I told you, now would it? Just be ready, mentally, to leave as soon as you get home from your last client tomorrow."

"Holston...hon...I really don't feel..."

"...like lifting a finger. I know. You won't have to. We'll do it all. Take Pearl to work tomorrow. I'll need Betty." He leaned over and kissed me lightly on the lips. "I'm going to turn in, now. Sarah was a handful today. If I know her, she'll be up bright and early, ready to go at it again. Come to bed when you get ready." He hit the remote button to restore the sound.

Where was I being dragged off to? Nothing too damned cheerful, heaven forbid. Disneyworld would send me screaming over the edge. All I needed was for one of those perky overstuffed rodents to come bouncing up to me. I smiled at the mental picture of neatly-pressed Disney theme park security guards pulling me, kicking and gnashing, off Minnie Mouse. I would be barred from Sea World, Universal Studios, and MGM theme parks, too. A thought worth entertaining; a valid reason to never have to visit south Florida again!

When I arrived at the Hill the next afternoon, Betty was parked on the front lawn, full of fuel, washed, and loaded for a road trip. Holston allowed me to eat a sandwich, change clothes, and use the bathroom, before he packed Sarah, Spackle, and me into the SUV. Shammie, in the height of her kitty golden years, had been elected to remain at home to guard the farmhouse. She watched us leave from her perch in the front plate glass window, a mixture of cloaked interest and feline disdain on her fluffy face. She'd miss Sarah, but would relish the peace of the empty house. Jake and Margie had been drafted to fill the food and water bowls, clean the litter box, and croon and fuss over her. Dogs have masters. Cats have slaves.

Our destination soon became clear. Dense hardwood forests gave way to the scrub oak and palmetto thickets marking the beginning of the Florida coastal plane. In two hours, we reached the entrance to the dual bridges spanning Apalachicola Bay to St. George Island. The quarter-mile strip of land separating the bridges was peppered with small signs warning motorists to reduce speed. From June to September, hundreds of migratory seabirds annually used the slip of land as a rookery.

As Betty crept along the narrow two-lane motorway, seabirds zigzagged across her path. A two-foot-high mesh fence separated the roadbed from the grass nesting grounds, but an occasional juvenile hatchling wandered precariously close to the asphalt. The pavement was littered with the feathered carcasses of the chicks unfortunate enough to tangle with the swarms of beach-bound tourists traversing the causeway.

"I feel like I'm crossing a battleground when I come down here this time of year. Amazing how many dead birds there are," I said.

"Reminds me of an Alfred Hitchcock movie. Hope they never decide to seek revenge." Holston braked and steered to miss a chick that was being herded into the grass by a protective adult.

By nature, I'm more of a mountain glen/coldwater creek kind of girl. Like a lot of native Floridians, I preferred to vacation in the Blueridge Mountains of the Carolinas. More than likely, we Floridians passed the Carolinians heading south to our beaches as we ripped a path to their hills.

Several years had passed since I'd planted my feet in the sugary white sands of St. George Island. Like many of the coastal paradises in the state, the island was undergoing development. A state-owned park preserved a large portion of one end of the island. The remainder of the high-priced real estate was being hacked into vacation home sites. Rows of tinker toy stilted homes loomed over the dunes, aching for a category three hurricane.

One particular tier of narrow, three-story, pastel-hued rental units had earned the title, *the Domino Houses*. If God possessed a sense of humor, He smiled down on the frenzied building folly, awaiting the perfect opportunity to shove the end unit with a big celestial thumb. His peals of laughter would echo like summer thunder as the spindly houses clanged into each other until the entire row lay at a thirty-degree angle to the ground.

At Jake's suggestion, Holston had eschewed the perfectly preened beach rental units for one of the few remaining oceanside bungalows, the historic Hadler House on the gulf beach side of the island. Constructed before hurricane-wizened builders had the notion to plop houses atop pilings far above the dunes, the gray tone-on-tone block and wood frame cottage was familiar and welcoming. Any poor slob who's scaled three flights of stairs carrying a heavy cooler could appreciate the ground level accommodations.

Inside the window-unit cooled cottage, the *artful and whimsical* (the rental brochure touted) décor was decidedly early fifties. Sunbleached shells clustered like museum displays on every available horizontal surface. The tiny bathroom continued the theme with mirrors encrusted with pieces of broken shells in orange and blue-gray hues. The plastic-framed print of Jesus walking on the water seemed to fit in, somehow.

The Hadler House wasn't the Hilton, but it felt homey — reminiscent of the old Florida of mom-and-pop roadside attractions and garish red-lipped painted coconut shells; the state I recalled from childhood vacations.

The best feature of the small house was the 20x20-foot screened porch facing the ocean. Wind chimes fashioned from small shells and lengths of hollow reed tinkled in the constant salty seabreeze. Four white painted wooden rocking chairs invited visitors to sit for hours, pitching gently back and forth in time with the crash of waves against the shore. The window ledges provided exhibit space for the scores of shells and sea flotsam — the legacy from previous renters.

Holston ordered Sarah, Spackle, and me to take our first stroll on the beach while he unpacked. The salt-laced breeze licked my face and body as I dipped Sarah's feet into the cool sand near the surf's edge. She squealed with delight when the seafoam tickled the tips of her toes. Spackle ran into the water, barking and biting at the waves churning to shore. After a few mouthfuls of salt water, he retreated to land to hack up the brine he'd swallowed, before launching another series of attacks. For the first time in weeks, I found myself laughing.

In the gray early morning light, the footprints in my wake filled with the gentle pulsations of the small waves nudging the sand. I left Holston and Sarah happily chirping to each other over cereal and bananas and sipped strong Colombian coffee from an oversized thermal mug as I plodded down the beach toward the end of St. George Island dubbed *The Plantation*. Compared to the multimillion dollar stucco monstrosities on the far tip of the island, the section around the Hadler House looked like a ghetto. Amazing — even on an island less than fifteen miles in length, segregation spurred by money reared its ugly, carefully-coiffured head, shaded by a custom-built beach gazebo, of course.

Staring out across the expanse of blue-green ocean water and then down at the infinite grains of sugar-white sand caused memories to float to the surface like flotsam. Void of the distraction of the daily make-a-living, fight traffic, routine grind, the underlying muck oozed to the top like clabber in spoiled milk.

I plodded onward, my feet sucking in the wet sand, tears trickling in a steady stream over my checks and the tip of my nose. Wet salt leaked from my eyes, reminding me of my body's close kinship to the sea. If science can be trusted, some fish-like slug named Irving, my first relative, had climbed unceremoniously from the ocean, looked around, and decided to stay awhile. It was a long time ago, and the details have gotten sketchy. The pull of the sea, the desire to be near it, in it, bubbled up from an ancient gene lodged deep in the pool.

By the time I returned to the beach in front of the Hadler House, Holston and Sarah were busy setting up a homestead in the sand. Holston had erected two beach umbrellas and was positioning coolers, chairs, and toys on a beach mat. Our daughter watched and periodically stuck fistfuls of sand into her mouth. Luckily, she hated the taste, or she would've weighed ten more pounds before the morning was over.

Holston smiled up at me. "Nice walk?"

"Yeah. Sorry I left you with breakfast duties. I just needed to…"

He squinted into the early morning sun. "No need to explain. Besides, Sarah's a much more cheerful cereal companion than you, love. No offense intended."

"None taken. Looks like you packed everything. Wow! Who would've pegged you for a beach bum?"

"Jake provided a list — down to the food. You owe him on this one, not me. He even picked out the bungalow. Said you wouldn't go for a fancy condo."

I nodded. "He knows me pretty well. We'll have to make sure Sarah has tons of sunscreen on. The rays aren't quite as intense this time of year, but she can still get a nasty burn."

Holston dumped the contents of the beach bag onto the mat. "I have SPF 15, 30, 50+, and 24 for faces. Also, a special baby sunblock for her."

There were enough sun protection factors concentrated on our beach mat — not only would we not burn, we'd probably draw in clouds for fifty miles. Being a child of the late fifties, before the sun became arch cancer enemy number one, I had caused enough damage to my skin to feed and clothe two dermatologists and their staffs for the next half of my life. As a teenager, baby oil laced with iodine (for stain?) was the favorite potion to prompt the golden brown luster that signaled summer health and well-being. By the time all of my girlfriends of that era and I pushed into our eighties, we'd be lucky to have one whole nose between us.

The late August morning held the promise of intense heat. One important difference between a Florida native and an out-of-state tourist: we know to go inside between the hours of 11:00 AM and 4:00 PM. The early mornings and evenings provide the most pleasant and least damaging hours to enjoy the ocean.

Inside the artificially cooled bungalow, I crammed half of a sweet roll in my mouth and washed it down with the remaining dregs of lukewarm coffee. Rummaging in the suitcase, I located a bathing suit and cover-up. Through some loving touch of the fashion Gods, the suit fit perfectly. It didn't pull, ride up, or bind anywhere, and actually looked halfway decent, and perhaps, attractive. Jake, fashion police ambassador, had accompanied me on the dreaded bathing suit buying expedition. Bikinis and two-piece creations were a distant memory. Even before the colon cancer surgery had decorated my stomach with a ten-inch vertical zipper, I had opted for the coverage of a tasteful one-piece tank.

The invention of the tankini, a two-piece creation with the coverage and illusion of a one piece, had come at the exact moment we forty-something's needed it. The tankini had to have been a woman's idea, or at least, a sensitive male designer who'd listened to women bitch, rant, and rave about having to peel off a wet tank suit in order to use the bathroom, only to have to smash and mold her extra flesh back into the damp sausage-like casing.

I dearly loved the new tankini. The lower portion was a kicky little skirted number that artfully concealed the lumps at the top of my thighs and the part of my derrière hell-bent on following the pull of gravity down the back of my legs. The upper section sported delicate spaghetti straps and a long waist-hugging midsection that covered my vertical scar and more-than-a-six-pack abdomen. I wasn't model material, but at least I wouldn't show up in the front of a woman's magazine under the title *fashion don'ts* with a black slash covering my face.

As I watched Sarah and Spackle experience the beach, the essential reason the world is blessed with children and animals came to light: to help adults remember the pleasure of simple things. Somewhere along the line, I'd lost the ability to have fun; not the expensive, diamond-and-pearls-dress-up, buy-a-ticket-in-advance type of adult amusement. The play I watched was pure joy at its most elemental. Sarah giggled at each crash of the waves, wiggled stubby pink baby toes in the sand, tried to eat fistfuls on several occasions, and patted wet clods onto Spackle's back until he stood and shook to unload. Spackle chased the retreating surf, seagulls, crabs, and my straw hat as it escaped the blanket in a gust of wind.

Looking down the expanse of pristine sand, I spotted the yellow warning flags marking a few remaining buried sea turtle nests. One nest rested a few feet in front of our porch, its boundaries denoted by four small caution signs outlining the fines imposed for disturbing the nest. Upon erupting from the sand, the baby hatchlings would travel toward the brightest source of reflected luminescence — the ocean's surface. The realtor had informed us of the importance of extinguishing outside lights at night. Without artificial illumination to disorient them, the baby turtles could follow their instinct-driven path directly to the sea. At this point in late August, many of the nests were vacant, but ours still held the promise of emerging new life.

Never has so little spandex strained to cover so much surface area. Strange suits with mesh-lined holes in cleverly-placed locations, blinding neon creations that could double as highway hazard warnings in the event of a roadside emergency, and thong bikinis squeezed between white cheeks peppered with butt rash; the display spread along the narrow strip of island beach..

I watched a herd of hormonal adolescent males jog by. "Jake would fall out if he saw some of these beach ensembles."

Holston peered over his dark glasses. "That well-endowed woman, the one in the dark and light green striped bikini...umm...the suit makes her look like she's sprouting two ripe watermelons."

I poked him playfully in the arm. "I hadn't noticed her. Suppose our focus is different."

"I didn't mean..."

"Oh, Holston...you're married, not dead, hon. Piddie used to say, *it's okay to look at the menu as long as you go home to eat supper.*"

UP THE DEVIL'S BELLY

His smile was the only feature I could see from beneath the brim of his tilted straw hat.

By Saturday evening, sand was wedged in every body crevice, and it took considerable scrubbing to get the two kids ready for sleep. With Sarah and Spackle bathed and finally tucked into their beds, Holston and I slathered ourselves in bug repellent and settled into squatty beach chairs to witness the transformation of the peach and orange sky to the blue and purple of evening. A picture-perfect full moon popped from beneath a scattering of high clouds; the kind of too-damned-romantic balmy evening that could cause a single woman to sleep with the wrong man. The reflection of the full moon painted a wide streak in the smooth water, sparkling like ice crystals on the sea foam of the gently rolling waves.

As the daylight waned, the evening sea breeze increased, sending the ever-present biting gnats wheeling further inland. *No-see-ums*, as the locals called them, were the nemesis of North Florida beaches; the pit bulls of the annoying insect clan. If they had a purpose, other than to increase bug repellent sales, I'd not heard of it.

"Yiii!" I kicked one foot into the air.

"Crab?"

"Maybe." I studied the sand beneath my feet. "Holston, look!"

A few turtle hatchlings were making their way toward the moonlit sea.

I started to stand. "The nest! The turtles are hatching!"

"No," Holston grabbed my arm. "They're all around us. Better not walk. You could crush them."

In a few moments, we were stranded in a solid wave of scrambling baby turtles intent on following the moon's illumination. As the human intruders blessed to witness the marathon, we honored the silence. After a few minutes, the show was over as the final stragglers found their way to the ocean.

Holston's voice was a whisper. "That was…"

"Incredible," I finished.

We sat, frozen, not wanting the night to end. The moonlight softened the hard edges of the world. I relished every detail: Holston's chiseled luminescent silhouette, the etchings left by the baby turtles in the shifting sand, my toes deep and cool in the dampness, and the fine tickle-dance of hair at the nape of my neck.

Checkout time for the bungalow was 11:00 AM Sunday morning. The last day of our mini-vacation dawned with the promise of heat and humidity. August was taking its last stab at creating human misery before reluctantly bowing to the balmy temperatures of fall. After scribbling a note for Holston, I slipped from the house, careful not to slam the screened door. The first few fingers of sunlight crept into the sky as I headed down the beach, portable tape player in hand. The beach was deserted this early hour. Perfect.

I walked along the edge of the surf as I'd done hundreds of times in my over-forty years. The internal psychologist patted her couch and invited me to recline for another rendering. The raw bitterness of the past month had dulled, exorcised by the emotions expanding and popping as they reached the surface.

In an undeveloped stretch of dunes between beach houses, I spread a beach towel on the sand and plopped down to enjoy the view. Because of the island's relation to the land, the sun slipped from the horizon directly behind me on the bay side of St. George, but the sunrises appeared over the beach. Orange and yellow pushed aside the purples of the night sky. The call of birds awakened by the dawn filled the air.

"Okay, Piddie," I said as I loaded the first cassette into the player, "I guess I'm ready to hear what you have to say."

UP THE DEVIL'S BELLY

After a few moments of silence, my aunt's clear Southern voice came to life.

"Well, gal…I saved makin' your tapes for last. I reckon I got more to say to you. Lord knows, Evelyn's heard a'plenty from me over the years.

"First of all, I wanna thank you. If you're hearin' this after my final hoo-hah, I know you had a tough row to hoe with Evelyn over the cremation. She can be down right peevish when she digs her heals in over somethin'. That's why I picked you to handle my affairs, over anybody else in the family."

Piddie chuckled, remembering. "You was always a headstrong gal, even when you was a young'un. If your mama wanted somethin' done, she'd set you on it, and you'd boss all the rest of your cousins into line, quick as a whip! And, you did it in such a fashion that none of 'em knew they's bein' bossed!

"I'm mighty proud of the way you've settled into yourself here lately. I reckon some of us take a few detours a'fore we reach the station.

"Your mama always worried herself 'bout you and Bobby not gettin' on. I'm happy he's found him a good partner in Leigh…and his fun side's comin' out again. He was a cut-up as a young'un…always pullin' practical jokes on ever'body. That first marriage soured him on the world for awhile.

"I want you to watch over Jake, honey. He's a sensitive, carin' man that has had more'n his share of grief. They's a lot of folks who waste their time passin' judgement on other folks instead of lookin' in their own lives for fault. I hope this town might have learned a lesson 'bout that…but you never can tell 'bout the evil that lurks in a person's heart. He leans on you a lot, gal…but, I'm sure pleased he's gettin' stronger by and by…and I just love that Jon Presley so much I could pinch his head clean off huggin' him."

Piddie sighed. "Ever'thing's fallin' into place, I reckon. Evelyn seems to be blossomin' with her clothin' design business. And, Joe, bless his heart, is takin' over the cookin'. He even mentioned to me not too long back — he was

202

entertainin' the notion of openin' a little breakfast and lunch diner uptown. Can you imagine that?"

Piddie paused and took a deep breath. "As to that gang at the Triple C, I know Elvina will keep them in line. They've been like family to me, and I know Elvina will need them as much as they'll need her."

Piddie cleared her throat. "Now, this is serious, so lissen up. I want you all to keep a close watch over that Hank Henderson. He's bad seed. I just feel it deep in my bones. I hoodwinked him, I'll confess it to you — let on I knew somethin' 'bout his affairs that'd ruin him in town. I do hope the Good Lord will forgive me that little sin. I only did it to help out Jake. Hank was causin' a problem with the city commission over the rezonin' for the mansion. I just couldn't sit on the porch and watch that blowed-up so'n'so throw his weight around. Jake and Mandy had their hearts set on openin' the Triple C, and it wasn't fair what Hank was tryin' to pull. That man has a load of hate festerin' inside him, and I pity the poor soul that gets caught in his crosshairs. Y'all haf to take up where I left off."

Piddie's voice grew soft. "My little Chinaberry…it hurts my heart to think of leavin' her behind. But, that's the way of nature. The babies come in, and us oldsters take our leave. Sarah and Josh saved Evelyn's sanity; I tee-totally believe that. Byron's boys are too far off up there in Ohio, and pretty much grown up. But, I'm here to tell you, I beheld a change in Evelyn when Josh was born. Then, you brought Sarah home. Evelyn's finally settled herself on the fact that Karen's gone from us…as a relative, anyways. Both them young'uns are a blessin'.

"I ain't leavin' much of value behind. Never was one, much, for jewels or finery. I've been rich in ways you can't buy from a store. So, I'd like to tell you some stories — recount my life for you — to save for Sarah and Josh in case they want to know what their old aunt was like, since the memories of my life are all I got left to pass on to y'all…"

UP THE DEVIL'S BELLY

The remainder of the first tape and the entire second tape were filled with Aunt Piddie's life story, starting with her first recollections as a poor country child in rural south Alabama. Often, her voice would crack with emotion and the strain of weariness.

"Whew! Well, I reckon I've pretty much rambled on and on for a good while now. I know I've left stuff out — Evelyn and Joe can fill in the blank spots for you. I love you, Hattie gal. You'll have a guardian angel watchin' over you and yours all the days of your life — if I have my way 'bout it."

The hiss of silence followed her last words. A wave of gratitude for my great fortune of family washed over me. God was in his heaven. At least for the moment, everything was as it should be.

A woman tends to marry the likeness of her father — so the saying goes. Mr. D's knack for invention and tinkering was mirrored in Holston's writing ability. He could take a report on leaf mold and create a page-turner. Like my father, Holston had a knack with children. He understood Sarah on a level I couldn't comprehend. They spent hours simply hanging out together. Though she greeted me with enthusiasm and affection, it was clear she was quickly becoming a daddy's girl.

Another trait common to the important men in my life surfaced on the beach trip. Holston hated sand in the bed and didn't much care for it on his person. I'd awakened several times to a frantic overhaul of the sheets — fits of frenzied brushing and linen shaking. This would satisfy him for a few hours until some of *my* sand grains somehow migrated to *his* side of the bed for a sneak attack, and another wave of sheet shaking would ensue.

Though I had become a regular beach bum as soon as I could legally drive, I could recall only one occasion when my family had visited the coast. On the see-Florida educational tour, a requirement for both Bobby and me, the family stayed briefly in a small beachside motel on Daytona Beach. No one slept a lot that night, with my father's sheet shaking and muttered curses. I suppose that's the reason my mother looked forward to the yearly mountain trip. The Carolinas provided a cool escape from the spirit-breaking heat of north Florida, and the mountain dirt had no effect on the family's sleep.

Before returning to the cottage, I perched on a small dune fringed by sea oats and gazed out over the calm ocean. A pod of porpoise dipped and dived parallel to shore in the deep water just shy of the first sandbar. Lines of pelicans sailed by on their way to feed on schools of minnows churning in the shallow water. Closing my eyes, I breathed deeply of the misty salt air. The gentle lap of waves provided a meditation mantra. I remained for several minutes before the need for caffeine sent me toward the Hadler House. The aroma of freshly-brewed coffee greeted me.

"Mornin', hon," Holston called out from the kitchen table.

"Loo-lah!" Sarah said. She was busy wearing breakfast. I'm pretty sure the inspiration for oatmeal facial masks originated from a mother watching her child try to eat with a spoon.

I smiled. "Sorry I left you guys for so long."

"We got your note." He motioned to the tape player in my hand. "You okay?"

I nodded. "Better than ever."

Beach 99.3 Oldies Station carried us across the twin bridges to the mainland. Two things I love most about marriage: I can pass gas and belch out loud if I need to, and I can sing without being in the shower. Holston's tone deaf, anyway. He thinks I sound fantastic. Piddie's words floated into my inner ear as he bleated out his rendition of an old Beach Boys song: *poor man…he's handsome and sweet as the day is long, but he couldn't carry a tune in a bucket!*

"When you been on this earth long as I have, you think you've just about heard tell of every hard thing one person can do to another. But, all it takes is tunin' into the nightly news to find out some poor fool's come up with some new way to inflict sufferin'. Some days, I think if I was the Good Lord, I'd be rid of the whole lot of us."

Piddie Davis Longman

CHAPTER TWENTY-TWO

September 11, 2001

The Hill: Hattie

LIFE SETTLED BACK in to the semblance of normal routine in the days following the Lewis family beach trip. Though I missed Aunt Piddie terribly, my interest in family and the daily dramas spicing small town existence buoyed me from the quagmire of sadness. Elvina shouldered the weighty responsibility of being town chief informant, keeping the second phone line at the Triple C zinging with updates on current affairs. Each morning around nine o'clock, she called the Hill to briefly check in before making phone rounds to her list of contacts.

As I schlepped my way through my forties, I grasped the wisdom of Piddie's words: *if something doesn't hurt when I wake up in the mornin', I figure I'm dead.* I shuffled into the brightly-lit kitchen, shielding my eyes from the glare of reflected morning light. Passing the dining table, I delivered drive-by kisses to Holston and Sarah and headed to the front porch with a mug of inspiration. Luckily, I could ease into the day at a leisurely pace with strong black coffee at my favorite spot — my father's old wood-framed woven oak-split-backed rocking chair.

206

The porch resembled a seasonal plant sale at Tallahassee's Native Nurseries. Pots of yellow and rust-colored chrysanthemums rested at the base of each support column. Ten hanging Boston ferns successfully blocked the majority of the view of the yard, and a newly planted butterfly garden partially obscured the bird feeders.

The plant-populated porch treatment had been compliments of Jake and Jon. Inspired by an overnight trip to Georgia's Callaway Gardens the previous week, Jake had gone hog-wild ordering flowering fall plants. Not only was the day spa overrun with the cheerful ambassadors of the cooler weather, Piddie's little house on Morgan Avenue and the farmhouse had suffered the overflow. Jon had dubbed Jake the town's *mum fairy*.

The worn split oak seat of Daddy's rocker creaked as it cradled my body. Spackle wagged good morning, licked my hand once, and flopped down on the floorboards beside the chair. Since he'd moved past the *lick-the-human-till-she-drips-slobber* puppy stage of his young life, he had become a welcome morning companion.

The solitude was interrupted by the squeak of screen door hinges. "Hattie...hon? You'd better come inside and watch the news." Holston's voice was tinged with shock.

Network news is no compliment to coffee or breakfast, and I normally avoided the daily recount of the worlds' woes and evils. Something in Holston's tone prompted me to leave the peace of the porch and follow him inside.

"An airplane just hit one of the World Trade Center towers," he said as we watched one side of the building boil with thick, dark smoke.

"What's that plane doing?" Barely had the question left my lips when the jet disappeared from view. A ball of flame erupted from the second tower.

Coffee spilled from the mug in my hands. "Oh, my God! It hit the other building!"

The ring of the phone made both of us jump.

"Hattie! Hattie! Turn on the TV!" Elvina yelled when I answered.

I held the headset away from my ears. "Whoa! Hey! Don't talk so loud, Elvina."

"I'm sorry, Hattie. Oh, God A'mighty! It's the Armageddon! We're bein' attacked!"

"Elvina…"

"Lord help us all!"

"El-vee-na?"

"Jesus…Son of God, Save us!"

"EL-VEE-NAAA!!"

"Yeah?"

"Try to calm down. We don't know yet what's really happening."

"I gotta go call some folks!" Dead air followed the hang-up click.

I stared at the phone like it held some clue to world affairs, then threw it onto the couch. "Holston…it just occurred to me. Don't you have friends who work in one of those buildings?"

Holston's face was ashen. He nodded. "89th floor of the North tower."

Sensing our frantic mood, Sarah started to whimper. Holston removed her from the highchair and cooed comforting words into her ear. We sat, huddled on the couch, requiring the warmth of human contact.

"This just in…." Dan Rather, CBS commentator, reported, "at approximately 9:48 AM the Pentagon was hit by a jet airliner."

Holston frowned. "What the…?"

The news broadcast continued. "FAA has ordered the immediate grounding of all domestic flights…"

As we watched, numb and frightened, the tragic drama continued to unfold. The damaged South tower collapsed at 9:55. Shortly afterwards, the news of a downed flight eighty miles southeast of Pittsburgh interrupted the stream of information. At 10:29, the North tower collapsed in a billowing cloud of smoke and rubble. A video stream of trapped employees jumping from the doomed buildings and scores of ash-covered refugees fleeing to safety reduced me to tears. Sarah wailed in Holston's arms.

"It's like watching a Steven Speilberg movie," Holston said softly. "It just doesn't seem like it could be happening." His eyes shut against the terrible images. "This time of day...there must be hundreds of people in there...just starting to work..."

The first time I witnessed my husband in tears was immediately following my cancer surgery. For the second time since I'd met him, Holston Lewis broke down and sobbed. With Sarah sandwiched between us, we held each other and rocked back and forth until the love we shared brought a degree of calm.

Hank Henderson stood beside the king-sized bed with his crossed arms propped on his distended belly. Two large Pullman suitcases lay opened on the burgundy comforter.

"This time tomorrow, counselor," he announced to the silence of the tomb-like bedchamber, "you'll be strolling down Miami Beach."

No more Chattahoochee with its small town politics. No more obligatory social functions, mind-numbing church services, or dip-shit secretaries with beans for brains. No more Daniel H. Henderson, attorney at law.

Hank allowed himself to slip into the well-rehearsed daydream. His tanned, lean body cushioned in a chaise lounge beside a kidney-shaped pool. Tropical plants dripping with exotic blooms. Young, fresh-faced, well-paid servants catering to his every need. He stroked his chin. Perhaps, he'd grow a beard to accentuate his face.

Hank smiled. Truly, money could open any door. The years of planning and scheming — now all coming together. The time had finally arrived — better than any Christmas morning he had ever dreamed of when he was a kid. He could put aside the shady business contacts and child-fondling perverts who grappled like vultures for his homemade videos. He could ditch the gut-wrenching worry over his idiot cousin's inept philandering.

Tomorrow morning, September 12, 2001, would be a day he'd stamp in his memory as the date of his official rebirth. He'd leave the office for a routine business meeting, never to return. Hank chuckled to himself as he chunked a stack of underwear into one of the suitcases. Wouldn't that get them all going in this town? *Did you hear? Hank Henderson just up and disappeared!* By the time the authorities started to search, he'd be on his way to his new home, deep in the tropical jungle paradise of Costa Rica.

The man leaving Miami airport would no longer answer to *Hank*.

"Stanton Brett Johnson, Jr." Hank repeated his new name. "Originally from Birmingham, Alabama. Made good in the tech stock revolution of the nineteen eighties...before the economy went sour. Relocated to Costa Rica. Retired to a life of leisure and scholarly contemplation."

Professionally forged documentation for Stanton Johnson — birth certificate, credit cards, driver's license, and passport — was carefully tucked in a manila envelope inside the leather briefcase. The thought of leaving the house his father built stirred no emotion. Other than a few pictures of his mother, little of the family homeplace was tagged for inclusion in his new life. With the exception of the antique dueling pistols, one Glock, and his new SigSauer, the cherished gun collection would remain behind, locked in the trunk of the Mercedes.

The automobile's new owner, the same business associate who'd procured his documentation, had transferred funds for the sale of the guns and Mercedes into one of Hank's off shore bank accounts. The fine German sedan would disappear from its designated spot in long-term parking within an hour of Hank's departure. Because of its inherent value, the vehicle would be spared the violence of being reduced to parts at a distant chop shop. Hank felt a slight twinge of remorse when he thought of his car in the hands of some prestigious south Florida drug lord.

No matter. The new Mercedes waited for him at the docks in Miami like an expectant lover. Following his inspection and approval, the sedan would be shipped to its final destination. Stanton Brett Johnson, Jr., after all, was known for his taste in fine automobiles.

Hank tried his new name on his tongue. "Stanton? Stan? No, Stanton…Stan sounds too much like faggot middle class."

The portable phone on the bedside trilled. "Yes?"

Maxie's voice was barely audible. "Mr. Henderson?"

Hank sighed deeply. "Maxie, I told you yesterday, you can take the morning off today. I won't be in 'till after lunch."

"Yes, sir…I know…I mean…"

"Why are you calling me, then? I'm in the middle of some very important business!"

"Umm…sir? I thought I'd check to see if you're watching the news this mornin'."

Irritation knotted inside of him, and he felt the familiar burn in the pit of his stomach. "Noooo…I've been a little too busy to watch television."

"You might want to turn it on. We're under attack!"

Without bothering to formally end the conversation, Hank threw the headset on the bed and reached for the remote control. As he watched the replay and aftermath of the terrorist attacks aired in continuous video from the Cable News Network, the impact of the nation's crisis upon his personal plans settled in.

"Well, I'll be got-damned!"

"It's easy as pie to let yourself fall into despair. There's plenty enough goin' on in this old world to warrant sadness, that's for dog-gone sure. But, myself, I like a challenge. Try my level best to keep a cheerful outlook about me. Keep findin' things to be happy about. I don't have to look very far to find a blessing."

    Piddie Davis Longman

CHAPTER TWENTY-THREE

Hattie

THE INITIAL SHOCK WANED, and the American people struggled to return to a wobbly sense of normality. *Go back to work* was the new media-endorsed battle cry. Routine activities provided a sense of focus at a time when everything seemed off center and blurry around the edges.

Though I would have gladly canceled my annual follow-up visit to Dr. Lucas Thomas's office in Tallahassee, I did the patriotic thing and kept my nine o'clock appointment for the sigmoidoscopy. One must make certain sacrifices. Any cancer survivor can attest to this fact; once a doctor facilitates your cure, he welcomes you into the medical family with open arms as if he's reluctant to see you go your own way. Following the colon cancer surgery, I had become familiar with my physician and his staff, to the point of calling them all by their first names and inquiring about their families.

After the procedure, I bid a fond farewell to the area surrounding the hospital and picked my way through midmorning traffic on North Monroe Street. The congestion was the aspect of city dwelling I missed least. A rush hour jam in Chattahoochee consisted of less than ten cars lined up at the signal light in front of the mental hospital after shift change. Luckily, I'd have time to grab lunch and beat it out of town before the deluge of food-seeking drivers hit the streets.

The woman in the car behind me was dancing in her seat, hands tapping out the beat on the steering wheel. When her lips began to move, I realized we were singing along to the same song on the local oldie stations. For three blocks before she turned onto a side street, we sang a duet — two middle-aged strangers living separate lives.

Signs of patriotic support had popped up everywhere, almost overnight, since the September eleventh attack. A monster 4x4 pick-up truck roared into the lane beside me. I craned my neck to study the driver, a young man with a day-old beard, his head wrapped in a faded red, white, and blue bandana. In the back of the vehicle, an oversized American flag was tethered to a wooden pole. Sensing my scrutiny, he glanced down and flashed a toothy grin before accelerating sharply with the green signal. The flag flapped in the breeze, making him a one-man parade. Two blocks farther down Tharpe Street, an elderly gentleman bumped along the narrow strip of yard bordering the pavement on his riding lawnmower, a small flag duct-taped to its bumper.

Could good come from such a horrible act of anti-humanity? Perhaps, we'd pull together like threatened cows in a circle, unified against a common foe. By setting aside our differences for a time, we might feel gratitude for a country that had historically welcomed cultural disparity.

Shortly after noon, I pulled into the parking lot of the Triple C Day Spa and Salon. Finding no empty spot, I negotiated the narrow delivery lane to the rear door and squeezed Betty between Elvina's Oldsmobile and Holston's Acura.

Holston glanced up from his computer screen when I entered the study. "Hi, hon! How'd it go over at Dr. Thomas's?"

I kissed him lightly on the top of the head. "Fine."

"Fine as in *I really don't want to talk about it right now*...or fine as in *all is healthy?*"

The concern on his face caused a flood of love from deep in my soul. "Fine as in...I don't have to undergo any more disgusting, invasive tests for a whole year."

His features relaxed. "Fan—tastic! Did you get anything to eat yet?"

I rested the backside of my hand on my forehead in my best Southern lady I-feel-an-attack-of-the-vapors pose. "Forced myself to stop at Hopkins for a chicken tetrazini salad."

"Poor baby. Wanda just left to pick up carryout from the Homeplace for all of us. I've signed on for the gut-buster special."

"Shame on you!" Julie's half-pound hamburger with its thick slab of melted cheddar cheese and homemade steak fries was known locally as *heart attack on a plate.*

"Good thing I've already had my cholesterol checked this year. I just felt the need for some good grease...you know?"

"Uh-huh. Where's the wild child?"

He motioned toward the salon. "She's hanging at the front desk with Elvina. You have any clients scheduled this afternoon?"

"Just one — at 1:30. I'll pick Sarah up afterwards. I've got to hit Steph up for some massage lotion. I'm running low."

"Didn't you order last week?"

"Yeah, but with the planes grounded for a few days, they sent the package by slow boat. Suppose it'll be here eventually."

Elvina was simultaneously talking on the phone and watching the cable news network on the small color television near the reception desk. Sarah played at her feet on a quilt. The baby waved her hands in the air, and I gathered her into my arms, nodding good afternoon to Elvina.

214

The hair salon was crowded with patrons in various stages of completion. All three dryers were going and several women perched on chairs waiting their turn at bat. Mandy held court around her workstation as she deftly snipped the damaged ends from Ladonna O'Donnell's bleached and permed hair. Melody leaned intently over the hands of her nail care patron, one ear tuned in to her client, one ear trained to the ongoing discussion in the hair salon.

"Well, hey there, Hattie. How'd it go over there in the city? Everything turn out okay?" Mandy asked.

I sighed. There truly were no secrets in a small town. Since the community had followed my surgery and recovery, their interest was only natural. "I'm good to go."

Mandy smiled. "I'm sure glad to hear that. We need all the good news we can get…what with all that's goin' on."

Josephine Waters grunted. "I think we oughta just load up a bunch of bombs and go kill that hateful *Osamer-ben-lauden*!"

The audience of women nodded agreement. It was a common sentiment. If the Middle East was accessible by automobile, mobs of deer-gun-toting Southern boys would be loaded up in the backs of fleets of pick-up trucks, bent on retaliation.

Elvina stood at the arched door entrance to the hair salon. "I ordered five more gas masks from the Army surplus fella. There's a mile-long waitin' list for 'em."

"Gas masks?" I asked.

Elvina nodded. "Heck, yeah. There're rumors that them crazy terrorists will use germ warfare on us! I, for one, am gonna stand ready!"

Mandy smiled. "Elvina, I hardly think a town the size of Chattahoochee will be a target."

Elvina propped her hands on her hips. "We're only forty-five miles shy of where the President's brother lives, I might remind you…and, by the way, Hattie Davis Lewis, I can't hardly believe you'd support the notion of Holston flyin' off to New York next week!"

I shrugged. "Some of his friends died in the attack, Elvina. Besides, it's probably safer to fly right now than it ever has been. And, I wouldn't begin to tell him what to do, anyway."

"Well…" Elvina scowled. "I'm sure not settin' foot on a plane, I'll tell you!"

Mandy dropped the section of Ladonna's hair she was studying. "Correct me if I'm wrong, Elvina. But…have you *ever* flown?"

The women turned to watch for Elvina's reaction.

"Well…no…but, I ain't about to start now!" Elvina's stare of death squelched the titter of laughter.

Evelyn floated into the room draped in a knee-length quilted cape of red, white, and blue. A small embroidered *God Bless America* logo embellished the upper right chest. She swept in a circle. "Well? What do y'all think?"

Josephine Waters clasped her hands together as if she felt a prayer coming on. "That is the most beautiful cape I've ever laid eyes on!"

"This some kind of new design line, Evelyn?" Mandy asked. "If it is, it'll be right on target with all that's goin' on."

"No…well, maybe later on I can develop some gowns and casual outfits…this cape's gonna be my contribution to the war on terrorism!"

Mandy smiled mischievously. "What'cha gonna do, air drop one over Bin Lauden's head?"

Evelyn smirked. "For your information, smarty-pants, this idea came to me in a dream. You know I can't abide the idea of a needle, so givin' blood's out for me. But, I can sew! I'm gonna be takin' orders for capes like this one. Then, I'm gonna send the proceeds after expenses to the Red Cross folks."

216

"You can put me down for three — two large and one small," Josephine said.

"I want one, and I know Wanda and Steph will, too." Mandy said.

"Lordy! Don't leave me out!" Melody called out from behind the nail treatment partition.

Evelyn threw her hands into the air. "Heaven help! I'll never remember all this."

"I'll start a sign-up and prepayment order sheet at the front desk," Elvina said. "That way, folks won't fail to pick them up once you finish with them."

"Thanks, Elvina. I praise the Lord every single day that Mama sent you to us to keep things in order. I never was much good at it. Well…I gotta get back to my sewin'. These capes ain't gonna make themselves! Call me to the kitchen when Wanda gets back with lunch. Mama always said, an engine can't run on thin air, you gotta give it some fuel!" Evelyn twirled around and scurried off toward her workroom, a whirling blur of patriotism.

"Y'all stop by the desk on the way out if you want to order one of them capes. I gotta go confirm Stephanie's massage clients for tomorrow." Elvina called over her shoulder as she left the hair salon.

"That woman's amazing," Mandy said after Elvina left the room. "Since she put all her meddlesome energy toward runnin' the Triple C, she's got us so organized; I'd swear to you…the supply room is in alphabetical order!"

The ladies chuckled and nodded in agreement.

"Gotta love her," Ladonna said. "You think I oughta start partin' my hair in the middle, Mandy?"

Mandy eyed Ladonna's bleached locks. "No, honey. I don't. Your roots would be more noticeable that-a-way."

Stephanie poked her head around the corner. "Hattie! I thought I heard your voice. Let me get you that lotion you asked for." She reappeared in a moment with

217

a gallon of massage lotion.

"I appreciate this. I suppose I could use plain oil, but I just hate to work with it. My order should be in soon, and I'll replace this. The commercial flights are moving now, so I imagine things will start to arrive soon."

"No problem, glad to help out. I ordered five gallons before the attack, so I have plenty to spare." She smiled. "Sorry I can't stay and visit with all of you. My client's settling in." Stephanie looked thoughtful. "You know what's strange? I figured folks would cancel out on massage after the attacks. They did, for the first couple of days. I guess we all just stopped dead for a while. But now...I've had people call me who haven't been in since forever — begging for a spot!"

"Beats drugs and alcohol as a way to calm your nerves," Mandy said.

"I suppose. Call me soon, Hattie. We'll plan to swap an hour with each other. If your shoulders get as tired as mine, you need it as much as I do."

"I can't argue with that." The semi-permanent stiffness in the left side of my neck twanged to remind me of my lack of self-care.

"See you all!" Stephanie called.

"You and Holston goin' to the candlelight service down by the river tonight?" Mandy asked. "We're all gonna go."

The planned interfaith service was reflective of memorials across the nation.

"We'll be there," I said.

Mandy's scissors snipped as she talked. "All the preachers are goin' to talk. I heard Miz Lucille's ladies choir's gonna do a special set of songs, too. And, Jake's invited an Islamic religious leader from Tallahassee...since we have a family of them here."

Josephine Waters spoke up. "I think it's just deplorable about Ram Patel's store. He and his family have been here for a few years, and they're just the nicest folks you'd ever want to know. He's from Saudi Arabia, you know..." She shook her head. "Whoever threw the bricks through his plate glass window uptown ought to be put under the jail."

Elvina appeared at the door and rejoined the conversation without missing a beat. "Jake and the rest of the uptown business association members have taken up money to help him replace the glass," she said. "I thought I'd stop by later on…maybe take a casserole."

I smiled at the traditional Southern fix-all: comfort food in a casserole container.

"Well…it's been fun shootin' the breeze with y'all. I have to run." I handed Sarah to Elvina. "Don't hesitate to give her to Holston if she starts being a pill."

"Don't you worry over the chinaberry," Elvina said. "She's part of the staff here." She crooned to Sarah. "Aren't you, sweetums?"

As I turned onto Washington Street, I couldn't help wondering how the grip of fear would affect the town. The antique shops and B&B's depended on the influx of northern tourists who migrated south for the winter months. Could Chattahoochee survive?

"Hey, Sister-girl! How're your privates?" Jake called from behind the counter when I entered the delivery door to the shop.

"Perfectly peachy, thanks for asking."

Jake grinned. His blue eyes twinkled. "You had lunch yet? I'm gettin' ready to send Jolene down to the Homeplace for French Dips."

"Thanks, but no. I ate in Tallahassee."

He picked a dead leaf from the potted philodendron on the table in front of him. "You *will* be at the river tonight, right? It should be beautiful and inspiring. We're doing the entire service by candlelight."

I walked toward the massage treatment room. "Wouldn't miss it."

UP THE DEVIL'S BELLY

Hank Henderson's Office

Maxie glanced up from the computer screen when her boss tossed an unmarked envelope on her desk.

"Your paycheck," Hank Henderson mouthed slowly, as if he was addressing an impaired toddler.

"Thank you, sir. But, it's not officially payday...yet."

Hank checked the time on his Rolex, 3:30 PM. "I'm leaving now for a meeting in Tallahassee. Actually, why don't you take the rest of the day off...after you finish what you're working on right now, of course."

"Wow!" Maxie's blue eyes sparkled. "That'd be great! I'll be able to make supper before the memorial down by the river. You gonna be back in time to go?"

"Huh? Oh...yeah, of course. Wouldn't miss it for the world." Hank smiled with all the trumped-up sincerity he could muster.

What the hell, he might as well leave her thinking he was the most incredible boss, ever. "Maxie, why don't you go ahead and take those couple of days off next month for your cousin's wedding. It's slowing down here a bit, and I can wing it a couple of days without you."

Maxie leapt from her chair and flung her arms around Hank's neck. "Thank you! Thank you! You're the best boss in the history of the world!"

"Yeah...well." Hank disentangled himself from Maxie's embrace. "That's just the sort of guy I am."

The final act of generosity would paint a lovely picture after his disappearance.

"I won't have my cell phone on during my meeting, Maxie. You'll have to leave a voicemail message if anything of importance comes up."

"Aye, aye, sir!" Maxie military-saluted him before plopping down in front of the computer, her red-glossed lips stretched into a satisfied smile.

Hank shook his head as he left the law office. Women were so got-damned easy.

After placing a call to Alfonso, he loaded the trunk of the Mercedes with two packed suitcases and a sealed box containing the twelve master video tapes he had sold to the highest bidder in Miami. Tameka's debut as a child pornography star would make it thirteen, but since he believed in neither superstition nor magic, that fact eluded him. The tapes and their incriminating contents would be out of his life forever. The perverts of the world would have to find another lackey film director.

Hank pitched the wilted remains of three daisy blooms over his shoulder with a muttered curse. The closer he inched toward Tameka's seduction, the more the daisy incidents increased. He found them so often now, he had stopped keeping count. They were only a figment of his stressed creative mind, he had told himself. For a few days, he had collected the blooms in a wicker basket near the bed. By morning, the basket would be mysteriously empty, and the floral infestation would start anew. He'd found no evidence of forced entry at the house or office. No perpetrator appeared on his video surveillance tapes. Doubling the dosage on the prescription anti-anxiety medication served to squelch his mounting fear of mental illness. The episodes would cease as soon as he vacated town. He felt certain of it.

As a result of seeing a cheerful daisy bloom in every nook and cranny, Hank had developed an aversion to the color yellow. In a wild-eyed fit of temper, he'd thrown every piece of clothing boasting even a hint of the foul shade into a yard trash bag.

The incidents of September 11th had thrown a kink into his well-laid escape plans. Since airport security had been dramatically increased, Hank shunned the notion of booking a commercial flight to Miami. Though it took some finagling and a few extra hundred dollars, he'd arranged to deliver the Mercedes to Miami himself. Screw the airlines. He couldn't take the risk of any unplanned hold-ups this trip.

UP THE DEVIL'S BELLY

Hank felt the excitement build as he thought of the immediate future. Miami was his kind of town — where everything had a price. Hank's lips morphed into a greasy smile. A hot Latino woman would solve the minor sexual glitch he'd experienced of late. Maybe he would rent an extra, just in case the first one lacked the required talent. Too bad he couldn't stay in south Florida for a few days. Miami was an immense, depraved theme park — difficult to soak it all in, given a single night.

Tarrying long was just too risky. He'd inspect the new Mercedes sedan, procure its safe passage to Costa Rica, kick up his heals on the strip for a few hours, then leave via chartered jet under his newly-assumed identity.

Alfonso's voice from behind shattered his reverie. "You goin' somewheres?"

Hank slammed the trunk. "No where you'd want to know about."

Alfonso rolled his eyes. "I got your page."

Hank glanced around nervously. "Come on inside." He led the way through the darkened house with the teenager shuffling behind him. When they reached the study, Hank motioned Alfonso toward the couch and closed the door.

"What you actin' all spooked 'bout?"

Hank frowned. "Cautious. I'm cautious — not spooked."

Alfonso crossed one long leg over the opposite knee. "You got me here. What you want?"

The insolence in the boy's voice made Hank's teeth clench involuntarily. "We're making the tape this evening."

"I done told you, I ain't doin' Tameka Clark. I don't go for none o'that."

"Oh, you'll go for it, once I sweeten the offer."

Alfonso smirked. "What you gone give me, your car?"

The idea made Hank laugh out loud. "Fat chance. How does…all the video equipment and the computer strike you?"

Alfonso frowned, studying the older man. "What's up with this?"

"I'm turning the business over to you, as of tonight. After Tameka." The lie developed nicely as he went along. "It's time for me to upgrade the computer, anyway."

"You want Tameka Clark pretty bad, huh? You a sick motha-fu..."

Hank lunged toward the teenager and pressed his face close to his. "Don't you even think about calling me that, you hear?" The icy menace in his voice was unmistakable.

Alfonso drew back slightly. "Yeah...whatever."

Hank stood up and took a deep breath. "All right. Here's the deal. I'll pick Tameka up around 4:30. She thinks she's coming to tidy up the house, so I'll let her work for an hour."

Hank smiled as he paced the room. "It's beautiful, really. The idea came to me after the terrorist attacks. We can use her innocence and patriotism to coax her into helping us make a film about..." He twirled around and spread his hands as if he was a big time director. "...a young girl in love with her police officer rescuer. The girl's apartment's close to the World Trade Center. There's danger everywhere! I'll get her to scream and act terrified. Then, you come in, and she'll fall into your arms. You can take it from there. The rest doesn't matter. No need for a plot — for your acting, anyway."

Alfonso shook his head. "I still don't think I can do no eight year old girl...the others, they were older..." He grinned. "Some of them told me later they liked it."

"Yeah... well, lover boy — you find a way! No Tameka tape, no equipment for you. Just think — you can make your own name in the wonderful world of video porn."

Alfonso stared at Hank, a mixture of excitement and disdain playing across his dark features.

"I don't much care if you fake the sex, as long as it looks convincing. If that will make your conscience feel better…since you're feelin' so got-damned virtuous all of a sudden!"

Steel cold hatred flashed in Alfonso's eyes. "What time you want me here?"

"That's more like it! I'll have her in the room by, say, 5:30. Your police outfit's behind the door." Hank hooted. "*You* as a policeman! Now, there's a stretch for you!"

Alfonso ignored the jab. "What 'bout Moses?"

"His grandma said he'll be at some youth thing at their church. He'll be tied up all afternoon after school doing yard work at the spa, and then he's supposed to go directly to the church from there. He won't know Tameka's been here 'til after the fact. She'll be on her way home, little Miz Red Riding Hood comin' back from meetin' the big, bad wolf — her little basket of goodies…all gone."

"You got it all worked out, don't cha?"

"Remember one thing, Alfonso, when you look back on all I've taught you. Success lies in the details. It's the small, seemingly unimportant shit that'll nail your ass to the cross every time."

"There's a calm before any storm. If I let myself, I get to where I worry when things are going too smooth."

Piddie Davis Longman

CHAPTER TWENTY-FOUR

Moses

"YOU CAN JUST DROP ME OFF HERE." Moses pointed to the corner of Lincoln Drive and Wire Road.

Jon Presley slowed the 4Runner before pulling to the curb. "You sure, Moses? I don't mind taking you on to the church."

"I want to stop by May-May's and get Tameka to go with me, first," Moses said as he opened the door. "Thanks for the ride."

"I'll see you at the memorial this evening!" Jon called from the window as he U-turned back toward town. The final two Hospice calls for the day were to a young breast cancer patient across the river in Sneads, and to an elderly cardiac patient near Grand Ridge. If everything clicked, he'd barely make it back to the river park by sunset.

Moses took the front steps in one bound. "May-May?" he called out. "Tameka?"

"Back here in the kitchen!" Maizie's voice rang out from the rear of the small house. She wiped her hands on the worn dishcloth hanging over her shoulder. "I didn't 'spect to see you 'til the service."

"I wanted to stop by here on the way."

Moses grabbed a warm teacake and wolfed it down in one bite.

"Lawsy, son! Did you even chew that cake?"

225

UP THE DEVIL'S BELLY

He wiped the crumbs from his lips with the back of one hand and gulped down a tall glass of water. "Hungry, May-May. Been puttin' down pine straw at the spa so the plants won't freeze this winter. It's called *beddin' them down*." Moses smiled, proud of his growing knowledge of landscaping jargon.

She patted her grandson on the back with a gnarled hand. "That's good, honey pot. You want me to fix up a warm biscuit with a piece of ham and wrap it up in a napkin for you to take? Ain't you due at the church?"

"Yes'm, I am. I'll get somethin' to eat after the singin'. They gonna have some food for us. You comin'?"

She nodded. "Miz Lucille's gone stop by and pick me and Tameka up and carry us to the park."

"Where's Tameka? I'm gonna let her go with me to the church."

Maizie plopped down on a worn kitchen stool. "Whew! My old legs just won't tolerate me standin' up much. Your sister's over at Mr. Hank's."

Moses felt his insides go stone cold. "What?"

"Mr. Hank called this mornin' askin' after her…to clean for a couple of hours."

"But…she just cleaned that house last weekend when we went over there together."

Maizie swatted the air with one hand. "He said he was havin' a little party and needed Tameka to tidy up a little for him. I told him she needed to be home by no later than 6:30 — on account of the memorial by the river. He's bringin' her home."

Moses forced his voice to stay even. "I can't believe you let her go over there without me."

"Don't be so worried after her, now. It's only for a couple of hours. It's the least we can do for him…seeing as how he was so nice to have a phone put in for us. Makes me feel better havin' a way to call out for help in case I turn bad. He even paid ahead on the bill. If we're careful, we'll be able to use it for free for six, maybe seven months!"

Moses kissed his grandmother on the cheek. His heart beat wildly with fear, but he tried to remain calm. No need to upset her. "Gotta go, May-May."

"I'll see you later on at the service. You sing good, now. Make me proud, you hear?"

The slamming of the front screen door was his reply.

Moses raced down Wire Road. Near the intersection of Lincoln, he spotted Malcolm Edwards and his older brother, Javon, pedaling their bikes up the hill toward the church.

"Hey, Moses! Where you headin'?" Malcolm called as he came closer. "Church's the other way!"

"Lemme have your bike!" Moses spat out between gasps for air.

Malcolm swatted the air with one hand. "Get outta here!"

"No man, I mean it! I need your bike! It's an emergency!"

Malcolm turned to his older brother.

Javon climbed off his bicycle. "Here, take mine. His is brand new, and Mama'd fry us if anything happened to it."

Moses mounted the bike. The frame was too large, and his feet barely tipped the pedals. "Thanks, man. I promise I'll get it back."

Malcolm watched Moses wobble for a few minutes before he gained control of the bike. "Wonder what's up with him?"

"Dunno. But, if he misses the service, Miz Lucille gonna be hot!" Javon motioned toward Malcolm's bicycle. "Lemme pedal, and you can ride on the handlebars." The boys took turns pushing the bike to the top of the hill, and then doubled up for the remainder of the way.

UP THE DEVIL'S BELLY

Moses pedaled furiously. He flattened his body over the handlebars like he had seen the racers do on the sports network and took the route with the least amount of hills. Hank Henderson's Mercedes was not in the garage when he reached the attorney's house.

"Oh, man! Where's he taken Tameka?"

He threw the bike down next to the garage and ran around to the back yard. The sedan was parked out of sight of the road next to the back deck. Alfonso Williams' battered motorcycle leaned against a tree.

Moses let himself in through the side entrance with the key Hank kept hidden from view. His footsteps echoed in the dark, silent house. A quick search of the study and guest bedroom held no clues. Moses stood in Hank's bedroom, his hands propped on his hips. They had to be here somewhere! The scent of cleaning solution wafting from the master bathroom caught his attention. Tameka had been here. Hank Henderson wouldn't lower himself to clean a toilet.

One possibility struck him. Moses had been curious about the large room off the garage. Though the exterior dimensions indicated a good-sized space, the washroom was cramped — big enough for the washer, dryer, and a set of storage shelves. Once, when he'd gone in search of cleaning rags, he'd spotted a small door partially blocked by the shelves. He assumed it to be a little-used storage room.

Moses ran to the washroom and tried the knob. Locked. A muffled scream emanated from behind the wall. His heart raced. Tameka! Tameka was behind the door!

Moses struggled to strategize. He glanced around for an axe or crowbar, anything to pry the door open. The keybox! Moses rushed back into the house to the study. A small wooden oak cabinet hung on the wall by the locked gun cabinet. He'd seen Hank retrieve keys to the outdoor storage shed from behind its doors.

Rows of gold and silver keys of assorted sizes hung in the cabinet. Moses heart sank. How could he ever find the right one? He read the tags hanging from each set. None were designated for the extra room off the garage. Only one key was unmarked.

Moses grabbed the unlabeled key and said a silent prayer. *God, please let this be the one.*

He was halfway through the dimly lit living room when a thought stopped him cold. Alfonso…Hank…if both of them were with Tameka — that was a big problem. He wasn't large or strong enough to overpower either of the men. Moses spun around, dashed to the master bedroom, and jerked the drawer open on the bedside table. Hank's SigSauer pistol glinted in the low light.

Moses' hands shook so badly, he dropped the key twice before fitting it into the keyhole of the partially hidden door. He heard the tumblers click as the lock disengaged. The handgun weighed heavy in the sweaty palm of his left hand as he turned the knob.

The door opened into a musty, narrow hall stacked with cardboard boxes. He picked a path through the clutter to a second door that stood slightly ajar. Moses held his breath and listened. His heart pounded wildly.

Muffled screams emanated from the other side. Hank barked an order in an angry, frustrated voice. "Go on! Let's get this over with!"

Moses closed his eyes, and took a deep breath. *Please help me, Jesus.*

He lunged at the door and flung it open, the handgun firmly planted in two hands as he had seen numerous times on television police dramas. The scene before him made his stomach lurch. The part of Tameka's dress that wasn't in shreds lay across her face. Alfonso straddled her supine figure. He was naked from the waist down. A navy police uniform shirt gaped open on his torso. He had one knee wedged between Tameka's tightly clasped legs.

"Get off her!" Moses shouted. He aimed the gun at Alfonso.

"Hey, man!" Alfonso yelled in surprise. He threw up his hands and dismounted, easing slowly to the edge of the bed.

"Tameka! Get up and get out of here! Run home to May-May!" Moses yelled.

His sister gathered her torn clothing and inched off the mattress. Huge gasping sobs shook her bare shoulders. "Moses?" she asked in a shaky voice.

"Go! Now!"

She scuttled past her brother, and then cowered in the dark corridor behind him.

Hank assessed the situation. The gun was loaded. He kept it that way on purpose. But, it would take more hand strength than the boy possessed to pull the trigger. After the first shot, it would be a different story. Moses would never get that far. In fact, this little drama could actually add spice to the video, if he worked it right. He discreetly bumped the camera in an approximation of the developing action.

"Now, Moses…," Hank said as he left his post behind the video camcorder tripod. "This isn't what it appears."

Moses swung the gun barrel toward Hank. "Don't you move! I mean it!" His index finger tightened on the trigger. The Angel of Death's chilled breath tickled his neck, and he shivered involuntarily.

"Take it easy now…let me have the gun before anything unfortunate happens here. I know you're upset, but we can talk this out."

Hank stepped toward him. Moses finger squeezed with greater force than he realized. He felt the gun discharge and recoil in his hands. The deafening shot echoed in his ears. As the bullet struck his left shoulder, Hank spun around and fell face down on the concrete floor. A puddle of blood formed in a glistening

230

halo around his upper chest and head.

Frozen in the aftermath, no one spoke for a moment.

"Lord almighty...you kilt him...you kilt Hank Henderson...," Alfonso whispered.

Tears formed in Moses eyes. "What I'm gonna do?" His voice was that of a young child who'd broken the cookie jar.

Alfonso ran his fingers through his hair. "This is bad. This is *real* bad. Black boy shootin' a white man. You in a heap of trouble!"

Moses heard the snuffled cry behind him. "Tameka! I told you to get on home! I mean it! Go!"

His sister fled the storage room.

Alfonso grabbed his blue jeans and T-shirt. "Give me the gun!" he ordered. "I'll get rid of it. We gotta get the hell outta here! If we're gone, they'll think someone just broke in and shot him."

In the haste to escape, Alfonso forgot the one thing his mentor had tried to teach him: *pay attention to the details. It's the simple stuff that'll get you nailed every time.* When he and Moses fled the storage room, the video tape rested in the camcorder, its ongoing recording providing an accurate, irrefutable account of the afternoon's heinous events.

Moses pedaled hard — harder than he'd ridden before the shooting. There was one safe place he could hide until he had a chance to figure things out.

"Elvina got me started watching them soda-poppers on TV every day. Law, if those folks don't have some problems, now. Why we need to have such shows is a wonder to me. Alls you have to do is look around – there's turmoil, pain, lust, and hatred enough – and all without forty commercials!"

Piddie Davis Longman

CHAPTER TWENTY-FIVE

Hattie

A CITY-OWNED RIVER PARK bordered the west bank of the Apalachicola River less than one mile below the Jim Woodruff Dam. The area provided a landing ramp for fishing tournaments and grounds for local festivities, the most famous being the annual Madhatter's Festival on the third Saturday in October. The setting seemed mystical, and I could envision Native American tribes holding ceremonies beneath the ancient Spanish moss-draped live oak trees. The air smelled of damp river mud with a faint scent of freshwater fish.

When Holston, Sarah, and I arrived, Jake and Jolene were scurrying around lining up metal folding chairs and putting the final polish on the fern and candle décor. Sixteen chairs, one for each civic or religious leader, formed an arch around the podium at the center of the covered stage. The performance area was flanked by four white iron stands of tall red, white, and blue taper candles and massive Boston ferns in white wicker planters.

Jake shuffled over when he spotted us. "Sister-girl! I'm glad you're here. Will you make sure the members of the boys' ensemble get the baskets of small candles to hand out as folks arrive? They're on the table behind you."

"Sure." I studied his attire. "Going with the whole patriotic theme, I see."

Jake's dress black pants and white tuxedo shirt were accented by a red, white, and blue bowtie and cummerbund. The cane for the evening was white with an ivory handle and silver trim.

"I had to practically bribe the guy at the formal wear shop in the mall for these accessories. You can't find a thing in these colors for miles right now! Although, I did spot a fetching red feather boa in the craft shop." He grinned. "I'd hate to upstage the ladies of the community, so I passed it by."

"You always were the considerate one." I looked around the park. "Where's Shug?"

"He's working. Should be here by the start of the service, or shortly thereafter. Well, as much as I'd love to stay and shoot the manure with you..." He hobbled off, calling over his shoulder, "it'll be sundown soon, and the whole county's bound to show up!"

Bobby, Leigh, and Josh arrived with two folding chairs and assorted baby accessories.

"I'm glad you thought to bring the Kiddie Corral," Leigh said. "Tank's all over the place, and I'd hate for us to spend all evening fishing him out of the river."

Holston and Bobby arranged the plastic fencing for the kids and spread an old quilt over the leaf-carpeted ground. Leigh dumped a generous load of toys in the center. We added the kids and arranged the folding chairs in a semicircle for the four adult referees.

The religious leaders were among the first to arrive. Amazing. It took a national emergency to bring the different sects together with a common goal, sans the usual jockeying for afterlife points for the acquisition of converts. The Protestant leaders, being the most numerous in Gadsden and Jackson counties, were out in force. I counted three Methodist pastors, six Baptist preachers, two Presbyterians, one Episcopalian, and a Catholic priest. One Jewish and one Muslim leader had carpooled from Tallahassee. The remainder represented small, independent sects from deep in the backwoods, all dressed in their best Sunday go-to-meeting attire.

A bus from the Morningside AME church deposited its payload of members from the Women's Faith Ensemble and boys' choir. After I made sure the boys' choir members were taking care of the candle distribution, I settled in to watch the swarm of locals arrive. The honorable Mayor Jimmy T. Johnson worked the crowd, pumping hands and slapping backs. Even at such a solemn occasion, I couldn't help wondering if he was politicking for the next year's city election.

Our group was soon engulfed in a moat of townspeople from Chattahoochee, Quincy, Sneads, Mt. Pleasant, and the surrounding countryside. The gang from the Triple C Spa arrived and arranged their folding chairs beside ours.

"Where're Evelyn and Joe?" Holston asked.

"Coming soon, I guess." Mandy replied. "Evelyn had to go by the house and get Joe. His truck battery was dead as a doornail."

Anyone watching the scene in front of us would assume we'd all been struck by the God of Patriotism. Men sported garish stars and stripes ties. Miniature flags were pinned on lapels and choir robes. The best I could do on short notice were T-shirts from Wal-Mart depicting a bald eagle superimposed over a rippling flag.

"Get a load of all the women wearin' Evelyn's cape!" Mandy commented. "You know, she stayed up past one the last few nights trying to complete all the orders she got. Course, it won't be much under sixty-five tonight. I'll wear mine when it gets a little cooler."

As if on cue, Evelyn and Joe appeared beside us. Joe unfolded two aluminum chairs with flag-inspired cushions and seat backs. I'd lay even money on the fact Evelyn would redecorate their house in red, white, and blue in the wake of the terrorist attacks.

Stephanie scooted over to make room for them to squeeze in. "We were beginning to wonder if y'all were coming."

"We'd have been here sooner if we hadn't had to wait on that dern cake Joe was making." Evelyn perched on the edge of her chair and carefully arranged the cape around her. "He just buries himself in his cookin' and loses all sense of time!"

"What'd you make?" Wanda asked.

Joe spoke up. "It's a new creation I call *Joe's Revelation* – light chocolate bundt cake with a mocha whipped cream filling, coated with rich, dark chocolate icing, and served with a fresh raspberry sauce drizzle."

I felt faint. "Oh, my."

Joe smiled. "I've invited a few folks over following the ceremony for a piece with freshly brewed coffee, if y'all are interested."

Mandy groaned. "The way I've felt lately, a chocolate fix might help cheer me up. I could just about eat the whole cake."

"Not if Hattie beats you to it," Holston said.

I crossed my arms over my chest. "I'll have you know, there's not one cookie or piece of cake in our house right now."

Jake stood behind our gathering. "Does that count the Tootsie Roll stash you always keep hidden in a plastic bag in the produce drawer of the refrigerator?"

"Ain't no secrets here," Mandy said.

"Where the heck is Elvina Houston?" Jake asked. "She's bringing Elvis."

Leigh laughed. "You're goin' to have that little dog here at the memorial service?"

Jake looked offended. "Of course. He's a local celebrity, and Evelyn's made him a little tux just for tonight."

"Speak of the devil...," Bobby said, pointing toward the grass parking lot.

Elvina Houston walked primly through the crowd, a red and white braided ribbon- trimmed straw hat perched on her head. Her dress was bright red with a large white star on the left shoulder and a horizontal blue stripe at the hem. Bobbing beside her on his bejeweled leash was Elvis, Georgia 2000 calendar dog for December.

"I'd better find some extra seats." Bobby hopped up and removed several folding metal chairs from the last row.

"Hey, all!" Elvina called out. "Elvis had a little trouble with his bowtie. He couldn't get it to lay straight." She settled on to the offered chair.

"You could've just tied a red bandana around his neck," Mandy said.

Elvina huffed. She patted her lap, and Elvis hopped on board. "That would be so ordinary. He'd think he was *just* a dog!"

"Nice hat, Elvina," I said.

"Why, thank you. I bought this old straw thing at the Dollar Store. Added the ribbon myself."

"I've been trying to convince her to develop a line of hats to match some of the outfits I'm plannin' for next spring," Evelyn said. "She has such a knack for it."

Elvina glowed in the light of praise. "It is true. I do have a way with them. And, I'd love to see ladies wearin' hats again."

Jake and Jolene lit the candles as the last few orange-red rays of sunset streaked the sky over the water. Five members of the boys' ensemble carried baskets of small white candles and passed them out to the crowd.

Jon Presley slid into the seat next to Wanda. "Did I miss anything?"

Wanda pointed to the stage where Jake was rearranging one of the plant stands. "The mayor just tripped and nearly took out one of the ferns, but other than that, no. They're just about to get underway."

I attempted a head count of attendees. At best estimate, there were over three hundred people, with more making their way from the parking lot.

"May I have your attention please…," the Mayor Jimmy T. Johnson's voice crackled from the speakers. "The Ladies' Faith Choir of the Morningside AME church will open our memorial service with the singing of the Lord's prayer. Then, we will all stand for the pledge of allegiance and the National anthem."

We exchanged surprised glances. The mayor had abandoned the opportunity to blather on and on in front of a microphone.

The chorus of black women sang a cappella. Their blended honeyed voices drifted through the cool evening air. Wanda's cell phone trilled softly, and I heard her rise to remove herself from the crowd. When she returned, she leaned over and whispered in Jon's ear, and they quietly left during the final strands of the song.

"Where'd they get off to in such a hurry?" Elvina whispered to me as we stood to say the pledge of allegiance.

I shrugged. "I have no clue."

Evelyn glanced around. "You know something? I noticed Miz Lucille's not here…and, neither are Moses and Tameka…or Miz Maizie, for that matter. You don't suppose there's anything wrong, do you?"

"I'm sure they'll come get us, if there is," Mandy said. "Could be Maizie's having one of her spells again."

Officer Rich Burns turned the police cruiser off Main Street onto Morgan Avenue, beginning his final sweep of town before his shift ended at 7:00 PM. His wife, Carol, had phoned to say she and the twins would save him a spot at the river park memorial. He looked forward to the evening off with his family.

The streets were calm. Most of the townspeople had already left for the service. Rich rubbed his tired eyes. He hated day shift. Nights were much better — the squabbling married couples were asleep, and for the most part, an occasional drunk was the only highlight of the average evening. The town was pretty and peaceful after sunset, especially during the fall season, when the monthly full harvest moon painted silver tips on the trees. The cool nights were a relief from the oppressive humidity of summer. He could truly understand why cats and wolves chose to roam in the dark.

Rich glanced briefly in the rear view mirror, then jerked his head back to study the reflection of the road behind him. A young girl was running erratically across Main Street. Rich slammed the brake pedal, executed a three-point turn, and accelerated sharply. He saw the terrified expression on the child's face when she turned to look behind her. Rich recognized the child — Miz Maizie's granddaughter, Tameka Clark. He slowed the cruiser to a crawl and pulled alongside her.

"Tameka?" he called out.

The girl seemed to not hear. She proceeded with a limping jog. Even over the noise of the idling engine, he could hear her sobs.

Rich pulled the vehicle to the curb and parked. He caught up with Tameka in a few strides and grasped her gently by the shoulders. Her flowered cotton dress hung in shreds from her thin brown shoulders.

"Wait...wait...c'mon, honey. It's okay now...I'm here to help you."

She hung her head and swayed back and forth with her arms hugging her chest.

"C'mon, now...let's go back to the car and we'll find out what's wrong."

At first she resisted. Then, she allowed herself to be led to the cruiser.

After several attempts to get the child to speak, he had an idea. "Stay right here. I've got something that might help you feel better."

Rich opened the trunk and removed a plush Teddy bear. He'd learned over the years that children often found comfort in the stuffed animals, and he carried two or three with him at all times.

"Why don't you hug Mama Bear and see if she helps."

Tameka looked up at him with an expression so forlorn, his heart ached. What in the world had happened to this child? Rich squatted down in front of her. "If you want to, you can tell Mama Bear why you're so sad. She knows how to listen, and she can tell me how to help you."

The ploy worked. Tameka cradled the bear tightly and rocked back and forth for a few moments. She began to speak softly. "Moses didn't mean to hurt nobody. They's bein' mean to me. He was tryin' to stop them."

"Who, honey? Tameka? Who was tryin' to hurt you?"

"Mr. Hank...he was nice before..." She shook her head. "But not today."

"Can you tell Mama Bear what happened?" Rich asked in a soft voice.

"Moses came to help me...he didn't mean to shoot Mr. Hank." She began to cry aloud. Tears rolled down her brown cheeks. "May-May told us never to touch no guns! She gonna be so mad! Moses done kilt Mr. Hank. Now, Moses gonna be in trouble!"

"Tameka, were you at Mr. Hank's house when this happened?"

The child bit on her lower lip and slowly nodded.

Rich stood, walked to the rear of the cruiser, and dipped his head to speak into the radio clipped on his shoulder. "Chattahoochee 220."

"Chattahoochee 220, go ahead," Denise Whiddon, the dispatcher, replied.

"220 en route to residence of Hank Henderson, Satsuma Road. 10-17. Gunshot victim, possible suspect on premises. Be advised."

"Copy 220."

He heard Denise relay the call to the 911 dispatcher for an ambulance. The second officer on duty reported he was en route as well.

Rich returned to kneel in front of Tameka. "Sweetie, why don't you and me and Mama Bear go check and see how bad Mr. Hank has been hurt. Then, we'll see what we can do to find your brother."

"What 'bout May-May?"

"I'll call your grandmother as soon as we check on Mr. Hank."

Tameka sniffed and clutched the Teddy bear to her chest. She allowed Rich to help her into the front seat and secure a seatbelt. Normally, Rich would not allow a passenger in the front with him, but he made an exception with Tameka. As he drove quickly to the Henderson residence, he continued to reassure her in an even, gentle voice.

"You don't have to worry none about getting revenge on a person who's wronged you. God looks out after that, all right. Every man gets his just desserts in the by-in-by. Nothing slides down the Devil's back that don't turn right back around and crawl back up his belly. And when it does, it bites hard!"

Piddie Davis Longman

CHAPTER TWENTY-SIX

J ON PRESLEY GUNNED the 4Runner's powerful six-cylinder engine as he pulled onto Highway 90 east of Chattahoochee. Long lines of cars and trucks waiting to turn onto the river landing road stretched in both directions.

"What did Lucille say…exactly?" Jon asked.

Wanda nervously bit a hangnail from her right index finger. "She said she stopped by to pick Maizie and Tameka up for the service. Maizie was upset and started to feel funny. She asked Lucille to call me."

"Funny, as in how? Dizzy? Faint? Sick to her stomach?"

"Lucille didn't say…other than Maizie was talking out of her head a little."

"Did she call for an ambulance?"

Wanda knew how her elderly friend mistrusted doctors and medical personnel. Maizie avoided them in fear of high bills she hadn't the money to pay and the knowledge the care of the children would be left to the generosity of neighbors and friends.

Wanda shook her head. "Lucille didn't say, but I'll bet they haven't."

"Then we'll call." He motioned to her purse. "Go ahead and dial nine-eleven and get them en route."

"Don't you want to check her first?"

"I'm not a doctor, Wanda. If she's having a stroke or heart attack, I can do little to help her. Best to get them underway."

They reached Maizie's house on Wire Road in less than three minutes and rushed up the front steps.

Lucille met them at the door. "She's bad off. She keeps tryin' to tell me somethin', but I can't make out the words!" Lucille wrung her hands. "She was real upset when I got here. Somethin' 'bout Tameka not bein' home on time...she asked after Moses, and when I told her he never showed up at the church, she went to pieces...started actin' real crazy. Then, she said she was feelin' kinda funny and said for me to call you, Miz Wanda. The number was right by the phone, there."

Wanda nodded. "I gave her my cell phone number in case she ever needed me."

Maizie lay propped on the small couch. One glance told Jon what he feared most — stroke or some other kind of obstruction to the circulation in her brain. The left side of her face hung limp with a line of spittle forming at the corner of her lips.

"Haa...haann...," Maizie struggled to sit up, then fell backward onto the pillows Lucille had propped behind her head. She waved her right arm in the air.

"Miz Maizie, we have help on the way, hon. Please try to stay as quiet as you can." Jon's voice helped to calm the old woman as he elevated her feet slightly to improve circulation and held her wrist to take a pulse. "Wanda, behind my seat in the truck, you'll find a red duffel bag. Please run and bring it to me."

She returned with the bag, and Jon took Maizie's blood pressure with the equipment he carried for his job. "It's dangerously high," he muttered.

The scream of sirens announced the arrival of the ambulance. Wanda waved to the driver from the porch and held the screen door open for the two paramedics. EMT Marney Sullivan rushed into the small living room. "Hey, Shug. What've we got here?"

"BP 200 over 120, pulse 110, aphasia, parathesia on the left side."

The second paramedic, Terrance Odum, keeled by the couch. "Do you know her history?"

"Diabetes…high blood pressure…not sure on medications," Jon said. "Wanda, go into the bathroom and see if you can spot any prescription bottles."

Maizie moaned and opened her eyes briefly.

"Let's go!" Marney said. Jon helped the paramedics ease Maizie's body onto the rolling gurney. They navigated the narrow door and porch toward the parked ambulance.

Outside, Jon and Lucille stood by the rear of the emergency vehicle as Maizie was loaded into the back.

Wanda rushed down the porch stairs and handed two plastic bottles to Terrance. "These were the only ones I could find."

"En route to TMH?" Jon asked.

"Yeah. Does she have any next of kin around here?" Marney shut the ambulance door.

"Other than the kids, no. She has one son living up in Birmingham," Wanda answered.

In the house, the phone trilled.

"I'll get that," Lucille said. "It may be Tameka or Moses."

"Better get in touch with her son," Marney called as she slid behind the steering wheel. "They'll need someone from the family to consult with, if possible." Marney nodded to Jon and Wanda, pulled the ambulance onto the street, and left for the forty-five minute trip to Tallahassee Memorial Hospital.

"Miz Wanda?" Lucille called from the porch. "It's a police man askin' after Maizie!"

"Let me talk to him!" Wanda rushed into the house.

When she replaced the headset on its base, Wanda turned to Jon. Her face was ashen. "Jon, will you drop me by the spa to pick up my car?"

"What's going on?"

Wanda sighed deeply. "They've got Tameka at the station. Moses is missing. Seems he shot Hank Henderson."

"Lawd have mercy. Devil's done his business this night," Lucille whispered. "You two go on now. I'll see if I can get aholt of her son James. I been knowin' him since he was a boy."

Wanda pointed to the rear of the house. "She keeps the address book in the table by her bed, Miz Lucille. No use trying to reach her daughter. She hasn't heard from her in over five years."

"Okay." Jon grabbed his duffel bag. "I'll drop you by the spa, then I'll follow the ambulance on over to the hospital." He scribbled a phone number on a scrap of paper. "Lucille, this is Jake's cell phone number. Please call him after you reach James and let him know what's happened. He's in the middle of the memorial service right now, so I'd give it about a half-hour before you call. I'd phone him myself, but my battery's dead and I left the charger in his van."

"I can do that. I'll stay on here, too...in case Moses shows up."

Tallahassee Memorial Hospital

Hank Henderson struggled to open his eyes. Where was he? His arms and legs felt leaden. For a moment, he entertained the thought that he was either dead or paralyzed. He wiggled the big toe on his left foot and reached his right arm up to feel the bandage covering his upper left chest and shoulder. A stab of pain and drug-induced fatigue forced him to drop his arm onto the bed.

Since his eyes weren't focusing, he trained his ears on the faint noises outside his immediate area. Muffled voices called out names and numbers — an indistinct cry or moan and the sound of doors opening and closing. A rustle of activity close-by made him attempt to open his eyes once more. A blurred figure moved to his right side.

"Oh, I see you're awake," a soft female voice said. "Mr. Henderson? Can you hear me?"

Her face swam briefly into focus. "Wha...?" His mouth felt dry as month-old bread, with a bitter metallic taste.

"You're in a hospital room in Tallahassee Memorial in Tallahassee. I am Jennifer Smythe, your nurse for this morning."

Nurse Smythe's face swam into focus. She was a pretty thirty-ish woman with hazel eyes and long, shiny brown hair pulled tight into a braid. "I'm going to tell your doctor you're awake as soon as I check your vitals, Mr. Henderson. Is there anything you need?"

Hank parted his parched lips to answer, but the flirtatious words froze in his mouth.

Two indistinct figures stood at the end of his bed. The one with the tall yellow-tinted beehive hairdo laced with daisy blossoms smirked at him and shook her head.

"*Tsk...Tsk...You've been a very bad boy, Hanky,*" the familiar voice said.

He shifted his gaze slightly to study the second figure. The elderly black woman seemed less sure of her surroundings. She glanced around the room as if she didn't know exactly why she was there. He recognized the aged features – Grandma Maizie. What was she doing here?

A third figure, a young woman, stepped out from behind the other two. Her eyes were compassionate…yet…so full of sadness. Hank struggled to recall. The face was so familiar. "Mama?" He reached his right arm toward the figure.

"Mr. Henderson? Are you alright?" Jennifer Smythe asked as she fitted the blood pressure cuff on the upper part of his arm.

To the left of the three women, a fourth ominous shape took form. The hardened, stern face of Hank's father came into full focus.

"Stay away from me!" he yelled. "Don't touch me!" Hank pawed the air and grabbed the nurse's arm.

"Let me go get the doctor, Mr. Henderson. Please let go of my arm!"

Hank gripped Jennifer Smythe's arm tightly as the ethereal figures circled the bed like vultures closing in for a fresh road-kill meal.

His blurred gaze rested on the small daisy-shaped clasp that held the stethoscope to the front of the nurse's uniform. Hank grabbed for the daisy, then circled his hands around Jennifer Smythe's neck and squeezed. As the nurse struggled to defend herself, she managed to snatch the emergency call pull. Within seconds, the hall door flew open and several staff members rushed into the room. With the help of two aides, a second nurse, and the police officer stationed outside the door, Hank Henderson was subdued, sedated, and placed in restraints.

"You don't get to choose your family. God sets that up for you. But, you do get to choose your friends, and they become your family. I like some of my friends better'n the folks I hooked up with because of blood and marriage ties. It's a sad feller, indeed, what doesn't have a friend."

Piddie Longman

CHAPTER TWENTY-JEVEN

The Hill: Hattie

S HE'S A BRICK SHY OF A FULL LOAD. *He's coming in on one engine. She's lost her marbles. His elevator doesn't go all the way to the top. She doesn't have both oars in the water. He's as crazy as a bedbug. Her lights are on, but nobody's home. The shelf life on his medication's run out. She's not playing with a full deck. He's not the sharpest tool in the shed.*

I had often wondered if folks from a town without a mental institution on the main drag had grown up with as many euphemisms for mental illness. The citizens of Chattahoochee were accustomed to seeing the effects of brain dysfunction, from the mild cases of delusion and paranoia in the hospital residents who freely wandered into the Washington Street shops, to the faceless screams of the firmly-controlled patients ensconced behind the gray-screened windows.

Hank Henderson's sudden descent into his demon-filled reality shocked everyone. People huddled over cups of coffee at the Homeplace, chatted at the hardware store counter, and ruminated at length in the hair salon at the Triple C. How could someone they thought they knew so well and saw every day – a man who handled Aunt Edna's will, for heaven's sake – be stark raving mad?

247

UP THE DEVIL'S BELLY

As the sordid details of Hank's undercover business endeavors came to light, the combination of shock and the shame of harboring such a person in the midst of Chattahoochee respected society kept all of us searching for answers.

The bedside radio alarm clock read 1:30 AM in glowing green numerals. The inside of my eyelids felt like sandpaper disks burnishing my tired eyes. My body ached with exhaustion, but someone forgot to tell my brain. It was going full tilt.

"Come over here." Holston turned on to his back and patted his chest. I rolled over and molded to his body, cocooned and warm in the circle of his arms. He lightly kissed my forehead. "Can't sleep?"

"Nope."

"Neither can I."

I snuggled into his smooth chest. "I can't stop thinking about this whole thing with Hank Henderson. Could we have stopped it, somehow?"

Holston sighed deeply. "I don't know."

"I mean, we had suspicions, but that's all they were. I guess everyone was just too intimidated by him to make accusations without solid proof."

"Especially in this day and age. A slander suit would've popped up immediately, particularly with him being an attorney."

"It makes me worry, Holston. It's not enough that we have the whole terrorist issue, now we have to watch each other, too. What if it was Sarah who fell under someone's evil eye? Would we know? Could we keep her safe? If sick people masquerade as law-abiding citizens, how can we tell who to watch out for?"

"I'm sure every parent in this town's asking themselves the same questions right now." He stroked my hair. "Sarah has two loving parents, and, I daresay... she's safer over here than lost amidst the discarded children at the orphanage."

"I suppose. Another thing that's getting to me — I just hate the idea that Maizie died suspecting that she'd failed to keep her grandchildren from harm's way."

"I can't help believe but there's a deeper understanding on the other side," Holston answered in a soft voice.

I listened intently. Holston seldom spoke of his spiritual beliefs.

"I'm sure she knows she tried to do her best by them. Without her, they would have been fending for themselves on the street in some drug-infested neighborhood…or selling to support their mother's habit."

I was silent for a moment. The sound of Holston's steady heartbeat provided a catharsis for worry. "Don't you wonder why Hank did all the terrible things he did?"

"Rough childhood, maybe…underlying mental instability. Who knows?"

"I'm glad Sarah and I are teamed up with you. God, Holston — let us keep our daughter safe."

"Since the terrorist attacks, I've begun to think our sense of safety is an illusion." He was quiet for a moment. "We'll do the best we can, Hattie."

Triple C Day Spa and Salon

Elvina rolled up her morning copy of the *Tallahassee Democrat* and chunked it into the magazine rack. "Well, Chattahoochee's back on the map, again. It's not enough for us to be infamous for beatin' up an innocent gay man, now we've harbored an international pornography king-pin in our town. I su-wanee!"

Mandy swept the tendrils of hair around the base of the stylist chair into a small mound and collected them in a dustpan. The gray and blond pile of curls reminded her of an aging Pekinese. "One thing in our favor this go 'round — the press is so busy with all the terrorist news that we probably won't be overrun with reporters like we were after Jake's attack."

"Yeah, well...I still get so fired up when I think on it, I can hardly see straight!"

Elvina stood to return to the front desk. "Do you know when Wanda'll be back in?"

"Dunno for sure. I betcha she'll be out the rest of the week, what with Miz Maizie's funeral and all."

"Is Tameka still stayin' with her?"

"Far as I know. Maizie has a son, James, who's drivin' down with his family. I'm not sure if Wanda's going to put in to have them all stay with her. She has a pretty good amount of room at her house, and it might be easier on Tameka to stay there 'till after the services."

"Is James goin' to take the kids back with him, you suppose?"

Mandy chased a herd of miniature dust bunnies across the counter. "I think it'll be best for them, don't you? I mean, maybe it'll be easier for both of them to put it all behind them if they're living up there in Birmingham."

"That's assumin' the police can find Moses," Elvina said. She blew out an exhalation of air. "Lordy, what a tangled mess."

Melody swished into the room. "Anybody called for me yet this mornin'?"

"Just one. I set Maybelle Peters up for a manicure at ten. She said to tell you to be on time. She's got to leave for an appointment in Tallahassee right after."

Melody shucked her oversized canvas purse and shoved it underneath the manicure table. "Jeeze, that woman! I was ten minutes late starting on her one time, and you'd'a thought it was an hour! You better believe I'll be ready for her from now on — just so I don't have to hear it. What else has been goin' on this mornin'?"

Mandy shrugged. "Not much. I've done a couple of cut and styles. Wanda's still out and Steph's not due in till around eleven."

"Coffee's on in the kitchen, if you want to juice yourself up before Maybelle gets here," Elvina said.

"Got any Jack Daniels I can spike it with?" Melody laughed. "That'd help me get through the appointment, for sure. I know she'll want to talk about all this business with Hank." She sighed. "It just makes me sick inside when I have to hear it."

Elvina leaned over. "You know anything new?"

"Only that they caught up with Alfonso Williams. He was hidin' out over in Marianna with some cousins of his. I guess he'd decided to try and leave the state. His motorcycle broke down close to a truck stop near Chipley, and a local sheriff saw it and ran the tag, and they caught up with him. I heard he's singin' like a bird now 'bout all he knows of Hank's business...and..."

"Don't stop now, sugar. Do tell! You know you can trust us to keep a secret." Elvina winked at Mandy from the eye Melody couldn't see from her vantage point.

"Well, I reckon it'll all come out in the papers in a few days, anyways, but you didn't hear it from me. J.T.'d be furious if he found out I let on like I knew the inside scoop."

"Datin' a cop has its privileges, hon," Wanda said. "He knows good and well you can't keep it to yourself. For one thing...it's news. For another...it's not healthy to keep it bottled up inside. You'll blow up!" Mandy cut her eyes toward Elvina, who nodded in agreement.

Melody pulled a director's chair over to the hair salon side of the room and continued in a low voice. "There's more dirt fixin' to come out on this case." She glanced around to make sure the three of them were alone. "Seems Hank's cousin, Lamar — he's a deputy over in Midview — he's been stealin' stuff out of the evidence room, gettin' it over to Hank, and then, Alfonso's been selling it on the street."

"Whoop!" Elvina slapped her thigh. "This is a scandal with a capital *S*!"

"And," Melody continued, "the FBI's in town. They've confiscated some videotapes from the back of Hank's car, and also, his computer. There's a boatload of contact information stored on it. This could be an international thing with those porno tapes."

"Lawd have mercy." Elvina jabbed a bony finger in the air. "All — right here — smack dab under our noses!"

"Another thing — they found all kinds of fake ID's, a birth certificate, and credit cards in Hank's luggage in the trunk of his car. He was gettin' ready to skip town and take on a whole new identity. There's off shore bank accounts and organized crime connections. It's a royal-tee mess!"

"I feel a book coming on for Holston to write," Mandy said. "Does the press know all of this yet?"

"They will, most likely soon. Alfonso's turned state's evidence, tryin' to save his sorry hide. I'm sure the newspapers and TV will just jump all over this."

"I can't help but to feel a little bad for Alfonso," Mandy said.

Elvina's eyebrows shot up. "Why? He's a delinquent! Has been for years!"

"Well…yeah…but, I'm sure he had more opportunities with Hank leading him. In a lot of ways, he's as big a victim as all the kids Hank's used for his video tapes."

"That kid's been evil seed as long as I can remember." Elvina pursed her lips. "Well…maybe he'll be able to turn his life around. Who knows?"

Mandy drummed her fingernails on the counter. "By the way, Melody dear, did you eat the leftover piece of Jon's lasagna I was saving for myself?"

"You know I didn't," Melody said. "I'm on a diet. Besides, I knew you wanted it, so I wouldn't have touched it for the world."

"Unless you turned your back for a minute," a deep voice broke in.

J.T. Smathers, deputy, Chattahoochee Police Department, stood at the entrance to the hair salon.

"J.T.!" Melody fingered her blonde curly hair nervously. "How long you been there?"

"Just a second or two. I was wonderin' if I might squeeze myself in for a quick trim, Miz Mandy."

"Sure thing, officer." Mandy patted the seat of her stylist chair. "Sit yourself down."

His leather gun belt squeaked as he settled into her chair. "I do so much appreciate this. Melody keeps threatin' to get the hedge trimmers out and take after me. I just haven't had a chance to stop by and make an appointment. It's been pretty busy, here lately."

"I can imagine." Mandy ran her fingers through J.T.'s thinning hair. "Want the usual?"

"Do the best you can. There's less ever' day for you to work with. I just can't fathom what makes a hair decide to just up and fall out, when it was perfectly happy to be on my head the day before."

"What you doin' this mornin', honey?" Melody asked.

J.T. sighed. "I'm on the way to stop by y'alls' back yard neighbor's house. Zelda Bunch swears someone's stealin' off her outside clothesline again. Actually, this time it's blankets, plus a tarpaulin off her wood pile."

Mandy shook her head. "What a fruitcake. She probably saw some of the government-type men uptown, and it got her all riled up again. The FBI and CIA desperately need old lady blankets, you know." Mandy chuckled. "I'll just betcha one of them G-men is usin' Zelda's tarp to cover his car up at night!"

J.T. grinned. "Yeah, she generally gets fired up a mite when things are unsettled. This terrorist stuff has given her a whole new set of things to get paranoid about."

UP THE DEVIL'S BELLY

Jake flitted through the salon carrying a fresh bouquet of daisies. "Hey, all! Mandy, Melody, Elvina, Officer J.T.!" He stopped mid-stride and struck a pose, his left hand propped coquettishly on his hip. "I do *so* love a man in a uniform."

J.T. raised one eyebrow. "Careful, Jake. I'll rat you out to Shug."

"A girl can't even harmlessly flirt in this town!" Jake snorted. "Y'all had any leads on Moses?"

" 'Fraid not. We don't think he had access to any money to speak of, so we're pretty sure he's hidin' out around here somewhere...or, he might've caught a ride out of town."

"Most of the local truckers I know wouldn't pick up a boy young as Moses with out askin' some questions," Mandy said, "unless he made it all the way out to the Interstate."

"J.T. says Zelda's on the rampage again, Jake. The government's stealin' her stuff," Elvina said.

"Poor old woman. Maybe I'll take her some fresh flowers, take her mind off everything. What have the aliens — or the FBI — taken from her this time?"

"A tarp and two blankets," J.T. answered.

Jake left the room briefly to place the daisy arrangement in the formal waiting room, then returned to the salon. "We all know that's just some kids buildin' a fort somewhere in the woods. Same thing happens every year 'bout this time. The kids like to act like they're campin' out and huntin' deer like their daddies. Heck, I used to have forts all over the woods behind the house here...not that I ever acted like I wanted to shoot poor defenseless animals for fun."

"You were just hidin' from your mama," Elvina said.

Jake nodded. "Well...yeah."

Elvina rolled her eyes. "Sugar, if my mama had'a been Betsy Lou Witherspoon, I'd'a built a castle with an alligator-filled moat in the woods."

254

"Careful, Elvina. You wouldn't want Mama's ghost to come back to haunt this place, now would you?"

"Especially since Piddie's already here. It could get crowded." Mandy added. "Well, there you go, sir." She dusted a large talc-filled brush across J.T.'s neck to remove stray hair.

"Thanks, Mandy. What do I owe you?"

Mandy patted him on the shoulders. "Call this one — on the house. It's the least I can do for you calming Zelda down before she works herself into a high rollin' boil."

J.T. stood and straightened his gun belt. "I'll catch y'all later on. See you at the house after work, Mel?"

Melody stretched on to her tiptoes to deliver a quick kiss to his cheek. "I should be home after five."

"I got up to get back to work a half-hour ago," Elvina said. "Y'all are a bad influence on me." She hurried off toward the front desk.

"We surely twisted your arm, Elvina!" Mandy called out.

Jake shook his head in irritation when he spotted the teetering stack of dirty coffee cups on the kitchen counter.

"Gah! I'm glad Jon and I will have our own place in a few weeks!" He filled the sink with hot soapy water and dumped the crusty dishes in to soak.

His leg ached with a pulse of its own. Maizie's funeral was a day away, and the memorial arrangement orders were rolling in. He and Jolene barely had time to stop to call out for lunch and take a few bathroom breaks. The casket drape, Jake's donation to the service, was nearly complete. Tomorrow morning, he'd add the yellow and white rosebuds before transporting the drape to the funeral home.

Though she was nearing seventy and had turned the majority of business over to the Dragonfly Florist, Minnie Blue at Silver Moon Flowers had been able to handle a number of the floral orders. Maizie Clark had lived in Chattahoochee most of her life. Though she claimed little in the way of material possessions, she had a wealth of friends.

Jake had seen both extremes in the years he'd worked with floral design. Some funerals were sparsely attended, the only flowers being on the casket drape. Others saw an outpouring of love and compassion so copious; the floral arrangements were barely contained in the allotted space near the casket. In the last few years, many families requested charitable donations in lieu of flowers. Still, the traditional salute to the family remained a popular way to show support and warm wishes for the bereaved. At last count, Maizie had received fifty arrangements, enough to fill the front of the small Morningside AME church and spill into the adjacent fellowship hall.

At least Jon had left a fully cooked pot roast in the refrigerator. The notion of cooking for one person held no appeal tonight. With the exception of Mandy, all of the staff was gone, and Jon wouldn't be home until well past dark.

"Lordy be!" he exclaimed when he uncovered the casserole dish containing the roast. One thin slice of meat, two potatoes, and a carrot floated in a pool of congealed gravy.

Jake snatched the casserole from the counter and shuffled through the reception area to the hair salon. Mandy was cleaning her workstation following her final patron.

"Who ate all the dang pot roast?" he asked in an angry voice. "There was plenty of meat and potatoes left over from last night!"

"Don't look at me! Elvina called out for pizza for all of us. We made Melody go pick it up."

"Well…then…who ate it? It didn't just suck itself clean out of the refrigerator.

And, don't tell me the ghost of my dear Piddie is stealing food out of this house!"

Mandy shrugged. "Maybe Jon stopped in and had dinner."

"No, he packed a sandwich this morning. How 'bout Evelyn? Or Holston?"

"Evelyn's been in Tallahassee all day. She took some of her flag capes over to the First Lady. Remember?"

Jake looked perplexed. "Yeah."

"...and Hattie, Holston, and Sarah had lunch at the Homeplace. He hasn't been back this afternoon."

He stared down at the casserole dish. "This is way weird. I'm sorry I snapped at you. I'm cranky 'cause I'm so hungry, and I guess I had my mouth all set for this."

"I'm sorry, hon. I can't imagine who could've eaten it. Maybe the same little piglet who ate the last piece of Jon's lasagna I'd been saving for myself."

"We're gonna have a staff meeting 'bout respecting each other's food...and, while we're at it, we'll have a little chat 'bout washing the dishes up so that they're not left stacked to the ceiling for you, or me, to wash at the end of a long day."

"Sounds like an idea to me. I'll get Elvina to pick a spot on everybody's schedule." She rested one hand on Jake's shoulder. "You look pooped. Want me to scrounge around in there and make you some supper before I leave?"

Jake smiled weakly. "No thanks, sweetness. I'll just sling myself up a fried egg sandwich."

Mandy stuck out her tongue and groaned. "I don't know how you eat those things."

"You don't know what you're missin'. I practically lived off them in the lean years."

"Favored peanut butter and banana sandwiches myself."

"Yuck."

"To each, her own..."

"Will you lock up on your way out?" Jake called out as he started back toward the kitchen.

"Surely purely," Mandy said.

Jake flipped the fried egg in a moat of butter and broke the yoke so that it would cook. Runny yolk in a fried egg sandwich was just plain creepy. He let his mind go blank as he watched the grease sizzle around the curling edges of the egg white.

A thought struck him so hard, he almost dropped the spatula on the floor.

The missing food. Zelda's stolen tarp and blankets. He took the hot griddle from the stove and flipped the power off.

Jake started out the mansion's back door, then stopped to grab a flashlight. He picked his way carefully through the garden, past the butterfly plants to the heavily wooded thicket at the far corner of the property.

"Moses Clark! This is Jake!" he called out. "I have a pretty good idea you're in there!"

His voice calmed the cricket calls for a moment. Except for the muffled swoosh of a car passing by on the street in front of the spa, the woods were silent.

"If you're listenin' to me right now — they're not after you Moses. Hank Henderson's still alive. You did not kill him! The whole shooting, and what was goin' on before, was all on tape...and they know everything...all the bad stuff he was up to."

Jake heard the faint snap of a twig. "The police know it was an accident, Moses! They need you to tell your side of the story to help put him away for a long time...where he can't hurt anyone anymore."

Jake's brain raced. "Moses, you know I've never lied to you, and I'm not about to start now. Please come out and talk to me! Let's go to the police. Tameka is staying at Miz Wanda's house. She needs you, too, Moses."

A wave of heaviness at being the bearer of sad news washed over him. He leaned his weight on his cane. "There's something else, Moses. Your grandmother. She's...there's been some trouble. Please, Moses...if you're in there, please come out."

Jake's words echoed in the solitude of early evening. A furtive movement caught his attention. Moses Clark stepped from the shadow of a large pine tree. "Is somethin' the matter with May-May?"

Jake swallowed hard. "Come inside with me. I'll fix us some hot chocolate, and we can talk."

Moses walked toward Jake. He circled his arm around the boy's shoulder, and they walked back through the garden to the mansion.

*"I'll just bet the good Lord gets a chuckle out of us sometimes.
We cry and moan when bad things happen to us. But, just let
life settle into a day-by-day, and we're griping that things are
dull as dirt. Humans just beat all. We ain't never satisfied.
Bet the Almighty wishes sometimes he'd never thought to make
Adam, let alone Eve."*

> *Piddie Davis Longman*

CHAPTER TWENTY-EIGHT

FOLLOWING THE CHURCH FUNERAL SERVICE and brief graveside memorial, the small fellowship hall of the Morningside AME church overflowed with the family and friends of Maizie Clark. Like the crowd attending Piddie's service, the gathering was a mixture of people of different races and ages. Many of Maizie's coworkers from her years in the custodial division of Florida State Hospital came to pay final respects, as well as the majority of the church congregation. Patrons of the Triple C Spa who had grown fond of Moses and Tameka stopped by and brought food for the post-funeral meal. All of the staff of the spa was in attendance, as were the Davis and Lewis families.

"I understand, now, what Mama always said about the services here," Evelyn said to Jake as she served a piece of cake. "That was one of the most beautiful funerals I've ever attended. Sad, but uplifting at the same time ...and the singing!"

Jake nodded. "I heard that. I kept checking for cracks in the stained glass window beside our pew when that one soprano — I believe her name's Rayleen — hit some of those high notes. Whew!"

"I didn't know Miz Maizie very well. Mama did, though. She went with Lucille to see her a few times now and again, after Miz Maizie got too sick to get out much." Evelyn smiled. "Last Christmas, Mama and Lucille took a big turkey dinner and all the fixin's over to the house. When Miz Maizie laid eyes on them with all that food, she said, *Good God Almighty!* Well...Lucille says, *Now, Maizie, you shouldn't take the Lord's name in vain.* Miz Maizie says, real quick, *I wasn't takin' His name in vain — He's good, He's God, and He's all mighty!*"

Jake stifled a chuckle. "Wanda and Maizie seemed to hit it off, right from the start. I think Wanda spent most of her time off over at her house. This whole thing's hit her hard, 'specially since she knows the kids'll be leaving with James."

"Lawsy, I do feel so sorry for those young'uns." Evelyn shook her head sadly.

"Their Uncle James is a good man, though. I'm sure they'll bounce back after awhile."

"Wanda's gonna be lost without them. She and little Tameka have really grown close."

"I know. Actually, Jon and Wanda have already discussed going up to Birmingham to pick them up for the Madhatter's Festival next month. I'll be up to my wahzoo in preparations, but they can take the 4Runner and drive up."

"James and Alicia are okay with that?"

Jake nodded. "James thinks it would help them to maintain a connection with us here in Chattahoochee. Anyone can see how much the kids are goin' to miss this place."

Evelyn pointed to a towering six-layered cake on the dessert table in front of them. "Just look at the Red Velvet Cake my Joe made. Isn't it something? He's really got a knack for cookin'. He's planning on opening a little bakery up town when he finishes his training."

"A bakery? I thought he was leaning toward a full-fledged restaurant."

"I don't think he knows what he wants, just yet. He doesn't want to cause any ill will by competing with the Homeplace, you know. Maybe he'll just cook breakfast. He's gonna bake bread, fresh pies, and cakes, for sure."

"The way Chattahoochee's thriving, it could support another eatery. Anyway, I'll order from him for the sweet shop, if he decides to do pastries."

"You should talk that over with him. He even has a name all picked out. He's callin' it *Borrowed Thyme Bakery*."

Jake smiled. "Cute. Where'd he get that inspiration?"

"He's *borrowin'* most of the pie and cake recipes from Mama's old recipes. And, he's gonna hit up the ladies in town for their specialties — wants to publish a little cookbook. The *time* part is spelled *thyme* after the spice. He says that time's all he has on his hands since he's retired from the hospital. Oh, he has all kinds of plans! If we don't end up in the poorhouse, we'll be all right."

"If this cake, here, is any indication of his talents, he's bound to do well. It's truly a masterpiece, Ev." Jake scanned the crowd. "Where did the kids get off to, anyway?"

"I saw them walk outside a minute or two ago."

Jake wiped his hands on a linen cloth. "You mind if I leave you for a bit?"

"Oh, sure. You go ahead. I may not be able to cook any of this, but I can sure as heck serve it up."

The children's play area for the church had, for years, consisted of a two-seat swing set and a rickety aluminum slide. Thanks to the playground fund committee's numerous bake sales, car washes, and Friday night buy-a-plate dinners, the area now held a new six-seat swing set, monkey bars, and an intricate treehouse-style wooden clubhouse with two plastic tube slides. For the toddlers, three colorfully-painted fiberglass circus ponies mounted on stiff springs stood amidst a soft landing site layered with white sand.

262

Jake picked his way carefully down the steep side stairs and walked toward the swing set where Moses was gently pushing his seated sister. "Mind if I join you?" he called out.

Tameka applied her toe brakes to stop the swing's momentum and patted the wooden seat beside her. "Sit right here."

"Whew!" Jake eased on to the seat. "It's nice out here, isn't it? I guess, pretty soon, the leaves'll be changing colors." He smiled wistfully. "I always liked the fall. It's my favorite time of the year."

Moses sat down cross-legged in front of them. The first few cool nights of late September had laid the church lawn dormant and the grass crackled under Moses' weight.

Jake looked at first Moses, then Tameka. "How y'all holdin' up?"

Moses shrugged. "All right, I reckon."

"I'm not," Tameka said. "We have to move to *Bird-ming-hamm* with Uncle James and Auntie Alicia."

"Yeah, I know. That's a drag. We'll surely miss you both. I don't know what I'm gonna do at the Spa without your help with the plants, Moses. And, Tameka, it's always been a joy to see your smiling face around the salon."

They sat together in shared silence for a moment.

"Wanda said Mr. Hank's bad off." Moses' voice was barely audible.

Jake squinted into the sun. "Yeah. He's healing from his shoulder wound, but…"

"Why you reckon he was such a bad man, Mr. Jake?" Tameka's face shone with the innocence of a child.

"I don't know the answer to that, Tameka. But, I can tell you one thing — sometimes, grown-ups are really just hurt children inside, and that makes them lash out at other people." Jake stretched to find the words. He tapped his cane on his injured leg. "Do you two know why my leg's like this?"

Tameka shook her head.

"I heard someone beat you up," Moses answered.

"That's right. A boy I barely knew hurt me really bad. I almost didn't make it. But, you know what I found out later that helped me to forgive him?"

The children watched him intently.

"The young boy who hurt me wasn't much older than you are, Moses. He was almost eighteen. Turned out, he had a terrible, terrible time trying to grow up. His mama hurt him over and over, and a lot of the other grown-ups in his life did, too. He grew up just filled with hate and meanness. It wasn't me he beat up. It was all the demons that were hurtin' him inside that made him do it."

Tameka's face knit with confusion. "So...Mr. Hank has demons inside him?"

Jake shook his head. "Not real demons honey. But, I'll just bet he has the make-believe kind, and they can hurt you pretty bad."

Moses frowned. "I don't reckon I can ever stop bein' mad at him. How can I just up and forget all he did, just like that?"

"I know it's not easy, Moses. Man, do I know it." Jake sighed. "Mr. Hank's pain and anger ate away at him until there was probably not a bit of good or loving kindness left inside of him. He's in a prison in his own mind, now."

Jake looked at both children. "Don't let the same evil that took away his soul, reach down and take yours, too. You gotta find a way to let it go...or it will fester inside of you."

Jake rocked gently on the swing. "You don't forget it...not all the way. But, you'll find a way to live with it...without the anger taking a big chunk out of your heart and soul." He looked first at Tameka, then her brother. "Does any of this make any sense to you, at all?"

Moses picked at the dried grass on his pants leg. "A little, I guess."

"You know, you both can call me, or Jon, or Wanda — anytime you need to talk. Your aunt and uncle are good folks, too. I'm sure they will be right there to see you through."

"You reckon Mr. Hank will ever get well?" Tameka asked.

Jake paused, amazed at the depth of her compassion. "Hard to say. The pain might've pushed him too deep inside himself...but, the important thing for both of you to remember – you didn't do anything wrong. Do you understand?"

"We hurt May-May," Moses said softly.

"Your grandmama was very sick. Her body was just plain tired and worn out."

Moses wiped a tear from his cheek.

Tameka looked upward toward the clear blue skies. "May-May told us lots of times...she might be called home to heaven. She said that God was waitin' 'till He had her place prepared."

"You believe that?" Moses asked Jake.

"I believe a person's spirit goes on...after the body can't anymore. And, I believe your grandmama's going to be your guardian angel."

Moses rolled his eyes. "Aw...you don't really believe in angels, do you?"

Jake smiled. "Sure do! I think it'd be a sad world indeed, if I couldn't believe in them."

Wanda walked toward the swing set. "There you are! I was wondering where you all got off to."

"We're jus' talkin'," Tameka said. She reached up and grabbed Wanda's hand and guided her to sit on the seat on the other side of her and Jake.

"I spoke with your Uncle James, kids. He says it'll be okay for Mr. Jon and me to come up and get you for the Madhatter's Festival next month. Would you like that?"

"Would we ever!" Moses smiled wide.

Wanda reached over and patted him on the head. "Piddie would've said... *you're grinnin' like a goat eatin' briars*! I guess that means you think it's a grand notion."

Tameka's face turned from joy to sadness.

Wanda grabbed her small hand. "What? What? Why the sad face? Don't you want to come back and visit us?"

"I won't ever be able to see our old house again," Tameka said. "Some other people will be stayin' in it."

Wanda rubbed her hand across Tameka's shoulders. "You can stay with me, honey. That way, we can have a good long visit, and I can cook for both of you."

Jake held up his hand. "I was going to wait to let this out...but, I'll tell y'all if you can promise to keep it to yourselves until it's a done deal." He looked hard at each one of them, and they nodded ascent. "Jon and your Uncle James have been talking 'bout your grandmama's place. Seems that it's a good example of a style of house called a shotgun house — very historical, and all that. Well, we're going to propose to the city that they buy the house from your uncle, and then we'll preserve it as a museum."

"Cool!" Moses said.

"So...you'll be able to visit the house when you come back and see us." Jake shook his finger. "Don't you let on I told you a thing. It's still in the talking and planning stages right now. Jon's a real history buff, you know. He knows a lot about these shotgun houses, and he's going to get in touch with one of the groups here in the South who tries to save houses like your grandmother's."

"I think Miz Maizie would like knowing her house would be used to preserve history," Wanda commented.

"You gonna stay with us 'till we have to leave, Miz Wanda?" Tameka asked.

"I'll be right here. I promised your aunt and uncle I'd help you two pack up

266

your clothes and stuff." She cradled Tameka's chin in the palm of one hand. "It's gonna be all right, honey. You and Moses have your aunt and uncle, your cousins in Birmingham, and your other family right here in Chattahoochee."

Tameka jumped up and hugged Wanda, almost knocking her off the swing.

Moses laughed at the two of them teetering in midair. The hard knot of anger deep inside melted a little around the edges.

"When we went on the Alaskan cruise last year, the young folks went on a trail walk with a feller that made the best salmon spread they'd ever tasted. Hattie described it to me, and we experimented till we came up with this recipe."

Piddie Davis Longman

Spicy Salmon Spread

1   6-ounce can of canned, boneless, skinless salmon, drained of the packing water
1   teaspoon lemon juice
2   splashes of hot sauce
3   sprigs of green onion, finely chopped
1   clove of garlic, minced
2   Tablespoons of prepared horseradish
1   8 ounce package of cream cheese, softened

Mash up the salmon a little. Add the rest of the ingredients and mix well. Keep in the refrigerator. Serve with toast or crackers.

CHAPTER TWENTY-NINE

The Madhatter's Festival

Hattie

AS I STOOD ON THE MUDDY BANKS of the Apalachicola River holding Sarah in my arms, I couldn't help thinking of my father. Mr. D. had been a tall, burly man with a growling exterior wrapped around a marshmallow-sweet middle. How ironic; my own parenthood was necessary to bring a full appreciation of the struggles of my mother and father.

268

I was born to Tillie Davis toward the end of her thirty-ninth year, smack dab in the middle of her Masters Degree studies at Florida State College for Women, known in years since as Florida State University. Like the women on her side of the family, she began to experience the hot flash mania of perimenopause shortly after turning forty, when I was close to four years of age. Without the benefits of hormone replacement therapy, she had to simultaneously endure an active toddler and female madness. The way I figured it, my father was the only reason I made it past five. I tagged along with him everywhere: service calls, dove hunting, and fishing.

Bobby was adept in the outdoor sports department. I was not. I smiled as I recalled the countless times my father had tried to teach me to bait a fish hook. Because I couldn't abide the thought of inflicting pain on a defenseless worm, cricket, or minnow, I was a fisherman's nightmare companion. As long as Mr. D. baited my hook and removed any fish I caught, I enjoyed the act of fishing. I just didn't like all the yucky stuff that went with it.

One late summer afternoon after a frustrating teaching session, he beached the aluminum johnboat on a river sandbar.

"Get out," he said, "...and take that bucket of minnows and your pole with you. When I come back, you'd best have a minnow baited on the end of that hook!"

He gunned the small outboard motor and putted down river, until I could no longer pick out the sound of its engine.

First, I sat down on the sand and cried at the thought of being deserted. Then, I figured out a plan. I carefully poured one minnow from the bucket, hemmed it between two pebbles, and pierced the edge of a fin with the tip of the hook — all accomplished without actually touching the little fish. I lowered the minnow into the bucket to keep it alive until my father returned.

A few minutes later, my father's boat appeared around the bend of the river. "Did you bait your hook, gal?" he asked as he pulled to shore.

I proudly held up the nylon line, the minnow dangling from its speared dorsal fin like a limp linguine noodle. The expression on his face will forever live in memory.

He shook his head, trying to hide a bemused grin. "Aw...just get in the boat, for heaven's sake!"

From that point forward, I fished often with my father. We cut a deal that worked for us both. I packed and served our lunch, snacks, and drinks, and he baited the hook and removed my catch. On a few trips, between ministering to me and navigating the river, he managed to land a few fish himself.

"Hey, there!" Patricia Hornsby's familiar voice snapped me from the past.

"Oh, hello!" We hugged and she pecked Sarah on the cheek. "I'm so glad you could come over today. Looks like we're going to have a banner year. Jake said we've already sold over a thousand tickets, and it's just barely started."

Patricia nodded. "Traffic's backed up past the hospital entrance on Highway 90."

I searched the crowd. "Where'd you leave Ray and Ruth?"

"As frightening as it is to me, they're in New York. A set of Ruth's abstracts are being auctioned off for the nine-eleven relief effort. They really wanted Ruth to be there to present her paintings, so..." Patricia shrugged.

We turned and walked toward the festival grounds.

"It's kind of eerie, really," she continued. "Ruth painted the pieces a few months back...before the terrorist attacks. We didn't think much of the images then. Ray had hung them in the dining room, and we walked by them every day. But, afterwards, we noticed their significance. Even though they're abstract, you can clearly see the outline of the New York skyline before, and after, the attacks.

The paintings have created quite a stir in the New York art world."

"She's always had multiple gifts. That heaven painting she did for Aunt Piddie — that was close to Pid's death."

"Oh! Don't let me forget. Ruth sent a new painting for you guys. I have it in the car. I'll transfer it to you before I leave today."

"What is it?"

Patricia shrugged. "I don't know. She wrapped it herself. Said it was for your family. That reminds me – did you see the article in the *Tallahassee Democrat* on that mural over in Quincy, a couple of weeks back?"

"No. I've gotten so depressed over the news lately, I've stopped reading the paper or watching TV."

"That's understandable. I may still have the article at home. I cut it out and stuck it God knows where. Seems this wall mural the local children painted five years ago on the side of the Sheriff's department building has one scene that looks like the World Trade Center towers...complete with a jet airplane approaching it. I stopped by to get a close look at it on the way over here. You can see faces painted in a few of the windows, and some figures appear to be leaping from the buildings! One of the deputies even pointed out what looks like a little demon with a pitchfork at the base of one tower."

"That is so bizarre. I'll have to stop and check it out next time I'm over that way. I'm sure it's been the talk at the spa. I just don't get by there as much as I'd like."

Patricia gestured toward the crowd. "Jake waved at me as I made my way through the festival grounds. He was flustered about something or other. You want to walk around and see the crafts with me?"

"Sure, maybe I can pick up a few early Christmas presents...and Jake's always in a fizz around festival time. There's the usual planning and stuff. But this year, Elvina and Evelyn are at odds over who's entitled to judge the Best Damn Chocolate Cake and Icing Contest, what with Piddie being gone. That's probably what's got him in an uproar. The two women were barely speaking to each other last week. Let's check out the booths, then we can stop by and see how the cold war is going."

Jake and Jolene had settled on a patriotic theme for the festival. Flags of assorted sizes were suspended from several of the low-hanging live oak branches, and the arts and crafts venders had followed instructions to decorate in red, white, and blue. The main performance stage was flanked with two immense wreaths of red and blue carnations tied with oversized white bows. *The 2001Madhatter's Festival* was printed in bold blue lettering across the banner spanning the stage. Between the booths, large glittering white paper stars on gold sticks were plugged into the ground like the discarded magic wands of migratory behemoth fairies.

As the city's contribution to the relief effort, a large portion of the proceeds from ticket sales and vendor fees were earmarked for the American Red Cross Victims Relief Fund. Evelyn and Stephanie had spent two weeks gluing silk daisies to lapel pins wrapped with strips of red, white, and blue ribbon to sell for donations. Most of the craft vendors had pledged a percentage of profits to the fund. The local women's quilters' guild offered an Americana-themed handmade quilt that was being raffled for five dollars a ticket.

Over sixty arts and crafts booths were scattered between the live oaks and down one side of the dirt and clay river landing road paralleling the bank. Unlike the first Madhatter's Festival with its scattering of local craftspeople, the annual event now drew vendors from as far away as Tennessee and the Carolinas. Intricately designed quilts, hand-loomed rugs, nature photography, watercolor paintings, wood carving, and pottery booths were interspersed with local church and civic groups hawking baked goods, fried fish dinners, southern barbecue, and powdered sugar funnel cakes.

Rich and Carol Burns stood beside the entrance to an inflatable trampoline room watching their twin girls bounce and tumble.

"If I did that, I'd loose breakfast," Carol said when she saw us. "Hey there, Patricia. You over here solo today?"

"On the loose with money just burning a hole in my pocket! Ruth and Ray are out of town."

"Glad you could come over," Rich added.

I took the opportunity to pump my police friend for information. "Anything new on Hank Henderson…that you can tell us, of course."

"I think Mr. Henderson, as we knew him, is gone from this world." Rich shook his head. "He's been sedated, pretty much, most of the time. When they take him off the drugs, he rants and raves and fights…sees things that aren't there. And, for some odd reason, he goes absolutely ballistic if he sees the color yellow. I doubt he'll ever stand trial. He's already in more torment than any prison sentence would hand out."

I shook my head. "Wow. What about Alfonso?"

"That whole thing's bound to drag out for awhile. He'll probably be tried as an adult. But, there's a faction who see him as a victim of Hank, too. It's hard to say which way things will go for him. As to Hank's cousin, Lamar…" Rich rolled his eyes. "They'll nail his butt to the cross for his part in cleanin' out the evidence room over in Midview. Although, some of the officers think he's a hero for providing them a nice break room. Go figure."

"I read a tidbit about the FBI's ongoing investigation in the paper," Patricia said. "Maybe they can use Hank's Internet connections to at least round up some of the jerks in the kiddie porn ring."

"We can all hope." Carol watched her girls for a moment. "You try to keep your kids safe, and you hope you're doing okay by them."

"Holston and I were just talking about the same thing the other night."

"At least we live in a small community where we can watch over them and help each other. Of course, that didn't stop the likes of Hank…" Carol frowned. "I just want to lock my girls in a room and throw away the key."

Patricia chuckled. "Save that until they're teenagers."

Wanda appeared beside us, flanked on either side by Tameka and Moses Clark.

Wanda patted the children on their backs. "Go on in there. But, you watch out now, Moses. You're bigger than some of the younger kids. Be careful you don't hurt anyone."

Moses nodded. He and his sister joined the squealing gaggle of bouncing children.

Wanda watched with her hands propped on her hips. "He's at a weird age. One minute he wants to act all grown up, and the next, he's a kid again."

"You enjoying your visit with the kids?" Carol asked.

"Yeah, a lot. It's been a little over a month since they moved to Alabama, but it feels more like two years. I didn't realize how much I'd miss them." Wanda's gaze drifted to the playhouse. She turned back to the adults and smiled. "I'm spending Christmas with them. James and Alicia have invited me up."

"Things goin' pretty well up there?" Rich asked.

"Seem to be. Alfred and Antwoin – you remember James' two boys? They were here for the funeral. Well, they're helping Moses ease into big city life. Moses told me he's thinking of trying out for the soccer team next season. Both of his cousins play. And, I believe Tameka's the little girl Alicia always wanted. She's buying her clothes and teaching her to behave like a young lady.

274

I think Miz Maizie would approve."

"No one's heard from the kids' real mother?" Carol asked.

"No. I doubt we ever will. James and Alicia are the legal guardians, and they're already discussing adopting them so there won't be any conflict – in case she does show up some day. James and Alicia will make sure they get an education, too. Moses is already talking about wanting to train in horticulture."

"Sister-girl! Yoo-Hoo!" Jake's voice was tinged with his normal festival-level panic. He hobbled to where we stood. "Your presence is needed at the Cake and Icing contest booth. You'd better come with me before Elvina and Evelyn start to slap, spit, and scratch."

I rolled my eyes. "Will you all excuse me for a bit? Patricia, I'll catch up with you in a few."

"What's the deal?" I asked as we waded through the crowd.

"Elvina's still holdin' out that she should judge the contest, on account of her taking Piddie's position at the spa...and, of course, Evelyn *is* Piddie's daughter... but, Evelyn swears she's had some sort of vision. I'm afraid they'll cause a scene!"

"It's perfect, don't you see, Jakey? It's like...Evelyn and Piddie used to snipe at each other...now, there's Elvina and Evelyn! I mean, how would we know what peace is...if we didn't have war?"

The national level implications of my flippant comment hit us both simultaneously.

Jake smirked. "You do so much have a way with words, Sister-girl."

I shrugged. "Sorry."

"By the way – mark your calendar for the first two weekends in November. We haven't decided who's what, just yet...but, Bobby and Leigh's cabin warming will be held on one Saturday, and Jon and my house warming will be the next."

"What about...?"

Jake smiled. "FSU football? Got that covered. We'll both have the game on in one room for the painfully sports-addicted people who get dragged out durin' game time. You and I can slip off and catch the score, ok?"

"Works for me. Our team's not doing so well this year. I'd almost rather watch it in bits and pieces. Less painful that way."

Jake sucker-punched my arm. "Now, come on. Don't be a fair weather fan. They'll rebuild. Heck, they graduated half the dang team last year!"

"I know. They really shouldn't let that happen."

With the exception of Joe, who was helping with the Baptist Church bake sale, the family was huddled around the Best Damn Cake and Icing Contest booth when Jake, Sarah, and I arrived.

Holston had an amused expression on his face. "Just in time, hon," he mouthed.

Elvina sat in the official judge's red velvet high-back chair, arms crossed over her chest.

"If you'll just let me tell you 'bout my vision, it'll all work out just fine!" Evelyn begged. "Will you just listen?"

Elvina's lips pursed into a pout. "It's just somethin' you've made up to cheat me out of my rightful place as contest judge, Evelyn Fletcher."

"No, I promise, it's not. Cross my heart and hope to die, God strike me down with a bolt of lightnin'!"

Elvina looked up. "That's a pretty safe wager...seein' as how there's nary a cloud in the sky."

"It was this-a-way," Evelyn lowered her voice a little. "I was near asleep last night. Joe was staying up to watch some TV, but I was plain tuckered out. I saw this vision of Mama standin' at the foot of the bed." Evelyn's eyes watered. "She was beautiful...her face all lit up with light...so peaceful. She said she was gonna

276

be leavin' us all, now. She felt like we could handle it on our own from here on in…she'd check in on us from time to time. And, of course, she'd see us all in the by-in-by. Said she was done with earthly concerns — that she had better things to occupy herself with…"

Evelyn looked toward the family, her eyes dreamy. "Mama told me she was proud of all of us — the way we'd come together, and that we were gonna need to lean on each other in the comin' tryin' times. But, she was sure we'd be alright — if we kept the faith."

She spread her hands in the air and wiggled her fingers. "She got all wispy-like, then…like she was fadin' out. She said one last thing."

Elvina, totally engrossed in the story of Evelyn's ghostly visitation, leaned forward. "What was it she said?"

"You and Elvina got to work on gettin' along. You're my only daughter, and she's my best friend ever. Tell her to lighten up a little, and that I said y'all should both judge the contest this year. This will be y'all's true test – 'specially if y'all gonna collaborate on Easter bonnets and outfits come springtime. As for the contest, now, two sets of taste buds are better'n one."

Evelyn gazed heavenward. "Then, Mama smiled at me — the most angelic look I've ever seen, painted across her face. Then, she was gone. Just like that!" She snapped her fingers.

Elvina smoothed a hank of hair that had escaped from underneath her red and white striped pillbox hat. "Well, I reckon we can rate them separately, then figure a way to reach a winner."

"Lord help! I'm glad that's all settled," Jake said. "I'm getting too dang old for all the drama!"

I poked him in the arm. "Only because it's not *your* drama."

He shook his cane in my direction. "Don't get fresh, Sister-girl."

UP THE DEVIL'S BELLY

Discovering the things I didn't like in life came easy: raw celery, lima beans, too much hairspray, rude people, traffic snarls, and shopping for bathing suits. Not until I was firmly ensconced in my forties had I recognized the things I held important: family, friends, a sense of community, and a balance between work and play, sorrow and joy.

My father, mother, Aunt Piddie, Maizie Clark – their absence in our lives left us searching for ways to heal. They had been given the blessing of many years, unlike the multitudes whose lives had been brutally snuffed out on September 11th, 2001. As many people across the nation had grasped, the best tribute to the loved ones who'd left us behind was to move forward with our lives in the best way possible. To do less would be unthinkable.

"You're gonna have bad times – keep you up worryin' nights. When you can't get to sleep easy, count your blessin's. They'll keep comin', the more you count, and besides, who wants a room full of sheep anyhow."

Piddie Davis Longman

AFTERWORD

Ruth Hornsby's latest painting hangs in a prominent position on a wall in the reception room of the Triple C Day Spa and Salon.

The scene depicts the hazy figure of a beehive-haired woman in a print dress standing in the middle of a vast field of yellow flowers.

A small suitcase sits by her feet. A faint smile lights her indistinct facial features. One hand is lifted in a wave.

I suppose it's left to the viewer to decide if the wave means hello or goodbye.

Goodbye is too final.

I like to think of it as a hello.

THE END

My prayers, in these years after the attack,
still include the families and their loved ones
who must carry on.

Rabid Press, Inc.

Up The Devil's Belly by Rhett DeVane at $14.95 each: _____

The Madhatter's Guide to Chocolate
by Rhett DeVane at $14.95 each: _____

The Closing   by Dagmar Marshal at $13.95 each: _____

Sales Tax (if applicable): _____

Shipping: _____

Total: _____

Please include $3.95 for shipping and handling for first book and $1.25 for each additional. Texas residents must include applicable sales tax. Payment must accompany orders.

Allow 3 to 4 weeks for delivery.

Name: _____

Date: _____

Shipping Address:

Street: _____

City: _____ State: _____ Zip: _____

Phone: _____ Fax: _____

Card Type: ☐ VISA ☐ MasterCard

Name on Card: _____

Card#: _____

Exp. Date: _____

Signature: _____

Make your check payable and return to:

Rabid Press, Inc.
P.O. Box 4706
Horseshoe Bay, TX 78657
www.rabidpress.com

Rhett DeVane is a true southerner, born and raised in the piney woods of the north Florida panhandle. Originally from Chattahoochee, Florida, she now lives in Tallahassee where she is working on the third book in a series of southern fiction novels. Rhett is owned by two cats, Sisko and Saki, and a rescued Florida Cracker Retriever named Shelly.